ELECTRA'S COMPLEX

A Bella After Dark erotic, romantic mystery!

Emma Pérez

Bella
BOOKS

2015

Bella Books, Inc.
P.O. Box 10543
Tallahassee, FL 32302

First Bella Books Edition 2015

Editor: Katherine V. Forrest
Cover Designer: Sandy Knowles

ISBN: 978-1-59493-440-7

Dedication

Para ti, Carol

Acknowledgments

I am indebted to Michael Nava for his exemplary Henry Rios mysteries. With generosity, precision and thoughtfulness, he has taught me, and a generation about writing as a brown queer. As always I thank my writing bud Alicia Gaspar de Alba, for encouraging me to pursue the mystery genre. Artist Liliana Wilson read scenes and offered reassurance. My beautiful sister, Yolanda Pérez, read the draft and pointed out that I should pursue an erotic angle. I thank Cris, Sonja and Joe Robert for being loving, supportive, fine-looking siblings. Macarena Hernandez, journalist and writer, also listened as I refined characters and plot. I give a heartfelt thanks to my bud Francisco "Frank" Galarte, who didn't mind being the model for a pivotal character. Antonia Castañeda and Arturo Madrid extended their "love shack" in Albuquerque where I revised key scenes. Through the years lesbians and queers have asked, "Why don't you give us more sex?" I want to thank each of you, including Catriona Esquibel for being a dedicated virtuoso of Chican@ queer/lesbian literature. I'm perpetually grateful to my co-parent Scarlet Bowen.

I'm also thankful for inspiration from: Norma Alarcón, Arturo Aldama, Adelina Anthony, Ahimsa Timoteo Bodhrán, Luz Calvo, Ernesto Chávez, Lucha Corpi, Dina Flores, Alma Gaspar de Alba, Macarena Gómez-Barris, Deena González, Virginia Grise, Jack Halberstam, Ellie Hernandez, Lorenzo Herrera y Lozano, Miranda Joseph, Katie Kane, Sandra Lane, KG MacGregor, John Márquez, Cynthia Pérez, Sasha Pimentel, Manuel Ramos, Maria Salazar, Sandra K. Soto, Michael Topp, Rita Urquijo-Ruíz and Evy Valencia.

Thank you Bella Books and Karin Kallmaker for publishing my novel and for your expert interventions. I was extremely fortunate to have the inimitable Katherine V. Forrest as editor. She offered meticulous, editorial guidance and asked the questions that needed to be asked to enhance the story. I'm inordinately grateful to this pioneer in lesbian fiction. The staff at Bella Books has been ideal and professional. Any and all transgressions at this juncture are my own.

Finally, Carol Brochin appeared in time to assist me with select scenes. Her proficiency with all things sensual improved many passages. *Te voy a mostrar*, Dr. Brochin.

PROLOGUE

"Drive a blade in my back and I'll return the favor."

I had just fastened my mouth to a woman's labia, a woman I'd barely met, at the Down Under, the sex club that I fell into weekly, when I heard a former lover's voice. I was poised topless in my black boots and jeans with the woman's legs on my shoulders, her body naked on satin crimson pillows that provided the necessary height. Her wrists were haloed above her head and tied with blue suede straps and the way her torso writhed encouraged me to pursue fresh techniques. I was looking forward to an hour of indulgence—she tasted like my favorite lavender soap—but when I heard the familiar voice, I tripped backward, gripping the woman's ankles to anchor me.

"What the fuck, Isabel?" I asked.

"You heard me." She spun around and darted out of the dungeon.

Isabel Cortez claimed title to the place that transformed every Saturday to this hip, queer sex club. After she introduced me to the place, I'd become one of the die-hard regulars in what was once a seedy but now brightly lit side of Chelsea in New York City. After a dreaded vacation, when she drove a metaphoric knife into me, twisting the blade until my entrails spilled and dragged on the ground, I'd refused to go anywhere with her ever again. Doesn't matter, I'd thought. I'm free of her.

I resumed my pleasure with the woman whose thighs ironed my ears, despite knowing full well that Ms. Cortez was capable of doing far more harm than good.

CHAPTER ONE

It was Monday morning. Two days after my weekly recreation at the Down Under and I had forgotten my ex-lover's hollow threat. Well, almost forgotten. Let me fill you in. There's more to me than occasional Saturday jaunts to the sex club in Chelsea.

I'm a middle-aged history professor at a financially fraught New York City college. On this Monday morning, I arrived on campus at six thirty a.m., long before high-level administrators, staff, faculty or students inhabited the hallways. As I entered the Administration building to deliver my application for a long over due sabbatical, I thought I saw none other than "drive a knife in my back" Isabel Cortez slithering past the dean's office. At first I thought I imagined her silhouette, but when I turned my head, I could have sworn her speckled brown eyes gazed upon me for a split second. But she was gone. It was as if a ghost in a baseball cap had flown through the hallway. Minimally rattled, I refused to believe she was anywhere near, so I ignored my imaginings and proceeded to the dean's office, planning to slip my yellow manila envelope under his door. The deadline for the application was five p.m. on the previous Friday. Since the dean's secretary left her office at four fifty each day to catch her five p.m. bus, she wouldn't have been present to receive my application. That minor technicality would grant me the evidence to prove the damn thing wasn't late.

As I approached the dean's office, I stepped in a pool streaming out from under the door. I wore my favorite black Italian leather boots and the idea of water ruining the shine pissed me off. I tugged my trousers up, hoping not to get them wet, and that's when I spotted a red sheen on the floor. It was blood. Blood had trickled from under the door, but more disconcerting was that the door was cracked open and I saw the dean's head lying on his desk as if he were taking a nap. When I drew nearer, his bulging eyes stared eerily at me. I tiptoed closer and tripped over a computer cord that jiggled his chair and as it rotated, his head plunged forward, dropping his chin on his collarbone. That was when I saw a wound in the vicinity of his heart. The blood was still damp on his cotton shirt and more blood dripped on the floor at the bloody pool's edges around his desk chair. His fly was open and his penis poked through his pants, which had a round wet spot near where the penis's head rested.

"Fuck," I whispered. "What the fuck were you thinking, Johnson?"

I fumbled for the office phone and dropped the receiver on his lap, splattering beads of blood on the desk. Impulsively, I snatched up the receiver and smeared cold blood on my palm.

"Fuck, fuck, fuck!"

I punched nine-one-one.

Before I could panic properly, the New York City police department arrived in droves.

A seasoned type began to question me, making me feel even more suspect than I already felt. What was it about authority that made me imagine I was guilty when I wasn't?

"Is this how you found him, ma'am?"

The older detective who grilled me resembled a caricature of Columbo, the 1970s TV detective. He wore a wrinkled, stained trench coat and attempted an unguarded manner. But

I wasn't fooled. His gray, bushy hair was uncombed and he squinted beady blue eyes that were set so close he looked like one of those one-eyed monsters in fairy tales.

"This is how I found him."

"Begging your pardon, ma'am, what's your name?"

"Electra. Electra Campos."

"Well, Miss Electra. Is it Mrs. or Miss?"

"Professor Campos."

"Ah. Excuse me, Professor Campos. What time did you arrive on the scene?"

"Exactly six thirty."

"You're sure?"

"Yes."

"Why were you in the dean's office at this early hour?"

"I was delivering a packet." I pointed to my manila envelope on the floor a few centimeters from the fresh blood.

"And this packet, why couldn't it wait until normal office hours?"

"I had to meet a deadline."

He looked at his watch. "At six thirty a.m.?"

"Friday afternoon's deadline."

"I see." Colombo snickered and shook his head.

"Am I under arrest, uh—?"

"Detective. Detective Swift."

"Detective Swift?" I nearly snickered.

"You college types love my name."

"I don't love it, Detective. Just amused."

"I get that a lot." He inspected me from head to boot. "How well did you know Dean Johnson?"

"As well as anyone on campus. I attended a few mixers at his home. He wasn't bad as far as deans are concerned."

I was lying. The man was duplicitous. But then again, I was prone to harsh judgment when I regarded high-ranking administrators.

"Anyone you know who might've wanted him dead?"

"Oh, any number of faculty from the sciences."

"Why's that?"

"Funding."

"Funding?"

"Funding."

"You want to say more about that, Professor Campos?"

"He funded a new building in the arts. That pissed off the scientists. Oh, the engineers weren't too happy either."

"Politics, huh?"

"Politics."

One of the lesser detectives approached him and whispered in his ear. Detective Swift walked back inside the office to the center of the crime scene, scribbled in a three-by-five notepad and returned to me. I stood outside in the hallway, avoiding the vision that was the poor fuck of a dean.

"My men said somebody tampered with the crime scene. You know anything about that?"

I was annoyed that he called his group of detectives "men" when the one who had whispered in his ear was obviously a woman. A striking Latina at that. I notice such details.

"That's funny," I said.

"Huh?"

"Your detective doesn't look like a man."

"I didn't say she did."

"My mistake."

He squinted, his eyes becoming beady blue slits. He must have been somewhat handsome about twenty years ago and his habit of squinting probably helped him get the girl. Occasionally.

"Like I was saying, Professor Campos, the crime scene was compromised. You say this is exactly how you found the body when you entered the room?"

"Not exactly."

"Not exactly?"

"Not exactly."

He sighed. "Would you mind telling me why you touched the body?"

"I didn't touch the body. I stumbled on a computer cord and the seat jerked and half-turned. That's when I saw blood. And his penis hanging out of his pants."

"You yourself did not move the chair?"

"I myself did not move the chair."

The Latina detective lingered at the doorway listening and I sensed her amusement each time I answered. I found myself answering too boldly. Trying to impress a female detective, I thought. Stop it, *pendeja*.

"Professor Campos, you got a murdered dean here. You want to give me some straight answers."

Unexpectedly, my gut churned and I sprinted across the hallway to the bathroom. Remnants of a meager breakfast emptied into the toilet. When I came out of the stall, the female detective blocked the bathroom door, her tight skirt highlighting curvaceous hips. Black leather knee-high boots gave her height, but she was probably no more than five-five in bare feet. The light-caramel flesh of her neck was so tempting I wanted to lick the vein that popped faintly above her collarbone.

"You all right?"

I bent over the washbowl and splashed cool water on my face. "Did he send you after me? That's embarrassing." I wiped my face with a coarse paper towel. "No, wait, he sent you in because he thought I would escape." I pointed to the window that was large enough for a toddler to squeeze through.

She grinned and my gut cramped, warning me to stay away. This woman was far above my pay grade. She came closer and I stepped back, but she sloped in tighter and wiped my leather jacket's lapel.

"Blood," she said.

"Huh?" My suave demeanor disappeared.

She gazed straight through me. "It's hard the first time."

"The first time?" I didn't know what she referred to. We'd barely met.

"A dead body. The first time I saw one I nearly lost my breakfast."

"But you didn't."

"No, I didn't."

"That's why you make a good detective and I'm a history professor."

"History, huh? Never was my favorite subject."

"Yeah, me neither."

She grinned again and I felt I was getting somewhere, until I realized I was coming on to a police detective in a college campus bathroom after seeing my dean dead with his dick hanging out of his pants. A knock on the door saved me from my cavalier antics.

"Hey, Quinn, everything all right in there?"

"It's all good, Dan." She stepped aside. "Ready to see the world again?"

"Quinn, huh?"

"Irish father, Latina mother."

"Ah. Pretty common, I guess."

"You're saying I'm common?"

"I would never make that mistake about you, Detective Quinn."

I opened the door and faced Swift, who barred the exit.

"Just a few more questions, Professor."

"Sure, but can I sit down somewhere?"

"I won't be long."

He wouldn't move and I felt Detective Quinn's breath subtle on the back of my neck, swirling inside my shirt collar.

"You say you tripped on a computer cord?"

"Yeah. I tripped."

"Where's the computer?"

"Must be in the office."

"There's no computer."

"I tripped on a computer cord, I know I did."

"You sure it wasn't a lamp cord, Professor Campos?"

"No. It was a computer cord. It was thick and white."

"My men," he cleared his throat, "I mean, my detectives can't find a cord or a computer. Makes me wonder how you tripped."

"May I go in?" I gestured toward the dean's office, which had been roped off with tacky yellow crime scene tape.

"Be my guest, Professor. Be careful not to disturb anything this time." I heard sarcasm in his voice.

I tiptoed into the office, apprehensive that I might bloody my boots again. I stood in the middle of the room and saw no cord and no computer.

"I swear I tripped on a cord, Detective Swift."

"Please, Professor, feel free to call me Detective. Just Detective."

I was being set up and this guy was more concerned with hierarchical formalities.

"Does this mean you're going to arrest me?" I wasn't feeling debonair anymore.

"Not yet. For now, we're trying to get the facts straight."

My body twitched in that scared shitless sort of way.

"I have one more question and then you can leave, but don't go far. We may need you again."

"I won't board a plane to Buenos Aires, if that's what you mean."

"Did you see anyone else in the building?"

"No."

"No one? Not even a janitor?"

"No."

"That's all for now, Professor. Here's my card." He rummaged in his trench coat pocket and brought out a grimy card, frayed at the edges.

"Seeing a dead body. Never easy," he said.

"So I've heard." I looked around and saw Detective Quinn whispering with other detectives. I turned to leave and had an urge to look back but didn't want to appear too eager. I knew her name and where to find her. What was I thinking? Okay, stop it, *pendeja*.

I was headed to the Administration building's exit when I heard footsteps behind me. Fuck. I wasn't sure why I hadn't told them about the phantom in the hallway. They wouldn't have believed me. Or they maybe would've thought I invented suspects to ward off suspicion.

"Professor Campos?"

Detective Quinn's steady hand caressed my shoulder. Okay, maybe not a caress.

"I know what you're thinking," she said.

"You do?"

"We aren't interested in framing you. We're looking for the right answers."

"As opposed to the wrong answers?"

"Look. Maybe we can talk later. Here's my card. Call if you think of anything."

Her card was clean, crisp and taupe with bold lettering.

"Did Swift put you up to this?"

"I don't just take orders, Professor. Someone like you would know that."

This wasn't good. Already she was charming me and disarming me. I'm in trouble, I thought.

"Thanks for the card. I've got to get to class."

I glanced at my watch and noticed that more than two hours had passed. It was close to nine thirty.

"May I walk you to class?"

"What?"

"I thought I'd walk you to class. You seem edgy."

"I'm not going to class yet. I'm going to my office."

"You said you had to get to class."

"I do. At noon." We had barely met and already I felt like she was being forward. She was a cop, for Christ's sake. I couldn't trust a cop. My father was rolling in his grave.

She hung back. "Don't hesitate to call. For any reason."

I scrunched my forehead, stumped because she moved faster than me. That was a come-on, I thought, and rushed across a chilly campus on what had become a bleak November day.

CHAPTER TWO

Police cars, ambulances and journalists swarmed the campus and I regretted turning down Detective Quinn's offer to walk me to class. I tried to make myself invisible, hoping no one would notice me leaving the Administration building. I turned immediately away from the pack. When Detective Quinn diverted the journalists' attention and addressed them, I couldn't hear what she said but I was grateful that microphones were being poked in her face and not mine.

I hiked across the main quad and saw students hanging about pointing toward the Admin building.

"Hola Profe. Did you kill the dean for us?"

"That's not funny, Brisa."

"Oh, come on, Profe. Nobody liked him. Not even his wife."

Brisa winked at me. I ignored her attempt to bond over a secret she thought I might reveal. Some students had a way of entering your world without earning access. Brisa wasn't one of those, but she crossed professional boundaries and I allowed the crossing until I stepped back and asserted my position as her teacher and elder. The thing is, she was a remarkably bright Latina from Colombia and I relished her sense of humor. And it didn't hurt that she was voluptuously proportioned.

"I'll see you in class."

"Profe, don't be mad at me," she yelled.

I shook my head disapprovingly but didn't feel disapproving at all. Brisa was right. No one liked the dean, which benefitted me somewhat since Detective Swift would be eager for a suspect. Who better than the person at the crime scene pretending she had nothing to do with the murder? He'll think I'm that clever, and I think he's clever enough to pretend that I'm not a suspect to give him enough time to entrap me. Damn. I was in trouble. And the detective wasn't aware of the secret to which Brisa referred. Once he did a little digging, he would suspect me.

I climbed the stairs to my office on the second floor and strolled past the "dead white men's club" of the History Department. These old men made the English Department's love of Milton seem trivial. Like most history departments, mine also accommodated a group of elderly men from European ethnic backgrounds, meaning very white, very pale, very committed to Jacobean traditions, that denigrated the revolutionary, gunpowder-toting Guy Fawkes and translated that historical event into their reason behind chastising student protestors at #Occupy Wall Street. The pasty men avowed the need to return to Victorian sexdrives, which they misread as celibacy. For women. (None had read Foucault's *History of Sexuality*.) They even revered Jack the Ripper, calling him an extraordinary celebrity while others in their club marveled at Hitler. Openly. In neo-Nazi reverence, they were fascinated with the dictator's ability to rouse the hearts and minds of millions into despising those they considered not "normal."

"We heard you were in the building when it happened." It was Sloan, the leader of the pack, accompanied by one of his sycophants, an assistant professor that Sloan owned. Sloan was squat, burly, pockmarked and pot-bellied. His shoulders bumped mine and I sensed that his squat height next to the likes of me miffed him.

"Not when it happened, Sloan. After it happened."

"I'm curious, Electra."

"How refreshing for you, Sloan."

"Why were you in the building? That early in the morning?"

I paused and glared at him. "Because I had paperwork to deliver." I thought I'd better tell the truth, if only an economical truth. I didn't want his club inventing lies about me.

"At six in the morning? That's unusual." Sloan stepped back, seemingly to de-emphasize our matching height.

"What can I say, Sloan? I'm an early riser catching worms."

"While you're here, let me introduce you to our new colleague, Hugh Roberts."

"We've met," I said. To goad me, Sloan pretended I hadn't met his protégé, when we both had battle scars from the department vote that hired yet another conformist, heterosexually obligated white man to teach more conformist, heterosexually obligated white male ideologies.

"Hugh will be teaching the new graduate seminar on 'The Forgotten Democracy of Andrew Jackson.'"

"It's forgotten all right," I said. "How many Seminole Indians did Sharp Knife massacre?"

"That's out of context," said Hugh. "Way out of context." He adjusted his tortoise frame glasses with a grimy, long, thin middle finger that resembled his grimy, long, thin body. Assistant Professor Hugh Roberts's middle finger poked out conspicuously from a dressing on the palm of his right hand. Sloan had a similar dressing on his palm.

"Do you two belong to the same club?" I asked, glancing at their hands.

"Handball," Sloan grunted. "We play at six twice a week. You should join us sometime, Electra."

"I'm not much for competitive sports, Sloan. I prefer games that perfect my inborn sloth."

I left them gawking at my back and spun around the corner, entering a short hallway that led to two offices with doors facing each other. I entered my office, closed the door behind me and locked it. Not something I did often, but this morning I felt apprehensive. Just as I was about to sit at my desk, I heard a quick, staccato knock and someone jiggled with the doorknob. Startled, I froze.

"Electra, I know you're in there, let me in. Please."

I hurried to the door, opened it and hauled the dean's wife inside.

"Virginia, what are you doing here?"

"I'm afraid, Electra."

Virginia kept a svelte, shapely body from weekly tennis at her dead husband's country club. With her lean tennis arms she unwrapped a wool white scarf from her neck and held it in her hands, pulling it tight then loosening it repeatedly.

"Do the police know you're on campus?"

"Of course they do. I ran here as quickly as I could." She pulled the scarf tighter, released it and the entire length spilled to the floor.

"Here? To my office?" I picked up one of the ends that had fallen to the floor and placed the white cloth in her hand.

"I had to see you. What am I going to tell them, Electra?" She pulled two ends apart and let it fall again. This time I didn't pick it up.

"The truth might be convenient."

"What if they ask about us?"

"Virginia, there is no us. There has never been an us."

"What if they find out we had a thing?"

"Why would they have to know that?"

"They might suspect you." She fidgeted with the end of the scarf still in her hands. Her big round sunglasses made her look like Jackie O eluding the paparazzi. In other words, she was easy to spot in any crowd.

"Who knew about us? Really knew?"

"Just Coxwell."

"You told your husband? Why did you tell him?" I was stunned. We had always agreed his knowing could hurt my career. Well, not anymore.

"I couldn't lie to him last night, Electra. I felt sorry for him. He was so pathetic begging me to explain why we never have sex anymore. I told him I preferred sex with someone else."

"Please tell me that someone else is not me."

"Of course it's not you. But your name might have come up."

"My name?"

"I might have confessed about that time in the hot tub."

"The hot tub? At your house, Virginia? When everyone was delusional, drunk or passed out?"

"Oh, don't get so ruffled. That wasn't the only time."

"But why mention the hot tub?"

"He mentioned it. He said despite being drunk he was sure I was splashing about, excavating someone in the hot tub."

"Excavating?"

"His words, not mine."

"He waited a year to ask?"

"Oh, he said he thought it was just drunken debauchery and it was better to pretend it never happened."

"A fine man."

"He's dead, Electra. My Coxy is dead. How can that be?"

"I don't know. It happens. People die."

"But he was murdered, Electra! Murdered!"

"I know, I know. I'm sorry, Virginia."

"I feel so guilty."

"Why? Did you do it?"

She scowled at me, which was answer enough, I suppose.

"He finally agreed to a separation."

"Ah. That."

"It's not that I don't love him."

"You mean, didn't."

"I did love him, Electra. I just couldn't stand to have sex with the man anymore. He got so big and hairy and…"

"Please, Virginia, the man is dead."

She removed her sunglasses to reveal a big bruising shiner on her left eye. I inched closer and examined her face.

"Again?"

Virginia shrugged.

I fingered the edge of the bruise and she jerked back.

"Talk of divorce made him a little angry."

"Was that before or after he hit you?"

"He did this and stormed out at four."

Virginia looked down at her shoes, almost sheepish. I wondered if she was lying. I wondered if she had socked herself in the eye to prove she was a martyred widow. I'd known her long enough and had witnessed her willingness to do anything to have her way.

"How could his killer be waiting for him, Electra?"

"You were the last person to see him alive, Virginia. The police will want to know about the bruise on your face. You'll be a suspect, you realize that."

"Me? You're the one who found him."

"Who told you?"

"The detective. Swinburne."

"Swift."

"Swift? That's his name, really?"

"That's his name, really."

"Electra." Her eyelids twitched as she said my name. I knew that twitch. It was her earnest twitch. The one that warned me that something I didn't like was about to be revealed. "Don't you think they'll suspect you when they find out about our thing?"

And there it was.

"Our thing was over a year ago, Virginia, and unless you tell them, they won't know."

"I wouldn't be so sure."

"Excuse me?"

"What if Coxy told someone?"

"Okay. Let's examine the facts here. You say he left the house at four. Who could he have possibly told between four and the time I found him, two and one-half hours later? Do you think he called the press? Could he have posted it on his blog? Or tweeted? Or better yet, Facebook? Did Coxy have a Facebook page, Virginia?"

"Don't be silly. You know what I mean. You're doing that thing you do when you get angry."

"What thing is that, Virginia?"

"Well, for one, you keep repeating my name and for another, you get overly sarcastic."

"Excuse me if I sound a little irritated, Virginia, but I have this sneaky suspicion that someone is trying to set me up."

"Not me."

"Oh, no. Of course not you, Virginia."

"Electra, I came to you. To be sure our stories don't contradict each other. Stop being so paranoid."

She reached for my hand and kissed my fingers.

"Okay, okay, I'm sorry. You're right."

Without warning, my left hand's middle finger was in her mouth and she sucked firmly.

"Virginia. What are you doing?" My voice softened.

She seized my right hand and placed it on her breast. I knew what I should do, but I couldn't fight her seductive trap. I stood immobile and felt the warmth of her tongue titillating my middle finger.

"Virginia," I whispered.

Her gaze was less than intoxicating with her aberrant black eye. I closed my eyes and massaged her breast, unbuttoned her blouse and excavated for warm flesh beneath her bra. I guess excavation was my expert vocation.

"We shouldn't," I heard myself say.

"Why not? Everybody knows. I'm no stranger to your office."

I slid to my knees and lifted her black pencil skirt. She wasn't wearing underwear. I shook my head as she pushed my mouth between her legs. I found her sex wet, metallic and divine. The woman was definitely attempting to distract me. Her moans became strident and although my office was far from the main hallway, I thought someone might hear. Despite being a little anxious, I couldn't stop myself. I got up and, placing my hands on her hips, turned her around and shoved her against my desk. Her upper body was spread over the desk, making access to her ass and vagina much easier from behind. I thrust my fingers inside her and she moaned lustfully, which should've worried me, but I was as lost as she was. Her skirt bunched up and I bent to bite her naked ass and suck on its flesh until I left a plump red mark shaped like a bee sting on her right cheek. On the left cheek, I bit down hard while thrusting three fingers inside her, then slid out slowly and nibbled until she moaned.

"Maybe we need to stop," I whispered with no intention of stopping.

"Fuck you," she moaned.

"Fuck you," I responded.

"Fuck me, El."

"I will." I unzipped my pants, grateful I had packed that day. I was wearing my favorite sky-blue dildo held snug beneath my blue briefs with a thin black leather harness that was loose around my hips. I pulled on the harness straps to tighten it and the sky-blue dildo popped out erect, brushing against Virginia's ass. I wanted to penetrate her anally but decided to start slow. I leaned against her body and grabbed a handful of her black hair and pulled her head up from the desk to hear her groan. With my other hand, I reached inside a desk drawer and pulled out a condom, then ripped it open with my teeth, making sure not to get any stickiness on my tongue. With the condom carefully placed on the six-inch implement, I spread her vaginal lips with its head and entered, rough and sudden. She gasped. Just as I had wanted. I pushed in further and stronger, my full body leaning into her until I retreated, backing out then inward bound again. I slackened my rhythm.

"Please, Electra. Don't tease, darling."

I grinned. She only called me darling when we were like this. I suppose I still enjoyed hearing her call me darling. Even if she could be a murderer. Measured and precise, I shoved in and thrust, more forceful each time, steadily easing out and as her moans grew more extreme, I grew more aroused. Right then, I didn't care if she was a killer.

I settled into a rhythm that suited us both as the desk beneath us rattled and jiggled until she called out my name at a palpable moment of bliss. I turned her around and covered her mouth with my hand, thrusting inside her again. Her hips heaved up and against mine as she grunted louder beneath my hand. I had always enjoyed Virginia's willingness to have multiple orgasms.

"Kiss me," she mumbled.

I pressed my mouth against hers and she pitched up firmly against my hips, seizing sky-blue in depth and length until all trembling subsided. Fortunately, my eyes were open and I noticed that the hallway light blinked three times. My colleague across the hall and I agreed to warn each other by blinking the hall lights in case the noise in either of our offices grew clamorous or suspicious. I was glad Adrían was in his office, because I needed his assistance.

"I'll be back in a minute." I pulled out slowly, wiped off the dildo with a tissue, loosened the harness straps, tucked sky-blue back into my briefs and zipped my pants.

She pulled down her tight skirt and reached into her black crocodile handbag. I assumed she was going to tidy up and touch up her mauve lipstick. Virginia never minded when I left her alone in my office.

I knocked on Adrían's office and when he opened the door, he hiked up his eyebrows.

"Never too early in the morning, huh, buddy?"

"I need a favor, Adrían."

"Just ask."

"Virginia Johnson is in my office. I need you to escort her through the basement door and to the Admin building without anyone seeing you."

"Consider it done." He winked a sly wink and asked no questions.

I could always rely on him. He was a newly hired assistant professor, but I had known him since he—formerly she—was Andrea. A transguy, Adrían and I had a solid friendship; in fact, he was probably one of my most trusted friends, not something easily achieved in any department at a college or university.

I assumed Virginia had put herself back together but I knocked on the door out of sheer politeness.

"Come in, Electra."

I opened the door and made room for Adrían to follow. Virginia's eyes lit up when she saw him. Adrían dressed in fine suits, designer cotton shirts with cufflinks and bright, vintage ties. His hair was usually slicked back and it gave him that suave, dangerous air that women like Virginia craved.

Poor Coxy, I thought. What was he thinking when he married a woman like Virginia? From an elite family that had lost all its money, she married into power and prestige thinking he would rise higher up the administrators' echelons, but he never ascended above the position of dean. He was, however, from a wealthy family and more recently had amassed more wealth from hedge funds and insider stock exchange tips. Virginia counted his millions like some people count sheep at bedtime. For her, money was the means to power, her chief aphrodisiac, and she was drawn predominantly to powerful men even if she didn't like to fuck them. Women, on the other hand, serviced her regularly and clandestinely. I had been one of the many women in her life happy to accommodate her when I too needed accommodating, and because she was married, we both understood what our thing was: a sexual fling and nothing more.

"Virginia, this is Professor Adrían Fuentes. He's a new assistant professor in the department. He'll take you to the Administration building."

"Professor Fuentes. *Que guapo*."

Adrían blushed.

"Adrían, meet Virginia Johnson, formerly Mendez."

"Is a handsome young man like you old enough to be a college professor?"

She was already mining for a suitor. Damn, the woman was fast.

"I'm thirty-one, ma'am."

"Ma'am? Where did you find this refined young specimen, Electra, and why haven't you introduced me before today?"

"Virginia, your dead husband, remember? Some people might get suspicious. Shouldn't you attempt to feign the grieving widow?"

"Don't be so old-fashioned, Electra. Of course I'm grieving but a woman can admire beauty anytime." She drew nearer to Adrían and wrapped her arm inside his. "*¿Listo?*"

As they walked out of my office, their backs to me, Adrían swiveled his head and with hoisted eyebrows gave me his customary "Damn, she's hot" satisfied, grateful look. I lifted my eyebrows and widened my eyes, suggesting "Yes, she's hot, but in a dangerous sort of way, so be careful." He understood.

Finally, I had a moment to review notes for my history on anarchist movements, which wasn't as popular as my course "Murderous Latinas and the Men Who Marry Them," but the current wave of #Occupy Wall Street had brought me some engaging student protestors.

As I retrieved my notes from my filing cabinet, I noted something irregular. Someone had been rummaging through my files. Folders were out of order and in the back of the filing cabinet, I saw a knife. Not just any knife, but a bloody knife.

CHAPTER THREE

My first impulse was to call Detective Quinn. She would understand that I was being framed. And Adrían was my witness. He knew Virginia had been in my office. Fuck, fuck, fuck. She was up to something. Virginia Johnson was nobody's fool. She probably killed him for his money. I bet he wanted the divorce, not her. Probably fed up with her sexual antics and so he confronted her. She probably tried to lie her way out as usual but this time to no avail. From what I remembered, she had grumbled more than once that he had forced her to sign a prenuptial agreement. A woman like Virginia wasn't going to be left with nothing. She had plenty of motive. I searched in my jacket pocket for Detective Quinn's card hoping I could talk to her before Detective Swift roped off my office. Maybe I could remove the knife. Plant it somewhere else. Why not put it in Sloan's office, I thought. *Electra, don't be stupid. You're getting in deeper. Just tell the truth.* Damn. Now both detectives will suspect my thing with Virginia.

I punched Detective Quinn's number on my cell phone. A recording answered. "This is Detective Carolina Quinn. Please leave a detailed message. I'll return your call as soon as possible." I hung up.

Nice name, Carolina, I thought. And a sexy voice too. Okay, what the fuck was I thinking? I started hyperventilating and my pulse raced. I sat on my desk chair and rested my head between my knees, breathing slowly and deeply, and within seconds, everything went dark.

* * *

"Electra, hey, buddy, wake up."

"Adrían." I was happy to see his glowing face. "What happened?"

"You tell me."

"I guess I fainted." I rubbed my head but felt no bumps. "what time is it?"

"Eleven forty-five."

"Damn. Only fifteen minutes before class." I rubbed my neck, feeling stiffness.

"Hey, you've been gone over an hour. How long was that walk to the Admin building?"

"Well, it wasn't just a walk." He pursed his lips in that way he did to express satisfaction.

"You didn't?"

"She said she'd forgotten something at her house, and the dean's house is practically on campus so I drove her there and, you know, one thing led to another. Damn, she's hot."

"I told you she was dangerous, Adrían."

"No, you didn't."

"Maybe I didn't tell you directly but I gave you the look."

"The look?"

"Yeah, you know, the look." I screwed my eyebrows and contrived concern to demonstrate.

"That's the look?"

"It's our look. Don't you remember? We agreed? The last time?"

He looked puzzled, then lit up. "Oh, yeah, the look. Okay. Right. I get it. I thought that was for emergencies."

"A woman whose husband was just murdered is in my office and you don't think that's an emergency?"

"Not really. And that's not the look you gave me, buddy."

I shook my head. "Wasn't Swift waiting for her?"

"She said she needed to go home first. I took her. We hung out for about thirty minutes then I dropped her off. Just like you said. You're not mad, are you? I didn't think you two were exclusive or anything."

"I don't care about that. She does what she wants, but be careful with Virginia."

"I'm always careful."

"There's something I need you to see. Over here."

I staggered from the floor, still queasy and Adrían, who had been resting on one knee, rose and followed me to the filing cabinet.

"Take a look."

I opened the cabinet and he peered inside.

"Yeah. Kind of messy."

"Look toward the back."

"Okay. Not as messy back there. Looks like you did some fall cleaning, huh?"

"No." I was growing frustrated, which was bizarre, because Adrían usually calmed me. I examined the filing cabinet. Only files. My files. And not a spot of blood in sight.

"I swear there was a knife in there. A bloody knife, Adrían."

"*¿En serio?*"

"When have I ever lied to you?"

"Never, but it's not there anymore, bud."

"This is getting serious. I swear someone is out to get me. Now I feel like I'm being gaslighted."

"Huh?"

"You know, that movie about the woman tricked by her philandering husband, who is after her money. Damn. I can't remember the actress right now. I love her. Nice lips. Was in *Casablanca* with Bogie. Her name starts with a B, I think."

"El, you really want to have this conversation now?"

"I know, I know. Sorry. I'm a little scared, Adrían."

"You wanna call the cops?"

"No. Not yet. I don't know. Maybe I better get to class and then I'll have a better idea about what I need to do."

"You've got five minutes."

"I'm the professor. I can be late."

I grabbed my folder for class and dashed through the main hallway. When I passed the dead white men's club, Sloan peered at me as I rushed by. That man didn't like me, and I believed my role at this institution was to annoy him. I waved and smiled, knowing my gesture would irk him.

"Late to class again, Electra?"

I looked at my watch. It was two minutes before the hour.

"Plenty of time, Sloan." I saluted him as I ran out the main entrance.

Campus was buzzing with the curiosity of the masses and as I forged through a crowd on the quad, there was a parting like the Red Sea, giving me a path, all of which made me very nervous.

"Hey, Professor Campos, how's the dean's wife?"

Startled, I scanned the crowd.

"Oscar, you're late to class."

"On my way, Profe."

"Well, come on. Walk with me." Oscar was the quiet type and infinitely smarter than most of the students on campus.

"Profe, can I ask you something?"

"You just did, Oscar."

"I mean about the murder."

"I don't have any answers about that."

"Students are gossiping. Saying you were nailing the dean's wife and when he found out, he was gonna fire you, so you did him in."

"What?"

It was only five and one-half hours after I had found Coxwell Johnson's limp body, which was now rigor mortis stiff and already false rumors pointed the finger at me.

"Who's saying these things?"

"I dunno. People are talking, Profe."

"And what was your question, Oscar?"

"Did you do it?"

We arrived at our building, and rather than answer, I wobbled my head in disbelief. I expect he thought that was my answer. We climbed the stairs to the second floor and entered the classroom, which was jam-packed today. No absentees. Unusual for this group.

Brisa, la Colombiana, was in her customary seat on the first row and dressed in her customary low-cut blouse. She had the habit of dropping her pen on the floor at the most opportune moments. As soon as I swerved back around from writing on the blackboard, she bent over to pick up her pen and I averted my eyes, making sure I didn't linger on her voluptuous neckline. The guys in class, however, gazed until she sat up and straightened the corners of her floral blouse to obscure her plump breasts.

I had barely begun to open my notes when her hand went up.

"Yes, Brisa."

"What's going on, Profe? Are the cops gonna arrest you for murdering the dean?"

"Okay." I sighed. "Let's deal with this. How many of you have heard about the dean's death?"

Forty-seven hands flew into the air.

"Here's the story. I went to the Admin building early this morning to deliver an application for a much needed sabbatical."

Fuck, I thought, where was my application? I paused and wrote a reminder in my notebook. I looked up and all eyes were on me. I continued.

"Who should I see but Dean Johnson, already dead. I called nine-one-one immediately. The detective in charge questioned me and that's it. Nothing else to report. Now, shall we all bow our heads in silent prayer for the dean?"

All forty-seven students snickered.

"That's settled. Let's move on to our discussion for today. Anarchists."

"Wait a minute." It was Brisa. "I thought we were reading about anarchist women?"

"We'll get to that," I said.

"Why's it always got to be about women for you?" asked Claude. Our Tea Party authority had spoken.

"You got a problem with women, Claude?" asked Brisa.

"Today's lecture will review anarchists, both women and men," I interrupted.

"What about LGBTQ anarchists?" asked Brisa.

"They were all mostly queer anyway," said Liliana. She was an Afro-Latina, five years younger than the rest of the students, and exceptionally brainy. She not only read everything assigned but often read the suggestions in the bibliography. She was my star student.

"Why does everybody have to be queer these days? Isn't anybody normal anymore?" asked Claude.

"Shut up, Claude," said Brisa.

"You shut up, drug trafficking girl."

"Oh no he didn't," said Liliana.

Brisa rose from her seat and stood in front of Claude. "You shut the fuck up, lame white boy."

"Ooooh," forty-five students chimed in unison.

He sank down in his seat and snickered.

"Brisa, your seat. Please," I said.

She returned to it quietly and glared at me.

"Everyone's a little touchy. Let's try to cool it." I paused. "Who didn't finish reading the *Sacco and Vanzetti* by Topp?" It was time to distract them with course material.

About ten hands went up, unabashedly. Thirty-five students dodged my gaze. That left two who had done the reading:Liliana and Brisa.

"We have twelve honest people in the room," I said.

They chuckled, but only in the way students chuckle when they want extra credit.

"Those of you who read the documents, can you tell me who these men were and why they are important to study today?"

Only one hand went up. It was Brisa again. I waited for a brief second, hoping another hand would save me, but when no one else volunteered, I called on her. "Yes, Brisa."

"I think these guys were cool. I mean, they were anarchists and everything. Too bad they got caught though. That wasn't so cool."

"The anarchists from the early twentieth century would agree with you, Brisa. Any other opinions?"

"I thought they didn't do it," said Rufus. "I thought that was the whole point of the thing. That they didn't do it and they got lynched anyway."

Rufus was Irish Catholic, blond and skinny. He wore thick eyeglasses. Probably from all his time in front of a computer screen playing video games.

"They weren't lynched," said Liliana. "They were electrocuted. In an electric chair. It marked the beginning of industrialization's modern killing machines."

"Whatever," said Rufus.

"Let's look at page thirty-two," I said. "How about the fact that they were misidentified? That they were nowhere near the place that was robbed? They weren't murderers either."

"Don't matter. They were framed by the feds," said Omar.

Omar was Dominican and disillusioned. He only came to class because his mother told him he'd have to move out if he didn't finish his BA. Omar worked at the nearby Starbucks at night and early in the morning before classes in a college parking garage. Maybe he saw the dean arrive early on campus. Maybe he saw who killed the dean. I needed to speak to him.

"So what? The feds were doing their job," said Rufus.

"Their job? They were innocent Italian guys who came to the land of opportunity to bust their balls making shoes for the man. And then they get accused of something they didn't do."

I was pleased to see Omar taking an interest.

"They were guilty Italians who didn't even believe in the American Constitution," said Rufus.

I intervened. "Well, they were part of the massive influx of immigrants from southern and eastern Europe, many of whom believed in anarcho-syndicalism. Does that mean they were guilty? For believing in a system that didn't exploit workers but rather allowed for communal ownership of their goods?"

"They were fucking communists, man. That's why they did it," said Claude.

"Communists and anarchists are not the same thing," said Liliana. "Am I the only one who did the reading? Look on page three. Anarchists believed in local, political control. Not some far away government telling them what to do, but a local one determined by their own community."

"Yeah, a community of communists," said Rufus.

Everyone laughed and Liliana also snickered and shrugged.

"Liliana is right," I declared. "Anarchists are not and were not communists, nor were they out to destroy government in the way you might imagine, nor did they believe in anarchy as a state of being. They did believe in local, community control through local, community decisions. The anarcho-syndicalists struggled to have their own trade unions to protect themselves in case they were injured and lost wages. Back in 1922, the capitalist robber barons like the Rockefellers, the Dohenys, the Carnegies and the Fricks didn't have workers' interests in mind. They revered profits, not people. The almighty dollar was their god. So next time you go to Rockefeller Center, Carnegie Hall or the Frick Museum, look around at the wealth, the riches, all put there with blood. The blood of workers who died so you could go skating at Rockefeller Center, or go to a jazz concert at Carnegie Hall or visit the Frick on a rainy afternoon."

Claude and Rufus rolled their eyes.

"Which reminds me, last week one half of you were absent while you occupied Wall Street. And today, you're all here. Why aren't any of you occupying today? Have you lost all faith?"

"Didn't you hear what the dean said?" It was Oscar who had been quiet up to now.

"Which dean?"

"The dead dean, Profe. He went to the Occupy site last week and he warned a bunch of us. Said he'd be sure we'd get expelled if we kept going back."

"He can't do that, Oscar," I said.

"Well, he said he could and we believed him."

"The dean's daddy was a big man at Golden Sachs," said Omar.

I didn't react to his sarcastic twist on the name of the Wall Street behemoth. "How do you know?" I asked.

"Oscar told me."

The students smirked.

"Oscar, how do you know?"

"My mom cleans houses. She used to clean the dean's house and the dean's dad's house too. On the Upper East Side."

I made a mental note of the information I'd learned and opted to end class early. Gradually, I was grasping that the dean had many more enemies than any of us had ever suspected. I had to talk to Detective Quinn and I especially had to find out what the fuck had happened to the knife in my file drawer. Not that I wanted it back in my cabinet, but I wanted to prove to myself I wasn't deranged. Twice in one morning, I had seen phantoms. First, a freckled-skinned ex-lover and then a bloody knife?

"Okay, folks. I'm going to let you go a bit early today, given the circumstances on campus."

"Five minutes isn't early," said Rufus.

"You need help finding who did it, Profe?"

"Let's let the police do their job, Brisa."

"Yeah, but you don't trust those cops, do you?"

"They aren't all bad." I was, of course, reflecting on Detective Quinn.

"Yeah, they ain't all bad. Did you see the Latina in leather? Damn. She ain't bad at all," said Omar.

"I'm touched by your concern, Brisa, but I can take care of myself. For our next class, let's discuss women anarchists."

Rufus and Claude exchanged the look of besieged comrades.

"Class dismissed."

CHAPTER FOUR

Students scurried out of the classroom and I erased my scribbles on the chalkboard. I was old-fashioned and used a chalkboard instead of PowerPoint presentations or clickers that computed one's answers via computer. Chalkboards gave me an opportunity to be spontaneous. My lectures bored me and if they bored me, I thought they were bound to bore my students.

"Hey Profe."

Brisa had waited until only she and I remained in the classroom.

"Brisa, *¿qué tal?*" I crammed my notes and books into my leather book bag.

"Are you going to Mamacita's tonight?"

"No, not tonight."

She pouted a sexy expression that compelled me to resist grabbing her around the waist and laying one on her, tongue and all. I endured.

"Too bad," she said.

"Can I ask you a favor?"

She ogled me as she touched the neckline of her blouse. Her breasts popped out as she took a deep breath, a sigh of sorts. "Yes, Profe. Anything for you."

"Well, it's like this. I'd prefer it if you didn't mention Mamacita's in class."

"But it's not in class. It's after class."

"I realize that. What I mean is—"

"Don't mention it at all, right?"

I nodded.

"I get it, I get it," she said. She tapped her forehead with a forefinger. "*No soy pendeja.*"

"You're anything but stupid, Brisa."

She grinned and sauntered out of the classroom, and I swear she was shaking her hips more than usual. Again, I resisted. I did my best not to commiserate with students, particulary after I had a snag with a particular one who wanted to have coffee with me and broke into my office and set my garbage can on fire after I refused. I had suspected she was unbalanced, since I had an instinct about students with potential for stalking. Most were just lonely and wanted a friend or counselor but every now and then an unstable one showed up and created disruption. In this case, enough smoke had entered the hallway to cause a raucous among my colleagues, leaving me to explain that a student must have committed the prank because she was displeased with her grade. I didn't think the poor kid needed to be disciplined. She'd just wanted attention.

After that I was careful. I never allowed any student to sit in my office for longer than twenty minutes at a time. Hence the reason for asking Brisa to avoid any mention of places outside of campus where she might have seen me. Especially not a queer bar. It's not that she was immature or stalking me. Not Brisa. Brisa was mature beyond her years and freely dictated her own desires. Brisa didn't have to stalk anyone. She was too self-assured for that. Nonetheless, I never knew who might be nearby, listening to my conversations and ready to report favoritism—that I favored the queer students and gave them better grades. Or that I favored the students of color and gave them better grades. Or that I favored all women and gave them better grades. Or finally, that I favored young white men who read Foucault or Marvel comics in their spare time. Inevitably, disgruntled students made their presence known. Since the garbage can incident, I'd kept my distance from anyone bearing gifts or baring breasts.

As I left the classroom, I ran into Detective Quinn roaming the hallway. She wore her signature knee-high leather boots and a tight black leather skirt with a loose silk white blouse that probably accentuated her breasts beneath her red leather jacket.

"You didn't leave a message," she said.

"I meant to."

"Here." She handed me the manila envelope with my application for sabbatical. "I thought you would want this."

"Isn't this evidence?"

"Why? Does it have the murder weapon inside?"

"No, no, you can look inside to see for yourself." Frantic, I handed her the envelope.

She grinned. "I'm joking, Professor. We looked inside and noted that you were at the crime scene. We don't need an envelope to prove that."

"Oh. Okay." Her matter-of-fact tone and information made me feel a bit deflated.

"Why didn't you leave a message, Professor?"

"Call me Electra, Carolina." I spoke her name deliberately.

"Why the hesitation?"

"What hesitation?"

"In my line of work, when someone calls and hangs up, she's holding back."

"Holding back?"

"Yes. Holding back."

"And what is this phantom caller holding back?"

"You tell me."

I decided to be serious. "Something came up in my office. Something inexplicable. I wasn't sure if I wanted to report it."

"Because it's incriminating?"

"How did you know?"

"Lucky guess. Or could it be that I've been a detective a little over a few days."

"Really? Fresh at it?"

"So fresh, you couldn't imagine."

Was she flirting? Damn. I was off my game.

"You're still rattled, aren't you?"

"Strange things are occurring and fingers point at me."

"Care to be more specific?"

"Can we speak privately? In my office? I can show you."

She looked at her watch. "Fine. I have a few minutes before I have to report to Swift."

"He's a real winner," I said. I was attempting to gauge her relationship with him.

We walked through the hallways until we reached the front door. Claude and Rufus, my less than upright students, stared but I ignored them.

"He's obnoxious," Quinn said, referring to Swift. "At first. But overall, a good detective. I've learned a few things from him."

"That's reassuring. He seems like a nitwit. No offense."

"You're referring to his bumbling Detective Columbo act? It fools some people."

"The young ones who never watched the TV show maybe."

"You'd be surprised. Most people assume cops are inherently idiots."

She stared at me accusingly.

"Not me," I said. "I have absolute respect for New York's finest."

We reached my office building and saw Sloan, leader of the dead white men's club, roving the hallway. He seemed more interested in my comings and goings than usual.

"Top of the morning to you, Sloan." I tipped my head, tapping an imaginary top hat.

He glared at me. "Good afternoon, Electra."

I refused to introduce Sloan to Detective Quinn and preferred to keep him guessing since he had nothing better to do with his life than indulge in speculation about mine. He followed closely behind us as Carolina and I climbed the stairs to the second floor.

"I thought you'd like it because it was bigger than the last one. Plus, you said you wanted dark brown," said Carolina.

"Huh?" I answered, confused.

"I got the dark brown one for you."

"What are you..." I trailed off when I saw a glint in her eye.

Sloan walked closer than necessary.

"You just didn't seem as excited last night. I'm a little disappointed," she said.

"Oh, well, I guess I need more practice," I said.

I stopped at my office door. Sloan raced past, face flushed. I was about to kiss Carolina's neck, thinking I'd seize the moment, when my office door squeaked open on its own.

"Now what?" I said.

I flung open the door and saw Adrían sitting on the small couch in the back of the office.

He scrambled up so fast he nearly tripped.

"Detective Quinn," he uttered.

"Professor Fuentes," she said.

"You've met?"

"He dropped off the dean's wife this morning. What was her name again?" She peered at me.

"Virginia," I said. "Her maiden name is Mendez, Virginia Mendez. I'm assuming she's a prime suspect?"

"Why would you assume that?"

"His millions. Don't you people go after money as motive?"

"I don't know what you mean by 'you people' but sometimes the money angle can lead us to the murderer."

"Virginia, a murderer? Can't be," said Adrían.

"Adrían is smitten," I said.

"Yes, I could see that this morning," she replied.

Adrían blushed, as he was prone to do, and said, "I mean, doesn't she already have her own money? That's what she told me. She doesn't need his."

"*Ay*, Adrían, Adrían," I sighed. "I love how preciously naïve you can be."

"We haven't taken her into custody, but don't worry," Quinn said, addressing me. "We're keeping an eye on both of you."

"Why me?"

"You were both the last ones to see him alive."

"You're welcome to come inside for *café con leche*, Detective. No need to sit outside all alone while you watch us."

"We won't be tailing you, if that's what you mean."

"Tailing me? Hmm. I kind of like the sound of that. Don't you, Adrían?"

"I like to be tailed," said Adrían. "But only by someone I know intimately."

"Okay, I can see the two of you are a team."

"Well?" Carolina Quinn gazed at her watch then up at me. "You had something to show me?"

"Yeah. Okay, come here and look."

I opened my filing cabinet and explained the phantom bloody knife.

"You're saying first it was here, then it was gone?"

"Exactly."

"And between the here and gone, you fainted?"

"Exactly. You're very good at detecting, Detective."

She raised an eyebrow, seemingly exasperated. "How long were you out?"

"I don't know. Maybe an hour."

"Did you have breakfast this morning?" asked Adrían. "You know how your blood sugar drops, bud."

"I had my usual buttered toast with espresso, Adrían. Don't be such a *papí*."

"He's right, you know. It's no wonder you fainted."

"Fine. Tomorrow, I promise to eat a scrambled egg. Can we get back to the bloody knife disappearing act?"

"I thought it was obvious," she said. "Someone is trying to gaslight you."

"You know that film? I love that film," I said.

"Of course I know that film. Who doesn't?" Quinn paused and searched through the file cabinet. "In any case, let me say it's good the knife disappeared. For now. Don't worry about it so much unless it reappears. I think someone who has access to your office is playing a trick on you, Electra. Maybe a colleague who doesn't like you? Or a disgruntled student? Who knows. Of course, we're not taking this lightly. I have to report the incident."

"You're reporting it? I didn't want you to report it. I just wanted your advice."

"I have to report it. It's my job. And my job is to protect you."

"You make that sound so alluring, Detective Quinn."

Her smile, lips upturned and fleshy, made my heart leap.

"Like I said, it's my job."

CHAPTER FIVE

After Detective Quinn left my office, Adrían insisted on lunch. Our chosen hole in the wall was a tapas bar a short block from the college. Adrían ordered sangria and I didn't object since we had already taught our classes and I thought I deserved to get drunk after the morning's events. We held up our full cups and toasted another day of survival far from our homes.

"You still miss *Tejas?*" he asked.

"You still miss Cali?" I asked.

And then we drank. Adrían ordered *papas bravas* knowing if I ate nothing else I would surely devour the Spanish potatoes that I could eat daily if and when available. I guzzled the last of the sangria and broached our established topic of conversation. Women. Adrían and I indulged each other in collegiate rituals like overzealous drinking while venerating all types of women. We had comparable predilections, as demonstrated this morning with Virginia, and that he denied a propensity for blondes made him easy to mock.

"You're mimicking the typical American male who loves blondes, Adrían."

"I'm not typical. And the only blonde I like is Marilyn Monroe. Mid-century is my era."

"She wasn't real, bud," I said. "She was the nation's imaginary sex symbol. A construction. Fabricated and imagined. She herself breathed life into that precarious Hollywood image and she was nobody's dummy. In that sense, Marilyn is alive and well. Right here and right now in the streets of New York City and in the backrooms of Hollywood where every bald agent with a hard-on is still trying to find her in some kid from the farms of Iowa. And it ain't gonna happen, Adrían. You know why?"

"Don't want to know."

"Well. I'll tell you. Because the nation is no longer blond. Look around you, Adrían. The face of the nation. It's becoming browner and browner. I ran into a Mayan Indian on the subway last week. A Mayan. Don't you stop to ask yourself, what the heck is a Mayan Indian doing on the subway in New York City?"

"Same as the rest of us. Going to work."

"To do what? Wash dishes?"

"Nothing wrong with that."

"So long as you don't have to do it."

"Like you do?"

"Ha. Anyway, that's not my point. My point is, forget blond. Blond is becoming brown. Brown is the new blond. In the twenty-first century, brown is the new blond."

"So you're saying now we have the dumb brunette stereotype. Some progress."

Our banter had purpose. As we debated the obvious—well, obvious to us anyway—we wanted to reassure each other. We both taught history and we both feared the same thing: our students didn't watch the world around them for clues and codes; they didn't observe their world with the kind of insight they needed for a future that was about to rob the young yet again. Many were aware of AIDS and some believed they'd been robbed of sexual promiscuity. A few were beginning to think beyond the limits of the crazy world they'd inherited. I placed my bets on those who saw the codes all around them. These were not hallucinations. Mayans on the subway were not a hallucination. Mexicans and the Indigenous from Central America and the South American continent had come this far north in the twenty-first century. Trekking through villages of mud huts, through urban dreams and suburban nightmares to arrive at a bigger village. The biggest of them all, the most notorious of them all: New York, New York.

"Hey, buddy, before you start your next lecture, can I ask you something?"

"You just did."

Adrían glared at me. "I hate when you answer like that. It's sophomoric."

"It's not sophomoric, Adrían. It's precise. I want my students to think about how they frame their language."

"I'm not your student, El."

"Yeah, yeah. What's your question?"

"Do you think Virginia did it?"

"Kill her husband? I don't know."

"Could she have planted the knife?"

"I thought she had, but after it disappeared, I wasn't sure anymore."

"Yeah, it kinda doesn't make sense, huh?"

"Yeah, it doesn't. You were with her the whole time, weren't you?"

"Yeah, I was."

"She had enough time to place the knife in my file cabinet when I went to your office. All she needed was a few minutes. But if she was with you, she couldn't have returned while I was passed out."

"Not to mention that she would've counted on you not being in your office."

"Well, that's not so hard. I do leave my office to go pick up my mail in the main department office way over on the first floor. Someone who knows my routine knew I'd be gone long enough. But they weren't planning on me being passed out."

"Maybe they didn't see you. You were lying behind your desk."

"You saw me."

"Yeah, but I was looking for you."

"Yeah, thanks, bud."

"Was your office door locked?"

"I thought so. Did you unlock it?"

"No."

"It's easy enough to pick open. And these old buildings, who knows who has keys to the offices. I'm sure the locks haven't been changed in decades."

"More like a century."

I signaled to the slim-hipped thirty-something waitress who was accustomed to seeing Adrían and me in the bar at least twice weekly. Mariana weaved seductively through tiny crevices between tiny tables with another pitcher of sangria. She had a short bobbed haircut that danced against the flesh of her neck when she bustled through the restaurant. From Spain, she and her brother ran the tapas bar they'd inherited from a deceased uncle.

"Which one of you bumped off the dean?" she asked.

"Not funny, Mariana. El found him early this morning."

I raised my glass to acknowledge her sudden discomfort and surprise.

"Sorry, El. I was joking." She poured quickly and neatly. Not a drop spilled on the dingy tablecloth.

"I heard the wife did it," she said. She tossed her head back in the way women with long hair toss their mane, leading me to believe she hadn't adapted to her short bob.

"Where'd you hear that?" asked Adrían.

He liked Mariana particularly because she had a boyfriend. Adrían, like me, preferred challenges and women with men were exactly the challenge neither of us could resist.

"Oh, you know, the usual. Some kids came in here and I heard them talking. They seemed convinced his wife did it. They also said that the rumors about you and his wife were probably true but they couldn't believe you were a murderer.

Promise me you'll let me know how this turns out. This is better than my *telenovelas*."

She left our table and dashed off to other customers. The place was miniature and could get packed in the early afternoon, which was lunchtime for the Spanish and anyone else abiding by those hours.

"That's comforting," I told Adrían. "They believe I'm a womanizer but not a murderer."

"Yeah. You're a lover, not a fighter," said Adrían.

"Well, I don't think the police know that."

"Maybe you need to prove it to them." Adrían boosted both eyebrows and I knew what he was suggesting.

"I'm way ahead of you."

"Oh, yeah? When?"

"Not sure yet, but I have her number."

"Seems to me you better start charming her soon."

"It's not like that. She's too smart to fall for charm."

"All women are too smart to fall for charm, El. That's not the point."

"What's the point?"

"That a woman likes to be charmed. And if you mean it, she'll like it more."

"Yeah, well. She's out of my league anyway."

"No woman is out of your league, buddy."

"Oh, I'm not deceiving myself with that charming statement. Plenty of women have been out of my league and she's another one."

"You always say that when you really like someone. That she's out of your league. You're avoiding."

"Avoiding? Avoiding what?"

"A meaningful relationship."

I coughed and spat some of my sangria. "A meaningful relationship? What are you talking about? Are you trying to choke me?"

"You're a romantic. Just like me. We both want meaningful relationships with that perfect woman who will love us no matter what."

"Yeah, well, you keep believing in that fantasy. I've had more than one of those meaningful relationships, and now at my age, I'm lucky to find meaning in my daily horoscope."

He shrugged off my cynicism. "You don't fool me. I know you're still looking for the woman of your dreams, the love of your life."

"That's where you're wrong. I've had many loves of my life and I appreciated each one, especially as she was walking out the door."

"You can't fool me." Adrían peeked at me over the broad black rims of fashionable eyeglasses. He had a way of speaking truths I trusted.

"Come on. It's already five. I've got to get home to build up the courage I need to call a certain detective."

"That's how I like to hear my buddy talking."

CHAPTER SIX

We left the tapas bar, walking in opposite directions. Adrían said he had to return to the office to pick up some folders with student papers. The difference between a junior faculty member and an old professor like me was that the junior would be conscientious and return for papers that needed grading. An old, whacked out professor like myself would delay the grading another week, especially because I had a belly full of sangria.

I headed toward my subway stop and despite the swarm of people I spotted her easily. Cinnamon-freckled-ex-lover was feasting on lemon rinds, lounging on a bench, having spread books, magazines and the *New York Times* all over it oblivious to the tired working people who needed to sit. Three months had passed since our fucked-up vacation and I had no desire to see her again, especially after her little announcement at the Down Under about driving a blade in my back. But there she sat all scrawny and tight-assed. She glanced at me as I moved closer, and sucked on lemon rinds as she tore through magazines. As the rinds curled in her mouth, she bit into the white mesh and then nibbled through to the yellow peel, sucking until she swallowed the entire shell. Never once did she pucker her lips from the bitter flavor. I had turned my back to her, having given up on sitting on her bench, when she said, "Angelina and Brad, what do you think?"

She kicked me, not a hard kick but a gentle, almost tender touch to my ankle.

"Angelina and Brad? What do you think?" She gazed up at me and I was satisfied I hadn't softened from the warmth of her coffee-colored eyes, although traces of our nights reemerged between us and I remembered how I had relished her freckled skin, so patchy and odd. I fought an ache in my fingers to graze her buttocks.

"What?" I asked, distracted.

"Do you think they'll last?"

"Who?"

"Angelina Jolie and Brad Pitt. If he stepped out before, won't he step out again?"

I shook my head.

She crossed her legs and tossed books from the bench and pointed for me to sit next to her. I tried not to step on *Das Kapital*, pushed it aside with my foot and used Adam Smith's *Wealth of Nations* for a footrest. She looked down and smiled. I was caught off guard. Closer to her face now, I could smell her tangy lemon breath.

"What are you doing here?" I asked.

She reached for a plastic sandwich bag filled with finely trimmed lemon rinds, all the same size, probably half an inch long and a quarter of an inch wide, offering the yellow shells to me as if she had offered me chocolate candy. I took one and put it in my jacket pocket.

"I don't think he's Angelina's type. I think he's too sweet and she's feral and fierce," she said.

I shook my head again and thought that human trafficking was on the rise, wars and global inhumanities persisted, detention centers all over the nation continued unconstitutional abuses, AIDS-related deaths had not subsided, #Occupy Wall

Street gathered and lost momentum—and she read meaningless gossip. I remembered one more of many reasons I didn't want to see her again.

She tossed auburn tresses that graced her shoulders and adorned her back then placed her hand on my arm. I felt a jolt in my stomach. Not a big jolt, more of a nudge, a warning.

"Look at this. Another dead white man in the headlines."

I inched closer and read over her shoulder, "Shakespeare in the Park! Yeah, I guess he's pretty dead." I said.

"I mean this." She pointed to a caption with a photograph of the erstwhile dean.

"Isn't he your dean?"

"Was. Was my dean. Is no more."

Unexpectedly, the thought of Isabel Cortez in the Admin building at six thirty a.m. overwhelmed my gut so brutally that our vacation felt more like a prayer meeting instead of Barnum & Bailey purgatory. Was she following me? Was she capable of murder?

She flung the magazine to the ground. Angelina Jolie's face landed on top of Heidegger. Crossing her legs again, Isabel positioned her right leg over her left with her back to me.

"What are you doing here?" I asked again.

"I live here. You know that."

"It's a big city. I've never seen you at my stop."

"Don't flatter yourself. I have a night class."

"Ah. These all your books?"

She nodded and looked toward the railway.

"What's the class?"

The A train squealed into the station. She gathered her books and pitched the rest of the magazines onto the cement floor, splattering a puddle of coffee. She jumped over the puddle and dashed through the subway doors. The lemon rinds on the bench shimmered bright yellow. I grabbed the bag, ran into the subway and followed the outline of her curls as she squeezed between two teen boys hugging skateboards. She saw me, smiled and said, "Yes."

"Yes?" I asked.

"Yes, I'll see you later tonight."

"Where?"

"At the Met."

"The museum or the opera?"

"*Carmen.* The second act. Look for me inside. In the lobby. Next to the red Chagall."

"You forgot these." I handed her the baggie filled with the yellow worm-like rinds.

"Keep them. I have more." She pulled out a large freezer bag filled with coiled lemon.

The subway train stopped and she snatched her book bag, rushed to the doors, flipped her auburn-haired mane and said, "Don't be late. The beginning of the second act."

On my train I swayed in the subway aisle, leaning against the doors, and popped a piece of lemon rind in my mouth, savoring the bitter aftertaste. At my stop, I strolled up the stairs and to my apartment in the Heights.

What was I thinking? I guess I wanted to see her again to prove to myself I was done, but mostly, the vision of Isabel Cortez creeping in the building at six thirty was gnawing at my belly.

CHAPTER SEVEN

I showered and dressed in a black wool suit with a wrinkled white shirt underneath. If I kept my jacket on I wouldn't have to worry about being seen in a wrinkled faux tuxedo shirt. At least the cuffs were clean and my cufflinks sparkled. The cufflinks were onyx pyramids with a red garnet at the crest. The garnet represented the blood sacrificed at the summit of Chichen Itza in Yucatán. For me Chichen Itza was sacred. I had bought my cufflinks on a research trip to the Yucatán Peninsula when I was conducting research for my dissertation on Mayan pictographs of the female anatomy. Like so many North Americans, I too idealized and idolized Mayan myths. It was as if I had a past life in Chichen Itza or Tulum and that a better life had been possible then. The cufflinks were my good luck totem. I wore them when I felt confident about a woman, and tonight I felt poised to kiss those lips again regardless of the overpowering impulse to run away as fast as I possibly could.

My cat, Mocha, watched me as I brushed my teeth and manipulated my hair with an assortment of gels and creams.

I let the cold water run and she stepped daintily on the sink, lapping the running water with her pink tongue. Mocha was chocolate brown with crossed blue eyes and medium length fur that glued to my black clothes.

I fed Mocha her evening treat, a spoonful of tuna, then sprinted out of the apartment and caught the A train to Columbus Circle, where I darted out and up the avenue until I faced Lincoln Center. Opera season was in full swing. I had always promised myself that one day I'd buy season tickets, but the only season tickets I could afford were to The Pearl Company Theatre in Midtown, where they staged good performances of *Oedipus Rex*, *Electra*, or *The Oresteia*. Greek tragedy was in my blood.

I strolled to the fountain and saw tourists taking photos of each other. When the lobby filled with elegant black suits and dresses, I realized intermission had been called. I stood in front of the ticket window and asked for a ticket to the cheap seats in the balcony. The attendant handed me a rectangular receipt and without examining the printed title, I skimmed for the location of my seat, pocketed the ticket and sauntered over to the Chagall painting, but still didn't see Isabel Cortez. The chimes alerted aficionados to return to their seats. I walked up the flights and found my empty seat next to a woman who looked like somebody's mother. An attractive mother too.

"Are you a Goethe fan?" she asked.

"As much as the next person," I said.

She winked and I thought for a second, *I do believe she's flirting*. A gentleman sat beside her and handed her a packet of peanut M&M's. She ripped open the bag and leaned toward me.

"Have one. Or more if you'd like."

She winked again. Her male partner studied the program.

"I love these," I said.

"Nothing like M&M's for the body and Goethe for the soul," she said.

"I haven't read *Faust* in a long time."

"You're about to have a refresher." She offered me more candy.

I was perplexed by her comment until the curtains opened

and instead of the set to *Carmen*, I saw the backdrop for *Faust*.

"Where's *Carmen?*"

She looked at me quizzically.

"I thought *Carmen* was the opera for the evening."

"You didn't see the posters outside? The advertisements?"

She was whispering in my ear and her breath smelled like sugar and peanuts. I felt her tongue graze my ear and the tingle was peanut butter erotic. I didn't know how to react and pretended she had done nothing out of the ordinary.

"I saw a lot of advertisements for a lot of operas."

"And you didn't see the one for tonight?"

"All I know is that a friend told me to meet her here for *Carmen*," I whispered.

"And she sent you to see *Faust*? Cunning friend." She winked again.

As I rose from my seat, she placed her hand on my thigh and drew me down. "Stay," she sighed. "The final scene is worth your while. When the shower of white snowflakes fall, it's pure bliss."

Her saccharine breath tickled my ear. Without warning, she snatched my hand and pushed it beneath the silk wrap on her lap and shoved my fingers inside her soft flesh. The sensual charge probably turned my face crimson. Nervous, I glanced across to her male companion, who had no clue what was transpiring because his eyes were closed, his chin rested on his collarbone and he breathed a quiet snore. My hand rested inside her for almost the entire second act. When she began to gyrate rhythmically, I pushed into wet lips that I personally would've preferred to have in my mouth but settled for fingers inside moist vaginal walls as I witnessed her face contort with eyes slit half-open. I moved my fingers in and out as my thumb fondled her clit, which seemed fleshier than most, and with that knowledge I wanted to drop to my knees and take her in my mouth, male companion or no male companion, and anyway, he was asleep. But I abstained, and sustained a moderate pace of shoving in and out while fondling her plump clit until her ass gripped firm and my wrist ached. I didn't want to disrupt her contentment so I waited until her ass's muscles relaxed again but as the seconds passed, her eyes blinked shut, my wrist hurt more and her male companion began to stir. Fuck, I thought. Ten more seconds and we might get caught. She continued to grip harder down into my wrist and this time no matter how much I tried to pull out, her ass clamped down.

"Ouch," I whispered.

In a flash, thousands of vivid, white snowflakes fell from the ceiling onto the stage floor and she opened her eyes and released me. My hand, now mine again, recovered sensation and overall, I had to agree that the finale had been well worth my while. I rose to my feet before the first curtain call, smiled at my evening's companion, thanked her for the candy and skipped down the red-carpeted stairs and out the front doors.

Annoyed that I had been stood up, I took the train in the direction opposite my apartment for a drink at a queer bar in Chelsea. Nothing like sweaty, youthful and not-so-youthful bodies on the dance floor to cure loneliness and frustration. But no such luck, no cure for me. I was lonely, frustrated and pissed because I hadn't seen Isabel.

She was back to playing games, her forte. A master at schemes, especially while accusing me of dramatic ploys, she pushed and pushed until the pushing took me to the edge of a precipice and hurtling into an abyss was far preferable to stumbling into her. What the fuck was I thinking? Why did I think I wanted to see her again? My life was being threatened and I was concerned with a woman who did nothing but threaten my life? Time to go home, El. That was when I thought I spotted her in a corner locking thin lips with a guy. Of course. So like you to be distracted by a man. Fuck you, I thought. Fuck you, Isabel. I didn't investigate further.

I ran to the bathroom and slammed open the door, bumping it against a woman who dabbed her lips with a tissue. In the mirror, her dark brown eyes glimmered at me and she didn't seem bothered that we were in close proximity. I took the initiative and inched closer when I reached for a paper towel. My hands weren't even wet. She pressed her green and black dress against me and I felt the front zipper brush against my arm. She didn't have to do that twice.

I locked the bathroom door, took her hand and led us into the stall. Her shoulder-length brown hair framed her face and her breath on my lips was warm. Leisurely, I unzipped her dress, reached beneath the open skirt and pulled down a black and red lacy thong, pushed her onto the seat of the toilet, giving me complete access to her naked vaginal lips. I sank to my knees, kissing her delicately at first, tickling her clit with my tongue. I lapped up her juices and licked as long as she allowed, firm and tenacious until her ass stiffened on the seat and she moaned loudly. Her hands caressed my head and tugged my hair gently.

I retrieved her thong from my coat pocket, placing each leg through, pulled the thong up to her waist and zipped her dress. I rose from my knees regretful that I hadn't kept the lacy underwear. We hadn't said a word to each other, and I was glad she wasn't one to have to know my name or volunteer hers. I walked out of the bathroom into the late night air and felt like I could breathe again.

"Fuck you, Isabel," I said.

A homeless guy on the corner heard me and yelled out an echoing, "Fuck you, Isabel," and all I could do was agree.

CHAPTER EIGHT

Back in my apartment, I brushed my teeth and ran the faucet for Mocha, who dipped her paw beneath the water and splattered the sink. It was well past midnight and I bit my nails while processing the morning's events. Was I going to be accused of murder? Was it too late to call Detective Quinn? Maybe she could reassure me. Or not. My phone buzzed a not so silent buzz. It was a text message from the Detective.

"Can u meet *mañana*?"

Nice, I thought, she sends bilingual text messages.

"*Sí*," I responded.

"*Ke bien*. Will drop by office. Ten a.m."

"Will be waiting."

An impulse to phone her overcame me even though I wasn't sure what I would say. She was coming to my office in the morning and I didn't want to appear too eager. Oh, fuck. I'm calling. I tapped in her number and she answered immediately.

"Professor Campos, I'm surprised you didn't hang up this time."

"Why would I hang up?"

"Earlier. You hung up."

"Is it a hang up if no one is on the other line, Detective?"

"Carolina. Call me Carolina."

"Call me Electra."

"Okay, Electra. Something I can help you with at this midnight hour? Have you found more bloody knives?"

"Should you be making jokes about a murder?"

"No. Sorry. I was teasing. I didn't think he meant that much to you."

"Fact is the guy was unpopular."

"So we've gathered."

"Oh, really? From whom?"

"Staff, students, other faculty. His family. No one really liked him; they just put up with him. Seems he was on his way out as dean."

"He was? Nobody told me that. But then again, I'm not that popular on campus either."

"That's not what I heard."

"Oh. What did you hear?"

"That a certain history professor is quite popular among a certain population."

"I'm not going to pursue that. Sounds like trite gossip to me."

"Trite gossip is what we detectives thrive on."

"So that's why you love your job."

"I love my job because I love to catch the bad guy."

"I'm not the bad guy."

"I know that. But others may not know that."

"Does that mean I'm a suspect?"

"Is that why you're calling? To get me to talk? I'm not easily swayed, Professor."

"No, I didn't call to get you to talk. I called because I wondered if you'd have coffee with me sometime."

"Actually, I would. Tomorrow morning at ten. Remember?"

"Oh. Yeah. But I thought that was official business."

"And you wanted to meet on unofficial business?"

"Sure, I mean, I wondered…"

"Not while I'm on your case, Electra. My boss, the Lieutenant, he's a stickler for rules."

"He wouldn't have to know."

"I don't operate that way. I'm honest to a fault. Sorry to disappoint you."

"This isn't even 'my case.' Just because it happened on my campus doesn't make it 'my case.'"

"It's your case as long as you're a suspect, Professor."

"So it's Professor now, is it? Okay. I get it, Detective. I'll see you in the morning. On official business."

"Now you're annoyed. Do you always get annoyed when you don't get your way?"

"Yeah. Don't you?"

"Yeah, I do."

"Good to talk, Detective. See you in the morning."

"'Night."

That hadn't gone the way I planned and now I was jumpier than before. She knew something she wasn't telling me. And since when were the police not corrupt? As far as I knew, she was pretending to be an honest cop so she wouldn't have to deal with me outside of "official business." Fine. I can take a hint, Detective Quinn. I grabbed my pillow, reversed it to the cool side, lay my head down waiting to fall asleep. I tossed and turned for nearly an hour before I dozed off.

My alarm rang and I woke fatigued, having barely slept three hours. Insomnia was common for me but last night I'd felt too much on the edge of wakefulness. I hated that feeling. Overbearing consciousness that doesn't let you fall into REM slumber sucks.

I stumbled to the kitchen and turned on the espresso machine to heat the water for my daily four shots, dropped gluten-free bread into the toaster and hopped in the shower. I dressed quickly in my usual jeans, black leather boots, black T-shirt and black sports coat. I checked the weather on my smartphone and saw the temperature was going to drop before I headed home from classes. I grabbed my black wool peacoat and, after gulping the espresso shots and buttered toast, off I went. I loved espresso. Without it I couldn't survive the streets of New York City. Without it I couldn't survive consciousness because I wouldn't be conscious. Without it, I'd walk the earth like a zombie waiting for the world to build more espresso bars on every corner of every street, even in hamlets with folks who only drank Maxwell House.

At the subway station, the standard horde waited for the nine-ten. We zipped through neighborhoods below ground, arrived at my stop, and I transferred to a train that took me to lower Manhattan.

I lumbered up the stairs to stroll the blocks to campus and as I came within a block, an unmarked police car zoomed past me, siren blaring. Carolina was the driver. It was only nine forty-five. She had plenty of time to make our meeting. *Ha! You do use your police privileges to get what you want, Detective.* At precisely nine fifty-five, I opened the door to my office and Detective Carolina Quinn sat at my desk searching through papers.

I frowned. She smiled brazenly.

"How'd you get in?" I demanded.

"The master key. The janitors all have copies."

"You couldn't have waited for me to let you in, Carolina?"

"No. This is serious."

"If it's so serious, why didn't you tell me last night?"

"New developments."

"Sounds ominous. Should I be worried?"

"Virginia."

"Excuse me?"

"You heard me. Virginia Johnson, formerly Mendez."

"Yeah? What about her?"

"The two of you were cozy."

"So?"

"So the Lieutenant wants you in for questioning."

"Why?"

"Really, Professor? I have to explain? You're having sex with the dean's wife, the guy ends up dead and you're the one to find him."

"Had."

"Excuse me?"

"I had sex with the dean's wife. No more."

"Had, have, what's the difference?"

"Past versus present tense is the difference."

"Oh, now you're giving me a grammar lesson?"

"Not a grammar lesson, Detective. I'm pointing out the difference. I haven't had sex with the dean's wife in well over a year."

I was lying, but I assumed she wouldn't know about the little incident in my office with Virginia twenty-four hours ago. Carolina peered at me suspiciously.

"I'm taking you in as a friend, Electra."

"A friend? You want to take me in for questioning and I'm supposed to think you're a friend?"

"Swift was ready to take you in in handcuffs. I promised him I would deliver you personally."

"Gee, thanks. I sound like a breakfast burrito."

"Well, you are from Texas, after all."

"In my neck of the woods, we say *Tejas*. I call myself a *Tejana*. You should go with me sometime. I think you'd like Austin. Everyone loves Austin. I love Austin. You'd love Austin."

I hoped I hadn't blown it entirely with her despite being wanted for questioning. Fuck. Could this get any worse?

"Stop trying to ingratiate yourself. I already like you. I just don't trust you, Electra."

"Yesterday you didn't think I was capable of murder. Now you're saying you don't trust me. What changed?"

She paused and gave me a once-over, which I found titillating. Then she said, "Let's get going."

Carolina placed her hand on the small of my back. I wasn't sure I liked the familiarity with which she treated me, since she was escorting me not to a bedroom but to a police station.

"You don't teach until noon. I promise you the interviewing detective will be gentle and swift."

"Oh, aren't you clever. I get the sense you've used that line before."

"I get the sense you've used lots of lines many times before."

We headed out to the same unmarked car in which she had zoomed into campus.

"This yours?" I asked. We stood before a black 2006 Buick with leather seats that were in decent shape despite overall wear and tear.

"Yeah, my baby's a Buick."

I opened the passenger door and saw candy wrappers lining the seat as well as the floor. I made a mental note: Detective Carolina Quinn was a fan of Italian Baci chocolate bonbons, the expensive chocolate with poetic missives inside the wrapper. I picked one up as I sat down and read out loud, 'Kisses mark the minutes on the dial of love.' You believe that?" I asked.

"Believe what?"

"The poetic proselytizing about kisses and love by anonymous."

"You're asking me?"

"Oh, here's another one: 'Sweet is the dawn that breaks upon lovers.' Also anonymous. Doesn't anyone claim these turgid tidbits of tenderness?"

She ignored me and scant moments later double-parked in front of her precinct, which, as it turned out, wasn't far from campus.

"We could have walked."

"I was trying to save you time, Professor. Are you always so critical?"

"Only when I'm being questioned for murder."

She perked up an eyebrow, the right one, and I immediately felt the same attraction as yesterday morning. I'd barely known her for twenty-seven hours and I was as lovesick as anonymous in those pretentious chocolate missives.

"Please, after you."

She opened the door to the station and the smell of coffee, donuts and sweat assaulted my senses, but not as much as the ear-splitting male voices overwhelmed my ears. They shouted ordinary conversation.

"Is it always this noisy in here?"

"You should have been here for the play-offs last month."

"What play-offs?"

"What play-offs? You're kidding, right?"

"Nope."

"What play-offs," she murmured. "Come on. Follow me."

"With pleasure."

My voice was somewhat sarcastic. She wore her routine black skirt and knee-high leather heeled boots and I reveled in the slice of heaven that was Detective Carolina Quinn until we arrived at a dark, windowless room with a shabby formica table and three chairs bolted to the floor.

"Have a seat." She pointed to the side with only one chair. "I'll go get the detective."

Our tax dollars at work, I thought. The table was grimy and sticky as if one too many Big Macs and fries had been served up with syrupy soda. I kept my hands on my lap.

Swift and Carolina appeared in the doorway of the dark, dank room but Swift lingered at the doorway, shrieking at the top of his lungs to a clerk. Carolina sat across from me and blinked so slowly her eyes seemed half-shut and I gleaned the beauty of her thick black eyelashes. Her gaze confused me. Was she warning me with that blink?

Swift shouted epithets to the clerk and promptly parked himself across from me next to Carolina.

"Professor, would you like some coffee?"

"Sure, why not. I'll have a cappuccino, two-percent, a sprinkle of cinnamon—but before you pour the steamed milk; otherwise the cinnamon will flatten the foam and nobody likes limp foam."

Swift ignored my attempts at levity and bellowed toward the open door, "Hey, Clark, bring in a couple of cups of black coffee." He turned to Carolina. "You having any, Detective?"

"No, thanks, Dan. I've had my quota today."

Swift shuffled some papers in a thick, grungy file. Papers fell from the file, which was visibly messy. He pulled a writing pad and pencil from his jacket pocket and wrote the time, date and year on the top line. I felt like I was dealing with a kindergartener. His scrawl wasn't legible beyond the dates and in my experience, kindergarteners took more time with their penmanship. He set the pencil behind his left ear, slapped the writing pad and reclined in his chair, which squeaked from his weight.

"Professor Campos, what can you tell me about Isabel Mendez?"

"I don't know anyone by that name."

"You don't?"

Carolina leaned forward, whispered in his ear as she opened the file and pointed to the middle of a page. Swift sat up, spread his legs wide apart and leaned his stomach on the table. He reached inside his jacket and pulled out his glasses, which were probably bifocals, and as he held up the piece of paper he attempted to focus by finding the tiny space between the lines of his bifocals that would allow him to scrutinize it further.

"I see." He faced her. "Thank you, Detective." Not in the least bit embarrassed, he positioned the page back in his tattered folder and addressed me again. "Professor, do you know a woman by the name of Isabel Cortez?"

"Yes, I do."

"What can you tell us about her?"

"We used to date."

"Used to?"

"Used to. As in no more."

"When did you last see Miss Isabel Cortez?"

He pronounced Cortez in a white, non-Spanish-accented way, and I'm not sure why but I thought he was being deliberate. Probably one of those English-only types, I thought.

"Professor?"

"Yeah? Sorry, I guess I was distracted."

"When did you last see her?"

"About three or four months ago."

"Which is it? Three? Four?"

"Three and a half, to be more exact."

"Here? In the city?" He tapped his pencil on his pad.

"No. We were at a beach resort. In Mexico."

"A vacation?" Tapping louder. The pad became his drum and noise rendered a rhythm that wasn't a rhythm at all.

"You could say that."

"And then you didn't see her again? After your vacation together? That's odd."

"Not odd at all. It didn't go well."

"I see."

He crossed his arms and rested them on his protruding belly. Why don't policemen go to the gym after a certain age? Or go for a jog or lift a weight now and then?

"And you say you haven't seen her since?"

"No, I haven't," I lied.

I looked at Carolina, who savored my growing discomfort.

"Thank you for coming in, Professor. Not necessary but good you volunteered."

"Volunteered? Huh?"

"You're free to go," he said.

"That's it?"

"That's it. Thanks for coming in."

"But what about..."

I decided not to mention Virginia and instead paused to see that Carolina's face was expressionless. Carolina leaned back in her chair out of Swift's line of vision. She stared at me with that glint in her eye.

"About what, Professor Campos?" he asked.

"Nothing," I said.

I peered at Carolina, whose face had reverted to a blank stare.

Swift rose from his chair and walked to the door but before opening it he spun around and looked at me.

"One more thing, Professor."

"Yes?"

"Do you know where she is, Miss Isabel Mendez?"

"Cortez," said Carolina.

"Sorry, yes, Miss Isabel Cortez. Do you know where we can find her?"

I took out my smartphone, googled her name for the New York City vicinity and boroughs and an address in Brooklyn popped up. I held up the phone to show him the results.

"I need to get me one of those," he said.

He walked back to the table and rested his glasses on his head as he studied the screen. "Very nice, very nice. How expensive is a phone like this? I mean, monthly?"

"It varies. Detective, don't you want to take down the address?"

"Oh, no. We have that address. She's not there anymore but I guess you didn't know that since you haven't seen her since June?"

"July."

"July?"

"July," I repeated.

"Why'd you bring me here, Detective? I don't understand."

"I thought you came on your own, Professor. Nobody forced you. Quinn, did you force the Professor to come here?"

"No, Dan. I did not."

He shuffled to the door and left. I peered at Carolina, who fought back an oncoming smirk. A big one.

I sipped cold, bitter coffee, put the cup down and got up, attempting to stay calm. I didn't storm out but I wanted to.

She followed me down the hallway. A few police officers, both female and male, nodded as she passed. Clearly, she was their superior in rank, but I could also see that they respected her. Right now, I wasn't feeling any respect.

"Let me drive you back to campus. I wouldn't want you to be late to class."

"I'll walk."

"Electra, let me drive you."

She placed her hand on my shoulder but I jerked away. "I said I'll walk."

"Why are you so upset?"

"You lied to me."

"I didn't lie to you. I told you the Lieutenant wanted us to ask you a few questions and Swift asked you a few questions."

"You led me to believe I was a suspect. I'm not, am I? That's sweet, very sweet. Why the charade, Detective?"

"*Charade*? Now there's a classic, huh? I can never make up my mind which of the two I'm more attracted to in that film: Hepburn or Grant."

"That's easy—Grant," I stated matter-of-factly.

"Grant? You surprise me, Electra."

"What can I say? I'm full of surprises. Seems you are too."

"Don't be annoyed. I was fooling with you."

"Fooling with me?"

"Yeah, fooling with you."

"For what purpose?"

"No purpose. Just wanted to fool with you." She winked.

I wasn't falling for her charm again that easily. We were on the steps of the precinct, making our conversation less than private, but I didn't care. I was too pissed to care if any of her colleagues heard me. And anyway, tricking suspects was part of the job, wasn't it? She'd tricked me into believing one thing when she wanted me for another, putting me off guard. It had worked. I had been off guard completely. But I hadn't told the truth about Isabel. That I had just seen her at the subway stop and at the bar.

"Why all these questions about Isabel? Do you know something you're not telling me?" I hoped to pry information out of her, thinking she might feel a bit guilty for her little ruse.

"I can't divulge that information."

"Wait a minute, Carolina. This isn't exactly fair."

"Fair? What do you mean, fair? Who said anything about fair? This isn't supposed to be fair. A man is dead and you're talking about fair? Tell that to his family, Electra."

"Oh, you're good. Turning the tables on me now, are you? Fine. Make it about something else. I'm sorry for the dean and for his family, but I had nothing to do with his murder and you know that. In your line of work you must come across murderers all the time and I'm sure you know I'm not a murderer. And I didn't have a motive."

"You fucked his wife."

"Is that what this is about? Are you jealous?"

"Oh, please, *Profesora*. Get over yourself."

"Given my low self-esteem, that's not a problem, Detective Quinn."

I rushed down the last two steps and turned the corner. She didn't follow and I was relieved. What was going on? We had barely met and already we argued as if we had been lovers for years and were frustrated with compromising, relentless, cumulative lies. Damn. Why wouldn't she go out with me?

CHAPTER NINE

My office door was cracked open and Adrían sat at my desk.

"What is this? Grand Central?" I slammed my book bag down. "Can I please have my seat?"

"Sure. Sorry, buddy." He rose abruptly and rushed to the door. "I'll see you later."

"No, wait. I'm sorry. It's been a rough morning."

"It's barely ten thirty and already a rough morning?"

"Yeah."

"You want to talk about it?"

"No. Yeah. I don't know."

"Okay. I'll be across if you need me."

"Wait a minute. Adrían, where were you last night?"

"Me? I went home. Slept a bit after all that sangria we drank. Then took myself to the gym for a couple of hours."

"In Chelsea?"

"Yeah, not far from my place."

"Any chance you might have dropped by the bar last night for a drink? You know, our usual bar on Twenty-fourth?"

"Last night? Nope. Too tired after my workout. Why?"

"I thought I saw I.C. there last night."

"La I.C.?" Mz Icy herself? I thought that was over."

"It is over. It's been over."

"Why do you care if you bump into her?"

"I don't, I guess. Still seems odd that all of a sudden I see her three times in one day."

"What? Three times?"

"I think I saw her yesterday morning. Prowling the hallway in the Admin building."

"Are you kidding me?"

"Nope."

"Have you told Detective Quinn?"

"Nope."

"You're protecting Ice Woman? What are you nuts, buddy?"

"I'm not protecting her. I thought I imagined her. It's not the first time I thought I saw her. The last three months have been kind of difficult for me to shake her. Sometimes I imagine she's in the same room or walking behind me somewhere and then there she is. She came up behind me at the Down Under the other night. It's like she's around and hasn't let go, which makes it tough."

"At the Down Under? She was there?"

"Yeah."

"Damn. Don't you want to tell the police?"

"Not really."

"They'll think you're protecting her or worse, an accomplice."

"An accomplice? Adrían, she didn't kill the dean. I can't be an accomplice to a murder she didn't commit."

"You don't know that. Not for sure anyway. And you've seen her three times in a few days. They're going to be suspicious."

"Huh? Oh, yeah. Three times. Now that I think of it, probably four."

"Four? You've seen her four times in a few days? Are you fucking her too?"

"No, of course not!"

"But you might?"

"Don't confuse the issue, bud."

"Okay, so you saw her at the Down Under, the Admin building and the Chelsea bar last night. What's the fourth?"

"The subway stop. Near campus. When I was heading home yesterday."

"You saw her hanging around your stop? Are you sure it was her?"

"Yes, I'm sure. We talked."

"You talked? You talked to Ice Woman? Why? This summer you said you never wanted anything to do with her again. *Nada. Totalmente nada*. I'm supposed to remind you, remember?"

"I remember."

"Okay, you talked. That's all right. You didn't promise her a ring or anything. You're good."

"Actually, we made a date."

"What? You can't. I won't let you, buddy."

"Too late. The date was for last night. At the opera."

"Wait. Now I'm confused."

"She stood me up. Then I dropped by the bar and saw her there. With a guy. Typical."

"Damn. It's like the whole relationship all over again in one fell swoop."

"I know, I know, but if you'd seen her. That cinnamon-freckled flesh. *Dios mio*."

"Okay, what happened to Detective Quinn? I thought you liked her."

"I do like her. What's your point?"

"Here's my point: you've got to stop obsessing about Ice Woman. Remember how she criticized you constantly? If you talked about your friends, she went off on you. If you barely said hello to another woman, she went off on you. And if that wasn't enough, she openly flirted with men and was obsessed with her ex-husband. Really, El, you deserve better. Ice Woman only cares about herself. She used you and she's not done. That's the only reason she's shown up in your life again. She's not done using you and you're willing to let her use you. You're volunteering to be used. I won't have it. Nope. I'll stop you whether you like it or not."

"I know, I know. Fuck. What am I thinking? I don't even like her."

"You're not thinking. You're obsessed and we both know what obsession means."

"What?"

I had forgotten everything we had ever spoken about and all the ways in which Adrían had counseled me. He wasn't the only one who had been watching the train wreck that was Isabel Cortez. My oldest friend, Alex, who lived in Austin, also had warned me. She had said, "First chance you get, when she's not looking, back away slowly, do not turn your back on her, keep backing away slowly and as soon as you know she's out of your sight, *RUN!* RUN faster than you've ever run before because believe me, this one is nothing but sheer unadulterated trouble. That's my advice. *RUN!*" And did I run? Nope. I hung around to see how excruciating the situation could get. And it did. Now I'm protecting her from the police—but why? I don't know why. Maybe I didn't think she was capable of murder. She had no motive. Why kill the dean? It made no sense. His wife Virginia? She had motive.

"And another thing," said Adrían, "Ice woman doesn't have a compassionate bone in her body. Didn't you notice everything was about her? And she talked about herself relentlessly? Damn. She loved to hear herself talk. Let some man make her the center of his universe."

Adrían was right. But even though he was right, even though he'd reminded me of all the despicable times with Isabel, I knew I would see her again. But I couldn't tell him. And I wasn't going to tell the police either, although if they were tracking me, I'd have to be careful.

"Promise me, buddy," Adrían pleaded, "promise me you won't go back."

"I won't go back but I might see her again."

"*Ay, pinche chingao.* Okay. Fine. Do what you gotta do. One way or the other, I'm here for you. We're buddies and that's what buddies do. Through the bad times and the good times, through the mean women and the loving ones, through the ones who leave and the ones who don't leave but instead stay to harangue us with *mierda* about taking out the trash and fixing the leaky faucets and having dinner on the table while she's out carousing with some tool."

"Hey, hey, Adrían. You sorting something out?"

"Yeah. Maybe. I'm worried, buddy. I'm getting off track, though, I know. But damn, do you really have to see Ice Woman again? Why?"

"I don't know. Maybe I'm curious. Maybe I have to find out if she was in the Admin building yesterday morning and I wasn't imagining things."

"Trouble, *mucho* trouble ahead, El."

"No, the worst is over. I swear. I won't be seduced again, I promise you."

"Yeah, yeah. Sure, sure. Do what you gotta do."

He walked out of my office, pursing his lips and shaking his head. I began grading exams. My office phone rang and I bounced in my seat, unaccustomed to the ring of a landline.

"Professor Campos? I'm calling from the vice chancellor's office. She wants to know if you have time to see her."

"Tell the vice chancellor I always have time to see her."

"Fine. She'll be waiting."

"Now?"

"Yes. In her office."

"I'll swing right over."

I picked up my book bag, stuffed it with ungraded exams and made sure to lock the door behind me. I had no intention of returning for the day.

Justine Aldridge had been appointed the Vice Chancellor of Academic Affairs, a title that 'caused her to be the brunt of jokes for the five years she held the post. She treasured her position but had higher ambitions. She wanted to crash through the glass ceiling of academe to join the ranks of the few women who became college presidents.

I arrived at the Admin building, which housed all administrators high up in the hierarchy. Vice chancellors,

chancellors, provosts all belonged here and they rarely mingled with us lowly professors unless they wanted something. I had a sneaky suspicion that Vice Chancellor Aldridge wanted something. The young secretary who had called me whispered into a headphone while she filed her nails. When she saw me she signaled with her nail file toward a leather couch and I sat dutifully. I wasn't sure why she looked so familiar.

On the coffee table directly in front of me was the morning newspaper with the headline about Dean Coxwell Johnson. I read the story and noted there were no details other than the fact that he had been found dead in his office.

The vice chancellor came out of her office accompanied by none other than Sloan, the leader of the dead white men's club and my nemesis in the history department. They shook hands and I treasured the sight of the vice chancellor towering over Sloan's Napoleonic body. Although he attempted to make up for brevity of body with a bigheaded attitude, he appeared lesser when he stood next to Justine Aldridge.

She wore sensible heels, not too high and not too low. In bare feet, Vice Chancellor Aldridge was six-one and with heels she surpassed many. Some of the Neanderthal men were not thrilled with the fact that she could look them straight in the eye when they talked, but in Sloan's case, she definitely looked downward.

I rose to my feet. I wanted to stand next to the vice chancellor while she peered down on Sloan.

"Electra, thank you for coming so promptly," she said. She turned to Sloan. "I'm sorry I couldn't be more help, David. We'll have to see how things turn out after the recent events."

Sloan nodded, looked at me and mumbled, "Electra."

"Sloan," I muttered.

I followed the vice chancellor through the glass doors of her office.

"Come in. Have a seat." She pointed to the couch but I opted for the wooden chair next to her desk, propped myself down and rested my right ankle on my left knee.

"Electra, how are you?"

"I'm fine, Justine." She always asked her professors to call her by her first name. "Thanks for the concern. How are you? Is the president of the college giving you hell? I guess he's pretty pissed about the events on his campus." I was as deliberately sarcastic as I could get without sounding like I was too involved.

"Mike must protect the college's reputation."

She wore a Chanel jacket and skirt, black and yellow, suitable fall colors despite resembling a queen bee. When she passed me, the fragrance of Chanel perfume had wafted from her hair and neck. Her hair was conservatively coifed in a bun resembling a schoolmarm but she was no schoolmarm. She was a generation older than me but I had heard rumors about Justine when she herself had been in college in the sixties. Even then, she had been ambitious and grabbed the microphone from college boys at protest rallies.

"Of course. The college's reputation."

"If you were in my position, you'd realize the importance of reputation, Electra."

Instead of sitting behind her desk, she sat across from me, crossed her legs and reclined, but only halfway. In other words, she didn't need the back of the chair to support her. Her back was so straight she looked like she was practicing her sit-up-straight posture for a beauty pageant.

"Why am I here, Vice Chancellor?" I chose to ignore her last comment.

She smiled, enjoying the title she had earned, which also gave her enough grief to want to lock away all the entitled troublemakers who came to her office ordering her to fix their complaints—and of those there were many. Especially from the dead white men's club.

"I'm worried about you, dear Electra."

She faced me head-on and her cloudy gray eyes bore through me. She paused. Her pauses were ploys for her culprit to offer more information and although I would usually play, I was in no mood today. She reclined further into her chair and stared at me. I slouched in my chair and stared back. A long minute, perhaps two, crackled the air between us but I was determined to let her speak first. Justine smiled, a half smile, which was also her distinctive manner. Justine never offered more of anything unless she absolutely had to and right now a half smile may have been all she had intended. I didn't care. She had called me to her office and I refused to talk until she told me what she wanted.

"Well?" she asked.

"Well?" I replied.

"I'm worried about you, my dear, dear Electra."

"Yes, you said that, Justine."

"Whatever are you going to do, dear?"

"About what, Justine?"

"About this dilemma."

"What dilemma?"

"Why, the murdered dean, dear. And now the gossip about you and..." She trailed off deliberately.

"What gossip?"

"The gossip, dear."

"I'm not aware of any gossip, Justine. You want to fill me in?"

"That's not important, Electra dear. What is important is that we're worried about you."

"We?"

"The college president called me this morning. He asked me to talk to you."

"Ah, Mike again."

"Yes, Mike."

"He couldn't tell me himself?"

"You know the life of a college president, dear: meetings, fund-raising and political intrigue."

"You would know that better than me, Justine. I'm just an ordinary, simple-minded professor."

"You are anything but ordinary, my dear Electra, which is why we're so disappointed with these recent rumors. We want to alert you that we're here to provide you with any resources you may need."

"I haven't been arrested, Justine."

I liked saying her first name because, although she pretended to want to be familiar with her professors, she despised being addressed by anything but her title.

"Electra dear, no one expects that you will be arrested but should the case take a turn for the worse, you can come to us."

"Us, Justine?"

"Why, the college lawyers, of course. We don't want our most trendy professor held for something she clearly did not do. You were, after all, fond of Dean Johnson and his wife. How is Ginny?"

I paused. That she had referred to me as "trendy" was annoying, but more irksome was her attempt to have me confirm the rumors she had heard.

"Dean Johnson and I weren't friends, Justine. I've probably been to his home fewer times than you."

"Oh?"

She leaned forward, squinting her right eye as if to say she understood. I refused to play and I refused to pretend we were confidantes. Just because she was a woman didn't make her my friend; in fact, her title came before her "womanhood" and I wasn't about to forget that her ambition blinded her to the rights and wrongs she had once passionately debated. Or maybe she had never been interested in righting wrongs. Maybe I gave her too much credit. But I liked to believe that, like many of us, she too had had certain ideals during the sixties and seventies. Of course, she had made it abundantly clear that she wasn't protecting students who staged protests on campus supporting #Occupy Wall Street, and she had also made it abundantly clear that Capital College students at #Occupy Wall Street wouldn't be allowed to return if they were arrested. The fact was she and the former dean had similar convictions, although I had learned more recently that his convictions were definitely about protecting his bank accounts. The considerable difference was that Johnson came from money. Justine Aldridge didn't, which made her blind ambition and upward mobility that much more abhorrent. If anyone had forgotten where she came from, it was Justine and although she fooled the plebeians at the public university, no one, not even Justine, could dupe the filthy rich or affect their elite class rituals and prejudices. Chanel suit or no, I had seen how she was often dismissed at the dean's house for her class status and at the president's home for her gender. But she insisted on abiding by their rules.

She placed her hand on my knee, wrinkled her brow and peered into my eyes. "Do not let our past misunderstandings taint our relationship, Electra. I am your vice chancellor. Please come to me when you need support."

"I don't hold grudges, Justine. The past is the past."

She squinted her right eye again, a speck of a grin upturning her mouth in an attempt to be more familiar with me than I had ever permitted. "That pleases me, Electra." She patted my knee and got up from her chair, holding out her hand to shake mine.

I stayed in my seat. "Oh, are we done?"

"I have another meeting, Electra, but let's have lunch soon."

"Lunch? With me? Wouldn't that be slumming for you, Justine?"

She had her back to me and waved her hand toward the door. She might as well have pushed me out.

I headed for the bathroom near Justine's office and strode inside. Despite the three shiny stalls, I reached for the lock on the main entrance for additional privacy and just then the young secretary flung open the door. Then I remembered. She was the woman with the front-zippered green dress. In the Chelsea bar. In her hand she held a bowl of ice cream with chocolate sauce, bananas and pecans, which confused me. I mean, we were in a bathroom. Of course, it was almost lunchtime but why bring ice cream into a bathroom? She wore a purple A-line cotton dress with a square neckline and her breasts protruded plumply through the cotton. Her legs were concealed in black leggings but her feet were bare.

"Want some?" she asked.

She held the bowl up to my face, spooned a portion of ice cream mired in chocolate and pecans and thrust the concoction into my mouth before I could object. I grabbed the spoon and dolloped a serving on her chest above the neckline. My tongue caught the drippings before the cream tinged her dress. I reached around and unzipped the dress, unclasped her bra and with my hand seized a handful of ice cream, slapped it in her mouth and kissed her, moving my chocolate, gooey hand down her breasts. I licked off more vanilla cream that trickled to her nipples. I sucked each nipple with determined obligation, then snatched the bowl and placed it on the bathroom counter. I shoved her against the counter, lifting her ass, and as she sat steadily, I pulled up her dress, separated her knees and, dipping my hand into the bowl, smeared ice cream on her vaginal lips, kissed and licked for at least twenty minutes, until her moans convinced me that lunch was over.

After my rendezvous, I practically skipped to the subway, reflecting on my meeting with the vice chancellor. What could she possibly want? She wasn't worried about me. And President Mike couldn't be bothered about me either. No, they were up to something. That she had referred to our past "misunderstanding" was a tactic to rattle me. She grasped full well that I had disregarded the way in which she had willfully humiliated me when I was first hired. She had been an assistant professor herself, meaning she was about as fresh and new on the block as I was, but little did I know we were not in any way similar despite our professorial lowly rank. When I arrived on campus ten years prior, Justine pretended to protect me from the potent "dead white men's club." Little did I know that she was engaged in clandestine dalliances with the club leader, Professor David Sloan.

As graduate students at Princeton, they had been friends and Justine revered Sloan's popularity among the upper echelon administrators who appreciated the not-so-golden boy who opposed admission quotas that sanctioned race. The administrators loved him. Of course, his C average didn't guarantee him a job at an Ivy League like Princeton and that he ended up at a poor public university with a majority of students from a variety of ethnic and racial backgrounds was the irony of his life. He was hired before Justine and enthusiastically recruited her when she opted to return to New York City instead of traveling to a Podunk middle-America town. She herself was an A minus student, but her area of expertise, fashion in Jane Austen's novels, wasn't in demand except perhaps by Hollywood costume designers. In any case, Justine had few job prospects and felt she owed Sloan her job, which was precisely why they sustained their ongoing "friendship," a friendship no one questioned, although more than once I had caught them in compromising situations having late night drinks in out of the way places. The "misunderstanding" to which she referred pertained to the first time I witnessed their chummy canoodling.

Shortly after I arrived on campus, I had to stomach Sloan and his dead white male cohorts, who vehemently protested my hire, stating that despite my degree from a reputable history department ranked top ten in the nation, in their minds, I hadn't earned my PhD but had been bestowed the title because I was "Hispanic." Sloan advised students to avoid my classes and if a student whined about how much I discussed "race," Sloan promptly approached the student, instructing him to file a complaint of "reverse discrimination" against me. Never mind I was hired to teach Latin American history and the difficulty of conveying any history without invoking "race" was impossible. In any case, a few students filed complaints and the investigations wore me down so much I approached Justine for advice. She advised me to alter my lectures and when I refused, she claimed I was being a reverse racist. She later apologized but that was only after I bumped into her with Sloan in the corner of a queer bar, cuddling. I guess they thought no one of consequence would see them, and they were probably right. I was incensed that they'd turned a welcoming place for me into their rendezvous point when the rest of the city was clearly for the likes of them.

Sloan was sheepish when he saw me, but he was mostly pleased with himself at his conquest. Justine blushed and then invited me to join them for a drink. I flat out refused. She came to my office early Monday morning and asked that I please not tell anyone since both were so happily married and not to each other. What did I care if they were fucking? I felt betrayed by a friend. She reasoned I was jealous and that I'd always had a "thing" for her, but anyone who knew me also knew that Justine in her Chanel suits was far from my type. Matronly, conservatively dressed women didn't appeal to me. Never had. Never would.

Almost a decade had passed since that spectacle and Justine alluded to the past every now and then to assess the climate of our friendship, which in my mind was nonexistent.

CHAPTER TEN

While ruminating about my meeting with Justine Aldridge, I spotted Isabel Cortez. I wasn't surprised. She sat on a subway bench and nibbled on nuts, not lemon rinds. Almonds, cashews, pecans and Brazil nuts from a small package. She took tiny bites from a cashew, miniature bites, such teeny bites that her chewing seemed more like sucking. I watched to see when she swallowed, if she swallowed, but I couldn't see her throat retract, ingest or gulp. No movement, nothing at all. Just smooth, slow sucking on a cashew. I didn't approach her. I preferred observing from a distance. I didn't think she saw me, or maybe she did. I made sure to stay back, waiting until she boarded the subway, then I ran into the car behind hers. She might have caught a glimpse of me through the adjoining glass doors. I sat quickly, evading her.

Still feeling humiliated that she'd stood me up, I hung out of sight to satisfy my own curiosity about what she was up to and where she was going. And anyway, the one who committed the transgression of standing you up should be the one to feel disgraced. Maybe she did. I didn't want to know. I felt too disgraced. What if she had forgotten all about me? What if sending me to the opera was her way of saying get lost? What if, what if? Okay, enough. At the next stop, I ran into her car.

She smiled but I didn't trust the smile since it looked more like a pucker from a lemon rind. She was back to sucking on lemon rinds. As I came closer I saw magazines scattered on the floor before her. I sat and waited until she spoke. She continued to leaf through *People So Unlike Us* rags filled with gossip about Hollywood starlets whose time was brief in the limelight. Abruptly, she shook her head and spoke.

"You stood me up," she said.

"I stood you up? You stood me up!"

"I did?"

"You know you did."

"Oh."

"That's it? *Oh?* How about an apology?"

"I'm sorry."

She pulled out a book from her book bag, opened to somewhere in the middle and read a passage out loud. I was familiar with the book and the passage. It was my book, just a little book, a sort of not-so-autobiographical fictional account of my former life.

"Where did you get that? It's been out of print for years," I said.

"I've had it for years."

"But where did you get it?"

"In a trash bin. At a bookstore that only sells used books. I felt sorry for it so I picked it up. Gave it a home, you could say."

"I guess I should be grateful."

"Aren't you?"

"No. I wrote that a long time ago. Now it's pedestrian."

"Yeah. It is."

"I appreciate your honesty."

"I know."

"May I?" I started to take the book from her hands.

"Not so fast." She gripped it. "Are you going to give it back?"

"It's your book."

"No, it's your book. I'm only reading it."

She handed over the book and I flipped the pages. I must have looked forlorn because she grabbed the book and stuffed it in her bag. I breathed a sigh and slumped over, my shoulders drooping.

"Well, I liked it," she said.

"I thought you said it was pedestrian?"

"You said it was pedestrian."

"You agreed."

"You wanted me to agree."

"I suppose so."

"Come on. Let's go have coffee together."

"Aren't you on your way to a class?"

"Not today. Besides, I owe you. After standing you up."

I tingled inside my skin. When she stood, she almost seemed tall, but she wasn't. I gazed at her breasts and she smirked but not at me, just in general. She assumed I wanted her and that aggravated me. I rationalized that I was investigating for the detectives.

"I have to make a phone call," I said.

"No calling girlfriends while you're with me."

"I don't have a girlfriend. I'm calling a friend."

"A friend? Which friend? The one who warns you about me? That friend? That's not a friend, Electra."

As we walked up the stairs from the subway station, the humid air hit our faces and she flipped her hair behind fleshy ears that were pierced from the lobe up to the thinner interior. Garnet studs lined the inside of each ear. I pocketed my cell phone.

"Why don't you like it anymore?" she asked. "Your novella?"

"I don't know. Maybe because it's trying too hard."

"To be profound?"

"You noticed."

"That's not a bad thing."

"To try to be something and not succeed?"

"Success? What's that?"

"You know: fame, money, canonization."

"We're here." She pulled my arm and I followed until we sat at a table the size of a postage stamp. Canisters of tea lined the wall. We sat on dubiously constructed chairs and as I wobbled on mine, she ordered tea and cakes.

"I thought we were having coffee."

"This is better for you. Just wait. You'll love it."

"I do drink tea."

"Of course you do. But not this tea."

The teapots arrived and she lifted the lid to check the color. After another minute, she poured the tea into thick, tiny mugs that resembled miniature stoneware for five-year-olds. I sipped and burned my tongue.

"If you had one line to write, only one, and that was the line that you would be remembered by, for all time, what would it be?" she asked.

"That's easy. To be or not to be."

"It has to be original."

"*Verde que te quiero verde*."

"From Shakespeare to Lorca. Not bad, but I'm beginning to think you think I'm stupid."

"I think anything but that about you."

She stared into my eyes and I thawed in that way I hated when I was with her. Damn, I wanted to fuck her.

"Everyone reads Lorca," she said.

"Everyone used to read Lorca. Now it's blogs, tweets and Facebook."

"A technology insurgent? Since when, Electra? I've never seen you go for the length of an hour without checking your Facebook page."

"Hey, Facebook is helping launch revolutions."

She sipped her tea and ate a piece of raspberry cake. "You want me.

"No. I don't." I mumbled, "Ice Woman."

"Fuck you, Electra."

"You might as well." I finished a cup and she filled it again. "So what is this stuff? Gunpowder?"

"Yeah."

"No wonder I like it."

"I live around the corner," she said.

My stomach wrenched and I put down the lemon cake I was about to bite into. My throat tightened and I swallowed to keep it from contracting but it was too late. I coughed and then sneezed. Coughed and sneezed again. She laughed and handed me a napkin. I wiped my mouth and felt stupid. Young and stupid. No, old and stupid.

"Come on," she said. "It'll take a second to get there."

I followed as she led me around the corner. I could have made an excuse, walked away and hoped I wouldn't run into her again. Many times before I'd walked out on her knowing where we would end up. First in bed, then the arguments, then more battles of wills until I could take no more.

We faced her doorway and I hesitated, peeking inside before I dared onto the threshold. I lingered at the threshold while she went about her business, rattling dishes in the kitchen, battering the refrigerator door, cutting and chopping vegetables and fruit. She came to the door and handed me a demitasse of espresso with a dash of thick, sweet canned milk. I accepted it and stepped into the room. Just one step, just one foot, one shoe. By the time I finished my coffee, I found myself in the middle of a room that served as living room and dining room. The bedroom was behind a door, safely hidden. She set a small square table with dishes and silverware. The dishes were exquisitely fancy with a yellow floral pattern and the silverware was mildly tarnished.

"Sit."

"I have to go."

"No, you don't."

"I do. I have an appointment."

"No, you don't."

I set the cup down on the square table. "I do, really."

"Have a bite to eat first."

"I'm not hungry."

She ambled toward me and eyed me.

"You realize that you're not going to stop thinking about me. From now until tomorrow when you look for me at the subway stop, you'll think about me so much that you'll begin to ache and yearn and you'll say to yourself, I should have stayed, I should have had a bite to eat, I should have—"

Abruptly, I placed my hands on her slight hips, brought her close and bit her bottom lip. She sucked on my upper lip. I kept hearing a song in my head by Alicia Keys. What was it? "Karma?" The tune played over and over, irritating me. I dropped to the floor, dragging her with me. Not until my head had pushed between her open legs and kissed her lips did the song finally cease. Instead, I heard a hum, a pounding drone in my ears. Her inner thighs covered my ears so the racket must have been in my head. I kissed and licked keenly, almost calmed by the buzz and then I found myself wondering if Isabel Cortez was capable of murder.

Just then, she lifted her head and said, "What?"

"Hmm?" I mumbled.

She sat up straight, throwing me off my trail and itinerary. I was barely getting started.

"What did you say?" she asked.

"I didn't say anything."

"You did. I heard you mumbling something."

"I was mumbling?"

"You were humming. Again."

"No, I wasn't."

"You were."

"Oh. I thought I'd stopped that habit."

"And no one has told you that you haven't stopped?"

"You just did."

She was fishing to see if I'd been with other women since we were last together. Surely she knew me better by now. Of course I'd been with other women, but I wasn't going to start naming names. Not right at this moment. It was inappropriate.

"Come here."

She caressed my face with both hands and I landed on top of her.

"Wait a sec," she said.

She rolled from under me and hopped up, exposing a bony, thought-provoking ass. She opened the bottom drawer to her bedside table and pulled out a red satin bag. I knew that bag well. From the bag she drew a long, black cat-o'-nine-tails. The whip. Ah, she's in that kind of mood.

Standing over me with sturdy freckled legs on each side of my torso, she brushed the leather strings across my face, down my neck and swept my nipples. I could see her vaginal lips shining from wetness. I lay on my back patiently. With her foot on my pubic bone, she slid her toes down and thrust her big toe inside me.

"Ouch."

"Out of practice?" she asked.

"Never."

She shoved the toe in and out of my vaginal opening, slower this time and I felt myself letting go and getting aroused. She grinned. I grabbed her foot and as she lost her balance she fell backward, landing on her buttocks. I pushed her down and climbed on top, pulled her arms up above her head and tied her wrists with the cat-o'-nine-tails. Tight.

"I see you're still a zealous pupil."

"I was never your pupil, Isabel."

"Weren't you?"

"No."

With her wrists tied and my body holding her down, she couldn't move. I dragged the bag of goodies toward me with my foot and plucked out nipple rings.

"Someone is feeling inspired," she said.

"Shut up."

"Anything you say."

I tightened one ring around her right nipple then the other around her left nipple, pulling each one with my teeth. She moaned softly. Inching my way lower, I licked and bit her abdomen. My bites were soft initially but then I sank my teeth into the fleshy part of her left hip and pulled hard on her right nipple ring. She let out a loud groan. I wanted to draw blood. She wanted me to draw blood. I waited and moved lower until

I gently bit her clitoris, licking around her vaginal lips, moving my tongue swiftly back and forth and thrust three fingers inside her while I tugged on her left nipple ring. In an instant, I turned her over, retrieved the orange butt plug from the fun bag and rammed it steadily into her ass while I bit her left butt cheek, leaving a bloody tooth mark. Her body heaved ready to orgasm. Pushing the butt plug farther in, I sprang onto her back and slid myself back and forth, gathering momentum until we gasped together for a lengthy twenty minutes before we stopped, both of us improved by multiple spasms. Finally, I heard her exhale faintly and I fell off and to my back, loosening the leather cat-o'-nine-tails around her wrists. She moved closer and bit my right nipple so viciously I had to hold back a loud objection for fear of waking the building.

"What the fuck, Isabel? That hurt," I whispered.

"I thought that was the point."

"I'm not into pain as much as you."

"So you say. I don't believe you. I mean, you always come back, don't you?"

"Fuck you, Isabel."

She smiled so smugly I wanted to punch her but didn't dare since she would've been even more complacent had I done so. Isabel and I were amateurs. We had no contract, no safe word, no real comprehension or agreement regarding our sex games. That would've meant a commitment neither of us was prepared for.

I didn't get up for the rest of the evening until her phone rang and woke us. I looked outside and saw a hint of the moon through a crack between the high-rise apartments. A digital clock on her bedside table read two twenty-four. She whispered into her cell phone, then got out of bed and slipped into the bathroom. I heard her voice rise as if she was arguing with someone in Spanish. All I could discern was "*No, no, mi amor, Vee, por favor, Vee.* And then she'd mumble again. Who was Vee? Probably just one of her many lovers wondering why he or she had been stood up. More likely a he, but what did I care, so long as Isabel was regularly tested for STDs? Which reminded me, the last time I asked her if she had been tested lately or if she'd been practicing safe sex with her playmates, she accused me of being unsafe. She emerged from the bathroom somewhat flushed and awkward and I sensed she wanted me to ask about her caller, but I refused to play.

"Sorry about that," she said.

"Everything all right?"

Okay, I couldn't help myself. I had to ask, but it wasn't as if I was angling for details. Not entirely anyway. I was curious about who might be calling at this hour, but I wasn't going to ask directly and if she wanted to volunteer, that was fine with me. I hoped she'd volunteer. I mean, who calls at two in the morning unless it's a family emergency or, more likely, a drunk-dialing dumped lover. Jealousy surged through my veins. The games had begun. She wanted to make this Vee jealous and I was the recycled fool serving her purpose, but I wasn't going to play this time. I got up and put on my jeans.

"You can't leave yet. You just got here."

"It's late."

"Stay the night. I'll make you breakfast."

"I don't eat breakfast."

"Just shut up and kiss me." She cocked her head slightly.

"You give that look and get your way all the time, don't you?"

"That's not what you were going to ask me," she said.

I stared outside at the street lamps to keep from looking at her.

"Well?"

"Were you in the Admin building?"

"What?" She feigned bewilderment.

"Two days ago? Were you in the Admin building?"

"What are you talking about, El?"

"The morning the dean was found dead. I saw you in the building."

"What are you implying, El? That I'm a murderer?" She sounded irate and sanctimonious. I was familiar with her manner of deflecting.

"I thought I saw you. In the building." I refused to let up.

"Yes, I was there, El, and I stabbed him in his fat belly too, but not before I sucked his nasty cock something fierce until I emptied it out."

"That's what I thought."

I got nauseated with the image, which had clearly been her intent. She pushed me and I fell on a pillow. She nestled her head in the crook of my arm and within minutes slumbered, but I lapsed between drowsiness and disquiet. Just as I became calm with the nearness of her body, a spasm of fear overwhelmed me and I stiffened but she sensed my discomfort and pressed down on my stomach with her hand.

I'm not sure why I rose before sunrise but I did. Habit, I suppose. Quietly, I tiptoed in the shadows and dressed. Isabel's breath was a sweet cadence, not the breath of a murderer, I thought. I was sure she had escaped to a faraway place and I wouldn't disturb her profound sleep but she sat up and watched me cross the room. I put on my jacket, picked up my book satchel and checked for my cell phone. My alarm was set for six thirty a.m. I felt her gaze on my back but neither of us spoke. It was as if we didn't want to spoil some distant magic we'd shared but I knew the spell had been broken with that phone call and the image of Isabel emptying the dean's cock was no help either.

CHAPTER ELEVEN

The trek from Isabel's apartment in Chelsea back to mine in Washington Heights and then back downtown to campus would've taken me over an hour. Ordinarily, I wouldn't have hesitated to go to my office at six but a killer was roaming the campus. Fortunately, the slasher targeted middle-aged bald white men who held the post of dean and not someone of my lowly rank—a middle-aged Chicana history professor from Texas.

The subway was relatively empty, with workers coming from or going to work dispersed throughout the car. Across from me sat a woman who had probably finished a waitressing shift. Her eyes were closed and her head tipped back. As the subway car swung around curves, her head lolled back and forth until a jolt opened her eyes and she glanced at my wrinkled attire, slightly grinning as if to say, "You been out all night." I returned the greeting, hopped up from my seat at the subsequent stop and spilled out of the car, running up the stairs in a burst.

I needed coffee. Fortunately, one of my neighborhood coffee bars was already bustling. The barista saw me and immediately prepared my usual double espresso with a dab of foam. I downed it and asked for another double. I'd barely slept a few hours and needed the boost to survive the day's classes.

That I had spent the night with a prime suspect for the dean's murder didn't unsettle me. I'd done my job and eliminated Isabel as the murderer. Okay, I was easy to convince, but I never suspected her in the first place. Fuck. Who was I kidding? I was under her spell again. One way or another, I was going to catch hell from Adrían as soon as he smelled Isabel on me. Damn, I should have taken a shower before I left her house. As soon as I arrived in my office, I plopped down my book bag and ran to the unisex bathroom, making sure I switched the plate to read Occupied. Students had mobilized to create private bathrooms for transgender folks and I took full advantage, opting for privacy after feeling uncomfortable more than once in the "ladies'" room.

A shower in the bathroom of my building had been installed years before to absorb overflow from a summer training camp for women's soccer. The college had received money from Title IX and instead of expanding the women's gym, the administrators complied by installing showers randomly in antiquated buildings, forcing female athletes to walk across campus from their gym. Overall, another discriminatory practice against the female gender.

I leaped into the shower and scrubbed myself with the liquid hand soap from the dispensers. I wasn't fond of that soapy public restroom scent but the aroma was preferable to Isabel's perfume. I dried my body with paper towels, a venture that was more time-consuming than I would've liked, dressed in yesterday's jeans and shirt, pulled on my boots and smoothed my hair. When I opened the door, I faced Cintia, the floor janitor.

"Cintia, *¿qué pasó?*"

"You're here early, *Profesora*."

"I have work to catch up on."

"*Bueno. Pero* be careful."

"You be careful, Cintia. Does anyone come in with you in the morning?"

"*Sí. Un grupo*. Don't worry about us. We stick together."

"Good."

I was relieved that Cintia and the other custodians had a collective. Then I thought someone in her group might have seen something on the day of the murder.

"Cintia, do you have any friends who work the Administration building early in the morning?"

"*Sí.* That's Estela's building."

"Was she there when the dean's body was found?"

"*Sí.* Said it was *poquito* strange but it didn't bother her. Estela is from Nicaragua, *sabés*? She's seen worse than that in her own country. And a dead white man, that don't bother Estela. She's seen whole communities massacred. Children too. *Bien triste*."

"Yeah, that is sad."

We stood in the hallway and Cintia flipped her mop as if dancing with a suitor. She was only ten years older than me, meaning early sixties, and having been a dancer of ballet folklorico in northern Mexico, she swayed with an elegance I envied.

"Did Estela see anyone suspicious in the building so early in the morning?"

"Sí, *profesora*. You." Cintia grinned.

"Gee, thanks."

"She talked to the police but she's hiding something, that's what I think. She don't like to talk to police in this country. Don't trust them. She's afraid they'll get in the way of her residency papers. She's been waiting. *Mucho tiempo*. Longer than me."

"I have to talk to her."

"The police already did. That woman, the one who wears those tall boots, what's her name?" Cintia gave me a look that said, "I know you know."

"Carolina. Her name is Carolina Quinn."

"Estela don't trust her. But she don't trust nobody who's with the secret police."

"It's not the secret police in this country, Cintia," I tried to reassure her.

"Ha." She twirled around with her mop and pirouetted down the hallway. Unexpectedly, she froze and whispered to me. She whispered so softly I had to walk closer.

"What are you saying?"

"*Ten cuidado, hermana.* The halls have *ojos.*"

"I'm always careful, Cintia."

She shook her head and I wondered if that gesture meant she objected to the assorted friends with benefits who indulged in extracurricular activities in my office.

"*Ese* Sloan. He don't like you. Be careful. He has *ojos*. Lots of them."

"Something you aren't telling me, Cintiacita?"

She grinned when I used the diminutive of her name, fully aware I was attempting to find out more than she wanted to reveal.

"No, no, no, *Profesora. No se nada*. I watch. He don't like you. He don't like Profesor Adrían either. He has secret meetings. In his office. Sometimes early in the morning. Before anyone except me is here. Sometimes *a la madrugada*. Five. When my shift begins."

"You've seen these secret meetings?"

"I seen 'em. *Y con el pobre dean.*"

"Dean Johnson?"

"*Sí.*"

"He met early in the morning with Dean Johnson? When?"

"The other morning."

"The morning Johnson was found?"

"*Sí.*"

"He could be a suspect, Cintia."

"*Ese* Sloan? Puh!" She blew air, exasperated. "*Ese* Sloan *es un pendejo*."

"He's not that stupid, Cintia. The police need to question him."

"I got nothing to do with it, *¿sabés?*"

"Okay."

"You talk to the police then they gonna ask you how you know he was in the office so early. Then they gonna ask me and I don't want nothing with the secret police. I don't trust them. Like Estela."

"Detective Quinn is okay. You can trust her."

"I seen her. *Bien bonita*. But too young for you."

"Everyone's too young for me, Cintia. You're the only one who isn't too young for me."

She giggled and lifted her mop high, balancing the tip of the handle on her palm like a circus performer.

"I'm too old for you, *Profesora* and besides..." She stopped talking, put the mop down and mopped speedily.

"Besides what, Cintia? I'm not your type?"

Cintia swiped the floor and as I drew closer I saw why she quieted abruptly. On the other side of the hallway perpendicular to ours stood Sloan and his coveted recruit. It was seven thirty but not early for the likes of David Sloan and his minion, Assistant Professor Hugh Roberts, specialist in Andrew Jackson, Indian killer.

"Handball, boys?" I asked.

I glanced at their hands but neither wore the wrap I'd seen on them the day before. Sloan may have seen me talking to Cintia but he couldn't have heard our conversation and even if he had, I didn't care. I didn't wait for his response.

"Excuse me, Sloan. I have to get to my office."

I was eager to call Detective Quinn to report what I'd discovered and after that I was going to visit Estela in the Admin building to find out what she'd seen. I guess I wasn't convinced Isabel hadn't been in the building that morning. Why did she have to mention his dick, or was I just being my tedious, jealous self? Ah, the power games, Isabel. When will they end?

CHAPTER TWELVE

With time before my noon class, I thought about what I could safely report to Detective Carolina Quinn. For starters, I wanted to make Sloan as uncomfortable as I possibly could without implicating Cintia. I could say I saw him with the dean that morning but that would implicate me. It would have to be Cintia's word. Damn. Maybe I had to delay that information until I convinced Cintia that Detective Quinn wasn't out to harm her or harm her chances of citizenship. Wait, Cintia had her papers. I helped her study for the citizenship exam three years ago. Damn. The woman was clever.

I punched Carolina Quinn's cell phone number, hoping to get an update while pretending to give her an update.

"You can't stay away from me, can you, Professor Campos?"

"You're irresistible, Detective Quinn. I can't stop thinking about you even though you duped me into coming to police headquarters yesterday morning."

"Electra, Electra, I didn't dupe you. You came willingly and would do it again."

"Yeah, well. I have a weakness for young women who wear knee-high leather boots."

"Face it, you have a weakness for women. And I'm not young. Who said I was young?"

"I did."

"Professor, I've been at my job for fifteen years."

"You started your profession young. How old are you anyway?"

"I asked first."

"No, I asked first."

"I'm the detective, I ask the questions here."

"Okay, fine. I'll play. I'm fifty-three. You?"

"I'm thirty-eight."

"See. You are young."

"And you're so old."

"I know. I feel old."

"Oh, stop. You're not old and you know it."

"Almost sixty is old."

"Not by twenty-first century standards. Haven't you heard? Sixty is the new forty."

"Yeah, which means that forty is the new twenty, making you too young for me."

"Okay, let's stop this little game. Why'd you call me, Professor?"

"Checking in."

"Did I ask you to check in?"

"No, but I'm dutiful. And I wanted to know if anything new had evolved."

"Like what?"

"I don't know. That's why I'm calling."

"And you thought I'd volunteer classified information?"

"Classified? Why would a measly murder on a college campus be classified?"

"Because a human life was taken and a killer is on the loose, which reminds me, how is Ms. Isabel Cortez?"

"Excuse me?"

"Did you have a gratifying night?"

"You're still tailing me?"

"Just doing my job, Professor."

"Oh, so you tailed me this time."

"No, I'm too busy. I sent the same policeman who tailed you to the opera. I'm surprised you didn't see him. He was practically on top of you in the subway. But then again, seems you were otherwise occupied. That woman has a real hold on you, doesn't she?"

I was silent. I'm not sure why I allowed such a long pause. I didn't want to reveal that much but there it was. The long, silent, revealing pause.

"Ah. It's worse than I thought," she said.

"No, it's not."

"Don't try to deny it. You're possessed. You're smitten and you can't find your way out."

"I was investigating and I can tell you for a fact that she's not the murderer."

"You don't know that. Besides, it's your clit talking, not your brain."

"My clit doesn't talk."

"That's not what I heard."

"Now you're making things up."

"Think what you want, Professor, but we've been interviewing a few women who seem to know your clit quite well."

"Fuck," I mumbled.

"Yeah, that's what they said."

"Okay, you've talked to Virginia Johnson, the dean's wife. She's the only one."

"Well, there may be more. They seem to be coming out of the woodwork, ready to talk. You're popular."

"I'm not popular, I'm easy. There's a difference."

"Easy and popular, I'd say."

"Look, I didn't call you to be indicted for my extracurricular trespasses but if you plan to question me some more, why don't we have dinner."

"Can't. I already explained."

"You can't because you're starting to believe what you hear and that means you are starting to be curious about me."

"That's what you think."

"That's what I want to think. I may not be right but the thought of you being curious about me boosts my ego."

"My curiosity is more about whether you are capable of murder, Professor."

"That again?"

"That again."

"I don't believe you. You know I'm not capable of killing anyone, not even an old white guy who abused his power. And the way I found him? Not my sexual preference."

"Oh, you mean because the guy had just undergone fellatio."

"Yeah. That should be proof enough."

"You have a point, Professor."

"I do."

"That still doesn't eliminate you. I mean, you could have caught him with his pants down and then stabbed him."

"Why would I stab him? I didn't like the guy enough to want to kill him. Look, I gotta go. I have class prep."

"Can I ask you something?"

"What's stopping you, Detective?"

"What's up with all this prepping? Haven't you taught these same classes for decades?"

"Some of us like to update. You know, read newly published works to inspire the classroom."

"Hmm. Interesting. Maybe if I'd had a professor like you I would've made better grades in history."

"A compliment. I'm flattered."

"Don't be. I was stating a fact. I'm not prone to flattery, Professor."

"So I've noticed."

"There's one more thing."

"Another question?"

"No, just some information I thought you'd like to know."

"You mean you're divulging classified police information, Detective? I feel privileged."

"Don't."

Abruptly, her tone changed. Her professional demeanor was so sexy.

"We found the computer."

"What computer?"

"The tripped on cord, remember?"

"Oh. That computer. It was in the room after all, huh? Thing is, who moved it and why?"

"Don't get ahead of yourself, Sherlock. We didn't find it in the dean's office."

"No?"

"No. It was in a dumpster. In Chelsea. Along with the cord."

"Wait a minute. Why would you come across a computer in a dumpster in Chelsea? That's not even your precinct."

"You're a quick study, Professor. You're right. Not our precinct but stolen items go into a computer log available to all precincts since burglars have a nasty habit of roaming beyond borders."

"Are you saying you think a burglar killed the dean?"

"No, I'm not saying a burglar killed him, given how you found him, but then again, who knows what kind of kinky sex games the dean liked?"

"What does kinky sex have to do with this case? It looked to me like he was doing the usual male thing of having his thing serviced."

"Maybe I've said too much."

"No, wait a minute. I want to know how you came across the computer in Chelsea."

"Use that vivid imagination of yours, Professor."

"Okay, I'm using it. Nothing comes to mind."

I wanted a detailed explanation because I had no inkling of how the police recovered the computer, particularly because we were both avoiding the obvious: Isabel Cortez lived in Chelsea, where the item had been retrieved.

"Dumpster divers found the computer along with the cord and when they couldn't hack in, they turned it in to the Chelsea police. No big mystery. You see?"

"Wait. That doesn't make sense. Anyone can go to a computer store and get a computer hacked into."

"Gee, you're smarter than I thought. That's exactly what happened. The poor schmuck who recovered it did just that. The problem was that the computer had a barcode linked to your dean's office. The guy at the store realized the computer was stolen and gave the police a call. That's when the schmuck talked fast and led the police to the dumpster and you know where the dumpster was?"

"I'm assuming you're going to tell me the dumpster was outside of Isabel Cortez's apartment building."

"No, that would be too easy. The dumpster was a few blocks from her apartment building."

"A mere coincidence, Watson."

"Not so fast, Sherlock. Not a coincidence at all. In fact, the way we discovered where she lived was precisely because of the lost and stolen computer."

"Huh? I thought you googled her address."

"I don't even google restaurants, Professor. Besides, we have our own data register as I'm sure you are well aware but we had no need to use it since she appeared on the sidewalk passing the dumpster in question."

"That makes no sense. How would you know that?"

"Because I saw her."

"Are you holding vigil at the dumpster, Detective?"

"No, not me."

"Oh, one of your men, right? Of course, you can't be bothered."

"Actually, I've done many a stakeout in my time and I thought I needed to polish up my skills."

"When did all this happen? It's only been two days since the murder."

"Three actually. It's been three days but I guess you were too occupied to notice that another day had passed."

"Okay, three days. But still, when did you stake out the dumpster?"

"Two days ago. Same day we were told about the computer. We have to act fast in cases like this and we had to know if the killer dumped the computer. Perps have a way of repeating patterns. We thought she might return to the same place."

"She?"

"Just a pronoun."

"Not just any pronoun. You suspect the killer is female. Admit it."

"Nothing to admit, Professor and the killer could just as likely be male. I like playing with pronouns. Don't you?"

"Swift must love you for that."

"Yeah, well, Swift is who he is. Those types can't be changed. They meander into the next century with old habits."

"Why do you like him so much?"

"He's the lead detective. I've learned a lot from him."

"Okay, fair enough. I know what it's like to have an old white guy as a boss. Thing is, yours isn't going to be found murdered."

"In our line of work, death is a breath away, Professor."

"Wow. That's too profound even for me, Detective."

"It's the truth. I only speak the truth. Or not at all."

"Funny, I never thought you'd be at a loss for words. Seems you speak whether you need to or not."

"Are you criticizing me, Electra?"

I had gotten a rise out of her. Nice. Now I knew her weak spot. The woman didn't like to be criticized. But then again, who did?

"I'm not criticizing you at all, Carolina. I wouldn't dare criticize someone who is quite nearly perfect."

"Sure. Nearly perfect. Like Mary Poppins."

"Mary Poppins? First Sherlock Holmes references and now Mary Poppins? Are you an Anglophile?"

"Indeed I am. An Anglophile from the colonies."

We hung up and I felt manipulated. Carolina got information out of me even when I asked the questions.

It was barely ten thirty. I settled on strolling to the Admin building to catch Estela, the morning janitor, before her shift was over. I stepped out of my office and encountered Adrían with that customary smirk on his face that said, don't even try to hide it—I know where you've been and who you've been with. I wasn't in the mood to be interrogated again but here it was.

"*Buenos dias, Profesora* Campos."

"Good morning, Profesor Fuentes. I'm going to the Admin building. You want to walk with me?"

"No, not really. Just checking in to see how you are, and your wardrobe says you're doing fine."

I stared at my wrinkled white shirt. Damn. In all the excitement with Cintia, Sloan in the hallway and my phone call to Carolina, I'd forgotten to change. I kept a laundered, starched shirt in my office for emergencies. I retreated from my own doorway and walked to my desk drawer to retrieve a pressed shirt from a box in my bottom drawer. Adrían followed me in and closed the door behind me.

"Turn around," I said.

"I'm way ahead of you."

Adrían and I sustained delicate physical boundaries. I respected his privacy and he respected mine. When we shared hotel rooms at academic conferences, we respected the margins of our mutual bashfulness. It also helped when our hotel room had two bathrooms. Adrían had expressed to me more than once that his life had been hell before he transitioned and that he finally felt like himself. I made it my obligation to listen for cues about his needs now that he was more himself. I mostly didn't want to treat him like his life was an exposé. I'd had my own uncomfortable history, having been forced in high school to abide by tyrannical dress codes, meaning I dressed in drag. This was before Stonewall's influence reached small-town Texas. As an adult, I finally eschewed my mother's dresses and became a somewhat fashionable butch. Now that I was older I favored easy jeans and Brooks Brothers shirts along with the occasional designer jacket. Adrían, on the other hand, had an incomparable style, and I never attempted to compete with his elegant double-breasted, 1950s vintage suits, handsome wing tip shoes and broad silk ties. I felt too old to dress beyond the parameters of my time-honored comfort zone.

I ripped off my wrinkled white shirt and pulled on a clean-scented pink one. As I buttoned, I saw I had donned a dress shirt with French cuffs. I rolled up my sleeves for a relaxed look.

Adrían faced the bookshelf with his head buried in Roland Barthes's *A Lover's Discourse*. He and a former love interest had shared an obsession with the book. They weren't the only couple in academe quoting romantic dictums from that text but I guess he knew that. I was still pissed at the way she had mistreated Adrían, but he'd reassured me he was over her. He put the book down without a trace of nostalgia on his face. I was satisfied. She hadn't been worth his time.

I stood before the half mirror that was tacked onto a corner wall. "Not bad for an ole butch."

"You're not old, bud."

"Today I feel old."

"Sounds like she wore you out?"

He smirked. I saw the glint in his eye and I thought, fine, let's have the conversation. I was in no mood to delay the inevitable. Adrían's intentional smirks were usually right on the mark.

"No. She didn't wear me out. She has never worn me out. I wish she would wear me out and then I'd be done with her."

"That bad, huh?"

"I guess."

"Regrets?"

"I've had a few."

"Then again..."

"Too few to mention."

We smiled, content we were in sync.

"Did she kill the dean?"

"No. I don't know. Maybe."

"And you slept with her knowing she's a murderer?"

"I don't know if she is. I mean, think about it. In any murder mystery, the love interest can never be the murderer."

"I thought the love interest in this case was Detective Quinn."

"Oh. Yeah. You have a point."

"Of course I have a point."

"But Isabel isn't a murderer. She's selfish, self-centered, narcissistic and arrogant but she's not a killer."

"Wow. You make her sound so appealing. And you're not over her?"

"I'm over her."

"Sure you are."

"Look, just 'cause I had sex and spent the night doesn't mean I'm not over her. I'm over her. I had anonymous sex with a gorgeous woman in Chelsea the other night. Then, get this: I had sex with her again in the Admin building. I'm over Isabel, okay?"

"All right, all right. I hear ya." He pulled back and held his hands up in front of him, then shook his head. "In the Admin building? Damn. You sure do get lucky, bud."

"I don't even think about her anymore."

"Whatever you say, El."

"Oh, fuck."

I threw myself down on my couch and buried my head in my hands. Adrían sat next to me.

"Hey, she's not worth it."

"I know."

"You deserve better."

"I know."

"She's always going to seem charming at first but it's like you said: she turns on you once she's got you again. She can't help herself."

"Why do I feel sabotaged?"

"Because she takes you along for the ride. I've been with women like that. Sweet and attentive for about a minute. Long enough to get us inside their webs, then *zas*!" He punched the air with his fist. "We're stuck. Trapped. The harder you tussle, the harder her pull."

"I'm an idiot, Adrían."

"Hey, you're human. You want to be loved and she's good at pretending. For about a minute. Then the drama. She hooks you then blames you for the drama she creates."

"Yeah," I mumbled.

"And when she's got you, she comes in for the kill."

"Don't say kill, Adrían. It makes me nervous."

"Sorry but I got to be direct or you'll keep going back there."

"I know."

"And none of this is going to matter anyway 'cause you're going back there."

"I know," I mumbled.

My face was still in my hands. After a moment of much needed silence, I rose to my feet.

"I'll walk you part of the way," he offered.

"Please. Keep me company. I'm a little nervous."

CHAPTER THIRTEEN

We stepped into the morning chill. Across the quad, two policemen stood watch as if innocently hanging out on an icy morning. I gazed up at the sky and saw a dark cloud heading our way. I elbowed Adrían and tilted my chin for him to witness the oncoming storm. Neither of us wore our heavy coats.

"A hard rain's gonna fall," he said.

"The iceman cometh," I replied.

At the steps to the Admin building, Adrían paused, pantomimed tipping the brim of a hat and walked on gallantly.

Inside the building I noted that Estela was at the end of the main hallway and a tall man was speaking to her. She kept a safe distance from him, grasping to her chest a bucket with cleansers and rags. He flapped his hands wide as if to be explaining or perhaps miming since he probably didn't think she knew English. The wider he flailed his already elongated arms, the farther back she shifted, probably fearing that one of his massive palms would crash into her. Moving closer, I saw that the man was actually none other than Mike Miller, the president of the college. He looked like a scrawny, elderly giant next to Estela, and I sensed he only made her more ill at ease. I scuttled toward them.

"President Miller. What are you doing among us plebeians?"

He turned and glared at me. "Ellen, how the hell are you?" He slapped his forehead to show surprise. "Ellen, do me a favor and tell this woman she has got to scrub that office again. I told her to wipe that blood off the floorboards, but she acts like she can't hear me. I cannot make her understand. Maybe if you tell her, Ellen. I'm sure she'll listen to you since you're both from the same part of the country."

"I'm from Texas, Mike. Estela is from Nicaragua."

"Well, I'll be! I never knew you were from Texas, Ellen. Fine country, Texas."

"It's a state, Mike."

He slapped his forehead again. "Now, Ellen, don't you think I know it's not a country. My word, Ellen, don't treat me like the other faculty. They all think I'm a brainless fool but I know a thing or two. Now tell this young woman here to please scrub those floorboards again."

I spoke directly to Estela in Spanish, knowing that her English was better than Mike's, but in his presence I addressed her in Spanish. I told her she needed to pretend she was scrubbing the floorboards again to convince the president she had done so because Mike was an idiot who needed to see women around him busy. He gave orders relentlessly and expected those within hearing distance to leap in response to his frivolous commands—and of those there were many.

Estela returned to the dean's office and got on her knees in front of the spot where I had initially found a blood puddle that soaked my favorite Italian leather boots, which reminded me, I needed to take them to my exclusive, women-owned shoe stand for polishing.

Mike plunked his lanky arm around my shoulders, practically leaning on me as he towered above. "Come with me, Ellen."

With his arm resting on my shoulders, he led me up five flights of stairs to his temporary office behind two sets of glass doors and a receptionist who wasn't the least bit attentive when she saw us advance toward her desk. She had been filing her nails, which seemed typical enough. I was intrigued with the nail polish lined up on her desk in tiny bottles of primary colors: yellow, red and blue. A bottle of black polish sat in close proximity. When the phone rang, she picked up the receiver, punched the blinking light and hung up. When the phone rang again, she repeated the ritual, careful not to smudge her freshly polished nails. I recognized something about her but I couldn't quite remember. To my astonishment, President Mike ignored her indifference and led me to his office. I hadn't managed to twist myself free from his massive arm, and after five sets of stairs, his arm weighed heavy.

It was well-known that his corner office sat empty because he preferred his business office in the Financial District. President Mike Miller treated his college campus engagement like a nuisance distracting him from his billion dollar plastics and video game businesses. In the 1980s, he'd invested in plastic bottles that became the water bottles in every gym, business office and home. By the time environmentalists pointed out that plastic wreaked havoc on the earth, he had begun investing in multiple video games, many of which condoned race-related violence, which he justified by announcing to critics who tried to shut him down that his games trained young boys to be superior soldiers. As a successful businessman, he'd been hand-picked by Capital College's regents to rectify the school's financial chaos, meaning the regents wanted someone who could eke out profits from a place intended for knowledge. For the regents, places of higher learning had a lot to learn from Walmart, the premier prototype of capitalism in which money and things mattered more than people. So far, they were succeeding.

President Mike pushed me down on a leather chair that faced a massive desk with a chair behind it resembling an ornate throne. His cowboy boots, which he clunked on top of his desk, had turquoise sleeves and upon closer examination I noted that the carvings on the desk, throne and boot sleeves correlated. The corner office had a view of the main quad and a minor park in the distance. I glimpsed a patch of blue from one of the windows. I envied any patches of blue amid the heavens that were increasingly gray.

"I'm glad you dropped by, Ellen. I've been meaning to give you a call. The vice chancellor told me she had a little talk with you and I was grateful to her. Damn, if she isn't a good girl, that vice chancellor of mine."

He never called her by her name. President Mike only addressed men by their names. The rest of us—that is, the female gender, the transgender folk, anyone other than a white het man who made oodles of money—were nonentities whose names he got wrong no matter how many times he was corrected. I no longer reminded him that my name wasn't Ellen. If he didn't get your name wrong then he didn't get your name at all.

"Ellen, do you know why I took this job?"

"No, Mike. I really don't." I sank into my chair because he was on the verge of spouting his famous monologue about pulling himself up by his bootstraps and making his first million at twenty-one.

"Not for the money, Ellen. I lose money working here as your college president. I do. I lose millions of dollars every year. If I'm not out there hustling cash, nobody is going to do it for me. But I made a promise to my friends on the school board."

"You mean the regents?"

"Yeah, yeah, those guys. I made them a promise, Ellen. I promised they'd see a profit by year's end. And now those little 'Occupy Wall Street' weasels are getting in my way. Everybody's getting a little bit scared. Can you believe that, Ellen? Those little pipsqueaks can't stop us from making a profit. Profit is what this country is about. Hell, it's what the world's about. Remember Reagan? Damn good leader that man was. Damn good." He gazed at his knuckles folded into fists.

"Here's the thing, Ellen. I want to keep my promise to those boys. I never go back on a promise to make a profit. That's who I am. Thing is, now we've got this messy murder on our hands and it's not good for business. Now, you were here early that morning and you found Johnson with his dick hanging out of his pants. Who do you think wanted him dead? I heard you were real good friends with his wife." He winked at me.

I kept my face blank. "I don't know who killed Dean Johnson, Mike. I just happened to be in the building at that hour."

"Now see, Ellen, I think you know something and aren't telling. I think you're protecting someone. Maybe yourself?"

"Are you suggesting I killed him?"

"Oh, Ellen, of course not!" He flailed his arms, slapped his forehead and buzzed the receptionist. He buzzed for a long minute but she didn't answer. Finally, he screamed out, "Trudy, Trudy, you get yourself in here or I'm calling your mother."

Through the frosted glass I saw tiny Trudy rise reluctantly and smooth her skirt with her palms to avoid messing up polish that had surely dried by now. She opened the door abruptly. "What do you want, Uncle Mike?"

"Be a sweet pea and go get me a cup of coffee. Black and sweet. The way I like it."

She sighed loudly. Neither one of them asked me if I wanted a cup. I would've declined because I loathed office drip coffee but asking me would've been a considerate, non-corporate gesture.

"I'm feeling unlucky, Ellen. Dammit. I don't like feeling unlucky. It hurts profits. Gets into my joojoo magic that brings me profits. The job is sitting there. Nobody wants it right now. It's jinxed, Ellen. Jinxed."

He peered at me, clearly concentrating, leaning forward and stomping his boots on the floor under his desk.

"You want the job, Ellen? It's good pay. A nice salary boost for you. You could help me keep those little sons-a-bitches at #Occupy Wall Street in order. They listen to you, Ellen."

"Mike, I'm flattered. But I'm not your man."

He didn't even blink when I called myself a man. "Why, sure you are, Ellen. You've been here what? Ten, fifteen years, right? You know the lay of the land. Faculty respect you."

"No. They don't, Mike. Most don't even like me."

"That's not true, Ellen. Even my vice chancellor thinks it's a good idea to appoint you. Think on it. It's a good way to get those police detectives off your trail. We give you the blank check of interim dean and you can do anything you want, Ellen. Don't you find that attractive? And a six-figure salary. Anybody else would be chomping at the bit for this job right now, Ellen."

I wondered why President Mike had appropriated an attitude that sounded as if he was a cowboy from the Wild West. He was actually from the state of Maine but a couple of recent summers on a dude ranch in Arizona and he was suddenly a cowboy. Since then he wore only cowboy boots and affected a cowboy twang, believing he sounded tough yet personable. He wanted to be liked. Faculty and students called him "Like-me-Mike" to aggravate him, but the guy was clueless and ignorant about academic life and its procedures, never having written more than a memo. I wondered why the nation's imagination was so invested in frontier images of alleged self-made men, because when President Mike started wearing cowboy boots and simulating a twang, he became even more esteemed by the regents. But I wasn't buying the whole performance. And I was even more suspicious of "Team Mike and Justine." Why target me for the dean's post?

"I think I'm going to have to pass on that offer, Mike."

He frowned and smacked his forehead. "I'm not taking no for an answer, Ellen. Why, you'd be perfect and it would only be for a few months, or until the end of the academic year. May or June or something like that. Don't come in if you don't want to. Work from your department. I work downtown in my business office and I drop in occasionally to that big ole fancy-dancy space in regents Hall with the vice chancellor and all them other bigwigs. Makes me nervous to be over there. This place is much better. Look at that view. Hey, why don't you use this office, Ellen? Nobody wants that bloody mess of an office where they found the dead body. Heck, maybe we'll make that a reception area or something. Yeah, use this office instead. Come on over here. Let me show you this fancy desk. I had it shipped here from South Africa. Feel this fine rosewood."

I got up, walked over and smoothed my hand on fragrant timber. The job was tempting for the desk alone but I wasn't fond of the space. Too many windows made me nervous. I was accustomed to one small window with the blinds permanently shut.

"I tell you what, Ellen. Once you're done with the job, I'll throw in the desk. I'll get it delivered to you. As a consolation prize. What do you say?"

I noted the engravings on the side drawers. They resembled women's long hair stirring in the wind. The handles were shaped like tresses and I grazed my fingers on top, feeling the dense, exquisite rosewood.

"Go ahead. Slide it open. You'll see how easy and smooth she is."

I opened the drawer and startled in surprise. Lying on top of a blue felt cloth was a six-inch knife. Just like the one that I had seen in my file cabinet.

President Mike picked up the knife and held it up to the light. "This is my favorite hunting knife, Ellen. Sure love the look of it. See how clean that blade is?"

He put his finger on the blade, admiring the razor-sharp edge. The knife had a pearl handle with a turquoise bead in the center of the handle. I hadn't seen the decorative bead on the knife in my file cabinet but then again the knife had been covered in blood.

"Here. Take a hold of it, Ellen." He placed the dagger in my hand before I could object. "Heavy, isn't she?"

I nodded and handed it back to him.

He held it up to the light. "Hmm. What's this?" Mike slid the tip of his nail over the turquoise bead and poked the setting.

"Something wrong?" I asked.

"Don't know where that came from."

"What?"

President Mike didn't answer. Promptly, he wrapped the dagger in a felt cloth and dropped it back in the drawer.

"What's it gonna be, Ellen? You ready to take over as dean?"

"I don't think so, Mike."

"Don't talk crazy, Ellen. You'll start in the morning."

He reached in his pocket, came out empty and yelled, "Trudy, Trudy, do you have the key to this office?"

"I'm busy, Uncle Mike," she yelled back.

Through the frosted glass doors, I could see a figure hovering over her. A boyfriend, I thought. Of course she was busy.

"Trudy, darlin', don't make me come over there."

She and the figure hovering at her desk whispered intimately. Trudy still ignored her uncle. President Mike Miller rose from behind his desk and flung open the door.

"Trudy," he said. "Ellen, come on out here with me." He held the door wide open. "Well, if it isn't our up-and-coming new professor. How are you doing, Hugh?"

Mike slapped Assistant Professor Hugh Roberts on the back. "Trudy, why didn't you tell me that this upstanding young man was here? Ellen, do you know Hugh?" He slapped his forehead. "What am I saying? Of course you do. You're in the same department. Good to see you, Hugh."

Hugh and I exchanged cordial looks without uttering a sound. He was probably annoyed because I openly disparaged his hero, Andrew Jackson, Indian killer. Trudy reached inside her desk and handed her uncle a brass key, which he shoved in my jacket pocket.

Damn, I thought. I'm a dead man.

CHAPTER FOURTEEN

I walked out of the Admin building to be greeted by thunder and sheets of rain. Perfect. The hard rain was here. I ran across the quad, slid and landed in a muddy pool. I got up, scanning to see if anyone had witnessed my tumble. My boots and pants were a muddy mess. The rainstorm had emptied the area except for two chumps in the distance holding up umbrellas and rushing from one building to the next. I brushed mud from the seat of my pants but only smeared more wet dirt into the cotton. I bolted to my office, hoping to avoid spectators. As I opened my door, I heard a voice behind me.

"Why haven't you called?"

It was Isabel.

"You like to leave a girl hanging?"

I faced her. "I had to get to work."

"At dawn? Who are you kidding, Electra? You were angry. Admit it."

"Angry? I wasn't angry. Oh, you mean because your boyfriend called you at two in the morning after I fucked you.

Why would that make me angry? That was a routine evening with you, Isabel."

"Let me make it up to you."

"You have nothing to make up to me." I pointed toward the end of the hallway. "Go. I have a class in an hour."

"Looking like that?" She peered at my muddy pants and shoes.

"I'll get cleaned up."

"You're angrier than I thought."

"That's your imagination. Now leave. Please. I have to prep for class."

"You never prep for class."

"Excuse me?"

"You don't. You told me you don't."

"Okay, let me clarify once and for all. I prep for my classes. What I told you is that I don't spend a week prepping for classes anymore. I did that when I was a young, insecure faculty member."

"Testy."

Sloan roamed the other end of the hallway, prompting me to seize Isabel's arm and tug her into my office. She rammed me against the wall and rummaged inside my shirt.

"What are you doing?" I whispered.

"Why are you whispering?" she asked.

I motioned my head toward the door.

"Oh, please. You worry too much."

She proceeded to plunge her hands deep inside my athletic bra and as she pinched my nipple, someone knocked on the door. I elbowed her aside and smoothed my shirt with my hands to ensure I didn't look disheveled. I cracked the door open to Sloan.

"I hear congratulations are in order," he said.

"Excuse me?"

"You're the new interim dean, I'm told."

"You're told? By whom?"

"I have my sources, Electra."

"I'm sure you do, Sloan. Excuse me, but I have work to do."

I shut the door, but his thick brown loafer jammed the doorway. What the fuck. My impulse was to bang the door and smash his foot, but I didn't want a lawsuit and the guy was capable of anything.

"Something else, Sloan?"

"I thought I saw you with the woman the police are looking for."

"Huh?"

"She's in your office."

"Who?"

"The police suspect."

"Sloan, if the police suspected anyone, don't you think they would have that certain someone in custody?"

I slammed the door and he yanked his foot out fast. I waited a minute, listening for his footsteps and when he was gone, I breathed deeply, comforted I hadn't lost my temper more than I had.

"Ooh. You're sexy when you're angry."

Isabel slammed me against the wall with more force and this time I accepted her rough games, but another knock on the door hindered our designs.

"Fuck," I whispered.

"I wish," she said.

She stepped aside and once again I cracked the door open.

"Carolina? What are you doing here?" The distress in my voice was apparent.

"We made plans, remember?"

"Plans? What plans?"

Isabel, hidden behind the door, groped my back.

"For lunch. You said to meet you here at twelve thirty. I'm early."

I stared and concentrated on the words coming out of her mouth while Isabel pinched my ass.

"I'm sorry. I guess I forgot. I'm kind of busy right now."

"Oh." She paused and looked at my shirt. The top three buttons were unclasped. "I see."

I ignored her observation, pretending I always wore my shirt in a way that left me half-exposed. "Can I call you?" I asked.

"Sure. Call me."

She backed away keeping eye contact and when she reached the end of the hallway, she twirled and disappeared.

"Who was that?"

"Police detective. And stop distracting me."

"You're having lunch with a police detective?" She moved back and away from me.

"Yeah, I mean, no." I couldn't remember making the appointment for lunch today.

"Why are you having lunch with a police detective?"

"I don't know. I don't remember." I stroked her arm but she pulled away.

"What's wrong?"

"I have to go."

"Go? Go where?"

"I have an appointment."

"No, you don't."

"Yes. I do."

"And you happened to remember after Carolina dropped by?"

"Oh. Her name is Carolina."

I ignored her comment, refusing to engage in fictitious jealousy.

"Call me. If you're not too busy," she said.

"Fine."

"Fine."

For the third time that morning, my office door banged shut and I felt shut out of all that could be a relatively wholesome time. This wasn't good. As soon as I became interim dean, my luck had changed for the worse. Or maybe I was paranoid. Me, paranoid? Ha! I'm always paranoid. I poked around in my pocket and found the key. The brass key to my new office in the Admin building. I felt like a sell-out. I tossed the key on my desk and scrunched down on my chair with my chin resting on cupped hands. I couldn't get my mind off Carolina. There was no lunch date. She was spying on me. I sat for a while and realized Isabel's hold on me was lessoning. I wasn't as fixated. Carolina has disrupted a moment of lust, causing me to hesitate and reassess a fixation that could kill me. Literally. Well, maybe not literally, but the way Isabel had tortured me psychically and psychologically made our sex games trite by comparison.

I thought about a phrase I had read in a novel. Something about the fissure inside a woman's yielding curves, the flesh when most desiring and desired. Carolina Quinn had walked backward calculatingly to obscure swaying hips and now I had to have her. Disrobed. Stripped of safeguarded logic.

But Carolina was her job and I was nothing more than an avenue leading her to answers to a puzzling case. She probably suspected that Isabel Cortez had been in my office and wanted me to call her to get more information about Isabel. Carolina wasn't interested in me. Not that it mattered. I would still pursue her now that I was hooked and there's nothing more seductive than feeling smitten by a woman who is only doing her job. Okay, there is one more seductive thing: a woman who never calls. Or, who calls occasionally to bestow friendly edicts that you detest because you were under the illusion that you had something but you grasp from the tone of her voice you were wrong all along. But I'm rambling. I mean, Carolina and I hadn't even kissed. But job or no job, suspect or no suspect, I planned to change that oversight. Soon.

I gathered up my books and lecture notes, stuffed them in my book back and walked to my afternoon class muddied and rejected but with renewed conviction.

CHAPTER FIFTEEN

After a heated debate in my class, "Murdering Latinas and the Men who Love Them"—inevitably a female student defended all Latinas and accused me of brandishing stereotypes, which pleased me because someone was paying attention—I hurried to my subway stop ready for reprieve from a day far more eventful than I had intended. Interim Dean of Arts and Sciences? Me? The faculty barely knew I existed. I was about to sit when an elderly man inched past me and fell into the last empty seat.

From the corner of my vision I spotted Omar, my student who worked in the parking garage. He smirked at my frustration. I lifted my chin and he stumbled over.

"*Hola* Profe."

"Going home, Omar?"

"Nah. Gotta go to work, Profe."

"At Starbucks?"

"Yeah."

"You like it there?"

"What's to like? All those hipsters." Omar's eyes were narrow slits, causing him to look distrustful of everyone and everything.

"How's your mom?" I was slowly making my way to questioning him about his parking garage job, hoping to disarm him with friendly conversation.

"Mami's all right. Works hard."

"So do you."

"Yeah."

"When do you have time to study?"

"In the morning."

"Before the parking garage job?"

"At the garage. It's pretty dead that early." He looked at me and squinted. "Why?" he asked.

I paused and he squinted harder. "Here's the thing, Omar. Did you see anything suspicious the morning the dean was found dead?"

Omar shifted his body and leaned into the subway handrail. He stuffed his right hand into his front jeans pocket and glanced over his shoulder. "Look, Profe. I never told you this." His head sidled closer. "That morning. I was studying. Like I always do 'cause there ain't much to do. Only ones who ever come into campus that early are the science profs and their flunkies. You know how they are. Anyway, this morning, I seen something I hadn't seen before."

He looked over his shoulder again then murmured, "I seen a strange truck. Like a moving van. I didn't think nothing of it. The driver flashed some kind of pass so I let 'em through."

"A moving van? What's so strange about a moving van?"

Omar quit tilting toward me and stood up straight. "Fuck, Profe. How should I know? I just thought it was kinda strange. Nobody moves at four thirty in the morning. You can't see nothing at that hour."

"Maybe someone was delivering the truck. Getting ready to load it or unload it."

"That's the other funny thing. It was empty when it came in and empty when it came out."

"Huh? So no loading or unloading?"

"Nope."

"How can you be so sure?"

"'Cause I followed it."

"You followed it? Why?"

"'Cause as soon as I let the driver through, the truck went out the exit and into campus."

"What's wrong with that?"

"It's my job to report anything not right and I thought it wasn't right. I mean, most moving trucks have some kind of logo on them. This was just a plain white van. And why drive through the parking garage?"

"But you said the driver had a pass."

"Yeah. Flashed a pass real quick through the windshield, but I wasn't sure if it was a real pass or not."

"Why didn't you stop him and check?"

"Why didn't I have coffee and donuts ready while I was at it? Then we could've had a nice long talk about the Yankees, who I don't even like, by the way."

"Okay, okay. So you followed. Then what?"

"Here's where it gets interesting."

"Omar. Wait a second. Why haven't you told any of this to the police?"

"First off, Profe, nobody asked. You're the first one. And second, I don't talk to no police. Fuck. Who you think I am? A snitch?"

"We're talking about a murderer, Omar. You're not a snitch if you report a murder."

"Well, I didn't see no murder. All I seen was a white moving van that rattled it was so empty."

"Where did he finally park?"

"In front of the Admin building. After that the driver went inside. But it gets kinda strange."

"Okay. I'm ready."

"It was a lady."

"A lady? Was she serving up high tea?"

"Huh? Fuck, Profe. Gimme a break. All I know is that when the driver jumped out of the cab, I saw a girl, petite-like, hair under a baseball cap 'cause the cap fell off and she had to stuff her hair back inside."

"How do you know it wasn't a guy with long hair?"

Omar shifted from one leg to the other and half closed his eyes. "Gee, Profe, maybe it was her tits that gave her away. Not big ones but I know tits when I see 'em."

"Okay, so she had nice breasts and long hair. What else?"

"Yeah, real nice. Those sweet babies were popping out of her tiny T-shirt."

"Young? Old? How tall?"

"I said she was petite, Profe. Too dark to tell if she was young or old."

"Oh, but it wasn't too dark to see her breasts?"

"Not hard to miss through that tiny T-shirt."

Omar grinned as he held out both arms in a forward sweeping motion, mimicking the contours of round breasts. The image was amusing but I wasn't amused because he was probably describing Isabel Cortez, whose breasts were not ample, hence her reason for flaunting them in tight T-shirts. And while Isabel had long legs, she was actually only a little over five feet tall. Dammit. Why, Isabel? What did you have against Dean Johnson anyway?

"I guess the police aren't looking for a girl shooter, huh?"

"First of all, there was no shooting, Omar, and second, they already suspect the wife and finally, sounds like the driver you're describing was a woman, not a girl."

"Oh. Yeah. Right. A Woman. Sure. I get it."

He emphasized the "wo" of woman, measuring how obnoxious he could get. It worked.

"Isn't this your stop, Omar?"

"Oh, yeah." He jumped out at Columbus Circle and yelled to me, "Hey, Profe, everything I told you, you can go ahead and tell that sexy babe cop. If she wants to talk to me, I'm ready anytime."

His arrogance irritated me, but I wasn't going to let on that he had irked me, and anyway, I wasn't going to share any of these details with Detective Carolina Quinn. If she was such a good detective, why hadn't she already questioned Omar?

A few stops later, I got off and walked ten blocks to my apartment. I needed to blow off steam from my recent encounter with Omar. I wasn't sure why I was so furious. Was it that he objectified Isabel's breasts or that he called Carolina Quinn sexy? One way or the other, the kid had too much information about my likes and dislikes. What made him think I liked Carolina and what gave him the right to talk about Isabel that way? Okay, he wasn't aware he was describing Isabel, but did he have to be so incredibly obtuse and insensitive about women in general? Twenty-something boys understood nothing about women.

Now I had more information leading me to believe that Isabel had been lying. Something was up with her and Dean Johnson; otherwise she wouldn't have been in the Admin building so early in the morning. It was almost as if they had something going on, some kind of agreement to meet that early. I didn't believe she was the killer but I did believe she was capable of fucking the guy since she wasn't too different from Virginia Johnson. Both loved men with money and power, and the fact remained that Dean Johnson had had money and power. Maybe the link was Wall Street and his father at Goldman Sachs. Didn't Oscar's mother work for the family? Maybe it was time to talk to Oscar's mom.

CHAPTER SIXTEEN

As soon as I walked through my apartment door, I punched in Detective Quinn's phone number.

"Carolina? It's me. Electra. It's time to question Oscar's mom."

"Way ahead of you."

"What? But how?"

"How did we know we had to ask the maid what she knew about the comings and goings in the dean's house? Gee, Electra. Call it female intuition. Or better yet, how about calling it good detective work?"

"You don't have to be so sarcastic."

"Me? Sarcastic?"

"What'd you find out?"

"Nothing worth repeating."

"Or nothing you want to share with me?"

"Maybe."

"Fine. I'll talk to her myself."

"I wouldn't advise that, Professor."

"She's my student's mother. I can talk to her if I want."

"You can do whatever you want, but I wouldn't advise speaking to her."

"Are you going to tell me why?"

"Obstruction of justice work for you?"

"Not really."

"Okay, how about just do me this favor and don't speak to her."

"Why would I do you any favors, Detective?"

"Because you like me."

"I do?"

"Yes. You do."

"Ah. I see. And is this precondition ever going to get me anywhere with you?"

"Where would you like to go?"

"I think you know."

"I think our relationship is strictly business, Electra."

"What ever happened to protect and serve? Isn't that your motto?"

"I'm fulfilling both."

"Are you? Because I don't feel protected, and correct me if I'm wrong, but I haven't been served."

"I get the sense you have."

"By you? No, I'd remember."

"Okay, Electra. You win. I'll let you in on one small detail."

"I'm listening."

"The dean was wealthy. Incredibly wealthy. So wealthy he could afford to make investment mistakes."

"Okay. And what does that mean, Detective?"

"What do you think it means?"

"That's easy. Follow the money. And Virginia Johnson will be at the end of that trail."

"You have motive as well, Electra."

"Motive? What motive?"

"You are the new dean."

"That's not motive. That's sheer insanity. The president of the college practically forced the job on me. Nobody wants it. I might as well wear a target on my chest."

She was quiet. I felt my blood pressure rising. I asked, "What about Virginia Johnson?"

She was still quiet.

"Hey, this is the part where you reassure me that there's no danger and I'll be fine."

More silence.

"Hello…Carolina? I'm still here…"

"Be careful, Electra."

"I am careful but nothing I can do if some wild-eyed killer decides to do me in."

"I'm not joking."

"Well, why not send protection?"

"I tried. But Swift doesn't think it's necessary."

"Wait. So trailing me to see if I'm the killer is acceptable but when I'm in danger, it's not necessary to protect me? I'm not understanding the logic here."

"I know, I know. Doesn't sound logical, does it?"

"Nope."

"You can call me anytime."

"If a murderer comes into my office and slices me up, I'm free to call you? I'll be sure to have you on speed dial."

"You're prone to drama, aren't you?"

"Hey, I'm the one in danger, remember? I think I'm allowed a little bit of high drama at the moment."

"Call me anytime, Electra. For any reason."

"Thanks, Detective. I'll keep that in mind."

I hung up without saying good-bye, regretting my impetuous behavior. I was about to call her back to apologize when my phone rang. It wasn't a number I recognized. I let it go to voice mail. I checked the time and saw that it was already after eleven. I was too angry to go to sleep. That's it, I thought. A certain someone deserves a visit. I grabbed my wool peacoat and tugged it on while Mocha gave me an agitated look.

"What? Not you too? I'll be fine. I'll be back in no time."

She made her habitual chuntering sound. Mocha couldn't be bothered to meow out loud like most cats.

I opened the fridge and unwrapped a package of wild sockeye salmon, tore off small bites and placed them in her treat bowl. She smelled it carefully before ingesting.

"You know I only give you the best, Mocha."

She ignored me.

"Fine. Be like the women in my life."

Into the night, I felt a cold wave greet my face. I loved the smell and feel of a crisp November, moonless night. I walked to the nearest subway entrance and hopped on a train to Chelsea.

I knocked on her door, loudly and repeatedly, until I heard Isabel scuffling inside.

"It's me. Open up."

"Me who?"

"Very funny. Open up, Isabel."

"Why should I?"

"Because I have to talk to you."

"I don't have to talk to you."

"No, but you're going to want to hear this."

After a few more minutes of clatter, she opened the door a crack. I could see her petite breasts popping out of a slinky ivory nightie but I quickly averted my gaze and focused on her eyes.

"What am I going to want to hear?"

"Aren't you going to let me in?"

"I don't think so. Not tonight."

"You don't want to hear about something that could change the course of your life?

"Not really."

"Isabel. Please. Let me in."

She shut the door, unlatched the chain and held the entrance wide open. As I was about to walk through, she shut it again.

"What the fuck, Isabel? I'm not here to play games."

"Aren't you?"

"No. This is serious."

"Our games are serious, Electra."

"Not to me."

The door flew open and I rushed in before she had an opportunity to shut it. I headed for the kitchen, reached inside the liquor cabinet and poured myself a tequila shot, downed it then poured another and downed that too.

"I see. It's one of those nights, is it?"

"What were you doing on campus at four thirty the morning the dean was murdered?"

"We've discussed this, El."

"You haven't given me any straight answers."

"Straight? You want straight? Now, you want straight? El, *querida*, are you asking me for vanilla sex, 'cause I can do that too?" She slinked up behind me and rubbed her breasts against my back.

I melted from their smoothness, struggling to remember I was fuming. I sidestepped and faced her. "You haven't answered the question."

"El. What do you want from me?"

"The truth."

"No, you don't. You want falsehoods and games. That's what you signed up for."

"I never signed up for that."

"Didn't you read the fine print?"

"What fine print? What are you talking about? See, that's exactly what I mean, Isabel. You love to distract me with your sexy *chichis* and your glib talk."

"I'm going to ignore that you called me glib and focus instead on the fact that you love my *chichis*."

"Isabel, someone saw you that morning. Driving a big white van."

"Lots of white vans in New York City, El."

"Not being driven by a petite woman in a baseball cap. Where is my cap, by the way? It's been missing for a couple of weeks."

Isabel leaned back against the kitchen counter, crossed one leg over the other, exposing flesh through the slit of her nightgown, and smirked. "I don't know what you're talking about."

"Which part? The part about the petite woman or the part about my missing baseball cap?"

"Take your pick. Neither of those items suit me."

She came closer and rubbed her breasts against my chest this time.

"Come on, El. Calm down. We both know why you're really here."

She took my hand and pushed it inside her nightgown and I felt her breast, supple and silky. I tightened my grip and pinched her nipple and slammed her torso against the kitchen counter while I yanked her hair with my other hand. I breathed into her face.

"I'm not playing, Isabel."

"I'm not either, Electra."

She heaved me against the kitchen table and unzipped my jeans, thrusting her hand inside me. I gasped. After she ripped off my pants and they dropped below my waist, she knelt before me and bit my clitoris hard. I almost screamed, but I didn't want her to get the best of me yet. When I didn't react, she looked up at me from her knees and smirked.

"Ay, El, El, El…when are you going to learn? *Eres mía. Totalmente mía.*"

She licked casually and I wasn't in any shape to debate the matter at that moment, particularly since I savored seeing her on her knees. It was an erotic view from my angle. With one hand, she jostled open a kitchen drawer and pulled out ruby red lipstick and a turkey baster. She uncapped the lipstick and applied the sinister red to her lips then gripped the baster and slowly shoved it inside me as she pressed her mouth inside my thighs ,smearing dark crimson on my flesh.

The turkey baster had a rough indented curve at the tip and I wasn't fond of the way it chafed but I wasn't going to complain. She found a rhythm that appealed to us both, shoving in and out, slowly at first until the eroticism of her mouth on my vaginal lips and clit was so acute I had to scream, rousing her to shove faster. I was on the edge of bliss when she stopped and grabbed my legs, causing me to lose my balance. I fell back and bumped my head on the table.

"Owwww."

"Quit complaining."

She climbed on top of me, and the kitchen table wobbled as her nipples popped out of her satin nightie. She teased my lips, moving her breasts side to side as I tried to catch one in my mouth until she allowed me to suck on both, which I squeezed together, until she moaned. I squeezed her breasts harder with my hands freeing me to suck her nipples as much as I craved—and I craved them. I always hungered for nipples in my mouth and I wasn't particularly particular so long as a woman was also eagerly involved. That is, so long as she pleaded for my mouth on her nipples and from the sound of Isabel's groans, she yearned for my mouth as much as my mouth yearned for her.

I opened my eyes to assemble her face and when I saw that her eyes were also wide open, I stared into her, hoping for a clue about something, anything. As I studied her, I realized she knew almost nothing about me but I had shared little, refusing to indulge in genealogies about boring past affairs. Isabel, on the other hand, was full of the past and inflicted her stories on the present when she thought I was losing interest. What she didn't bother to consider was that her past affairs with men and women were mind-numbing. Initially, her stories amused me and I think she shared anecdotes to deflect from the reality of who she was and where she came from. That I didn't trust what she told me was inconsequential, because her fabrications were alluring and succeeded in luring me into her web of trickery, which seemed premeditated. Isabel Cortez ensnared my imagination even when I began to lose interest. I wondered if her latest maneuver, showing up at the Admin building the morning of Dean Johnson's murder, was her way of inching back into my life. Because if it was, it had worked. Here I was invariably sprawled on her kitchen table sucking on nipples that enticed me, when I had only come over to check out Omar's tale about that morning's activities in the parking garage.

"*¿Qué?*" she asked.

"*Nada.* I was just admiring the view."

Just as I was about to take her nipple into my mouth again, I heard a bang coming from her bedroom. She shoved the turkey baster deeper into my vaginal cavity. Despite her insistence, I sat up and pulled the kitchen utensil out from me and saw a drop of blood. I tossed the baster aside, pulled up my pants and proceeded to her bedroom door. Isabel tugged on my leg but I managed to shake free and, shoving the door open, I fell upon the bed next to a hairy-chested, half-bald man in boxers. His headphones accounted for his not having heard me when I pounced in.

"Hi! Hi!" he said. He grinned big and didn't so much as feign jealousy despite my having been in close proximity fucking Isabel.

"Oh," I said.

"I was listening to *Pagliacci*. Here. Try them on."

He handed me his earbuds and I put them in and discovered that he was indeed listening to opera. He didn't strike me as the type but then again, who was the opera type? Was there a type? I suppose I had typecast opera aficionados as much as I had typecast Isabel's lovers and this guy seemed as typical as any.

"I know what you're thinking," he said.

"No. You don't."

"I'm Isabel's cousin. Dominique."

"Her cousin?"

"Yeah. She's never mentioned me? Isabel? You never talk about me? I thought we were close, you and me."

By this time she had entered the bedroom and was sitting beside me. We made an adorable picture, I'm sure, the three of us lounging on Isabel's bed deliberating about family matters.

"Yeah, why haven't you ever mentioned Dominique, Isabel?"

"Electra, meet my cousin Dominique. Dominique, Electra. There. Are you two satisfied?"

"More like are you two satisfied?" he asked.

Isabel punched his arm in a way that led me to believe they were indeed cousins, although I still had doubts because she was prone to lying about everything and anything for the sake of duplicity. She couldn't help herself.

As I scanned the room, I saw my pink baseball cap hanging from a naked nail on the back of the bedroom door. Yes, I had a pink baseball cap. I was exceedingly butch. I got up and plucked the cap from the spike on the door, holding the brim up high to make a point.

"Fine. Take it," said Isabel.

"I will."

"Hey, you two gonna fight over a lousy baseball cap?"

"Who's fighting?" I said.

"Yeah, who's fighting?"

"Never mind." Dominique rose from the bed and headed into the kitchen. "Isa, you got any real booze in here? All I see is this lousy tequila."

"That's my tequila and it's not lousy," I screamed out.

"Your tequila?" said Isabel. "Why is it your tequila?"

"I left it, remember?"

"Oh, that tequila is long gone. Someone else left this bottle." She smiled and yelled out to her cousin, "There's brandy in the cabinet, Dom."

"Brandy? Brandy? That's so girly. I need a man's drink."

"Well, then, help yourself to the tequila," I yelled out.

"Yuck. That's too manly even for me," he said.

"Okay. I'm out of here," I said.

I stuffed the brim of the baseball cap into my back pocket. In the middle of the kitchen, my peacoat lay strewn and Dominique tiptoed around it in his bare feet as if the coat were a carcass he refused to touch. I kicked the coat and propelled it upward to land in my arms. He whistled as if impressed. I made my exit without kissing Isabel good-bye. Something didn't feel right about the situation, but that was usually the way I felt when I left Isabel. Uneasy. Unsettled. Anxious. In a panic. Deceived. Used. After I closed the door behind me, I could hear Isabel yell, "No, not with the turkey baster."

Oh, well. Her apartment. Her body. Her life. Her cousin. Or not.

At one forty-five, I walked into my apartment and Mocha greeted me with her sweet chuntering as if I had stayed out too late and she was the offended paramour.

"All right, all right. I'm sorry. I know I said I'd be home earlier." I cracked open the refrigerator door and reached for a can of kitty food. I spooned the mush into her food bowl but she only sniffed and strode away.

"Be that way. I'm going to bed."

I threw myself onto the bed facedown and fully clothed then sat up, removed my coat and tossed it on the chair beside my bed. The baseball cap protruded like a lump in my back pocket. I retrieved the cap and inspected the inside mostly to whiff her hair. I was still addicted to the smell of her hair conditioner, an aromatic saccharine vanilla. I breathed in and inhaled, my eyes shut.

When I opened them, I spotted a miniscule dark stain. Like dried blood.

CHAPTER SEVENTEEN

Dammit Isabel. Why was my baseball cap stained with a spot of blood? I couldn't ask her. She'd lie. I had no choice but to destroy the cap, since I would be the one implicated. One more clue earning me the title of prime suspect. Fuck. She had distracted me again and this time with her alleged cousin and that damn turkey baster, which had 'caused my vaginal walls to feel just a tad raw.

I dropped my pants and sat on the toilet and with my index finger probed my vagina.

"Ouch!" I screamed.

Mocha scurried across the kitchen and into the living room.

"Thanks for the moral support," I yelled.

Blood smudges on my underwear were routine after our sex play but the rough-edged turkey baster had instigated the evening's bonus bloody specks. Damn. Blood, blood everywhere. I flung my underwear into the sink and ran cold water over the blood, lifting the stain, which made me wonder: why hadn't she washed the baseball cap? She must have seen the bloody fleck.

I couldn't prove she intended for me to find the cap but I sure suspected I had fallen into a premeditated trap.

Or maybe she cut herself shaving her legs. Yeah, right, that made a lot of sense. What the fuck, Isabel? I finished washing my underwear and hung them up on the shower curtain bar. The pink cap was strewn on the bed. I snatched a lighter in my nightstand and grabbed the cap. Holding both over the bathroom sink, I lit the cap and watched flames engulf the pink and turn the color a dark brown until pieces charred. The fire crept up to the brim, scorching my fingers. I flung the burning cap into the sink and listened to the singed sounds from the water trickling onto the scorched cloth. Unexpectedly, the fire alarm on my bedroom ceiling blasted into a piercing sound. It was two in the morning and the screeching was sure to wake my neighbors.

"Fuck, fuck, fuck!"

Mocha skid through the living room and into the bedroom closet to escape both the alarm and the pounding at the front door. I poured water over the half-scorched cap, closed the bathroom door and darted to answer the front door.

"Hey girlfriend. You got a fire going on in here?"

It was my neighbor, Sasha, the drop-dead gorgeous African-American woman from across the hall. What kept me from pursuing our acquaintance further was her boifriend, a transguy named Wally. When they moved in two years prior, I welcomed them with a bottle of tequila and we drank shots into the night. Wally knocked out immediately but Sasha and I threw back shots and shared childhood horror stories until the sun rose. She was from the South, Louisiana to be exact, and I was from Austin, meaning I recognized the Cajuns and Creoles she grew up with. Sasha worked the late night shift at a nearby hospital as a psychiatrist but she was still an intern, hence the reason for the hours until she proved herself, she said. Already in her mid-forties, Sasha had lived a jam-packed life and returned to school to get her MD in psychiatry, which intrigued her, she claimed, after traveling the world and observing human behavior.

"Sorry, Sasha. Did I wake you?"

"Girlfriend, you know I'm up at this hour. Just got in."

"Still got you on those long night hours, huh?"

"Yeah, me and the other woman of color. I don't know why the white boys get to have their choice of any shift they want."

"You don't know?"

"Hell yeah, I know. Don't get me started."

"Did somebody say, 'white boi?' Wally peeked from behind the door. "You two want to come in?"

"Wally, get in there and turn off that damn alarm."

Sasha grazed Wally's collarbone and he was off and running. Within seconds the blaring stopped, and I heard Wally shut the bathroom door. Damn. The burnt pink cap.

"You think I woke anybody up?"

"In this building? Hell no. These folks might as well be in a graveyard. Even when they're awake, they're asleep."

Sasha sauntered into the kitchen swaying accomplished hips. "Where's the tequila, girlfriend? You got a bottle hidden around here?"

"I thought you had to get back to work tonight?"

"No, honey, not tonight. Tomorrow—well, later today." She studied her Tag Heuer watch. "In exactly twelve hours I'm due back. Got plenty of time for a little tequila shot and a long nap." She rummaged through my cabinets. "Honey girl, where's the good stuff? I know you hide it."

Behind her, I skimmed her green scrubs purposefully and got a whiff of her neck. Damn, she smelled good. The aroma was a mixture of honeysuckle and fine-looking woman sweat.

"Excuse me," I said.

My arm coiled around her body and again I inhaled her neck's scent, coveting the polished flesh. I wanted to bite her. She seemed to intuit my thoughts and half smiled. Maybe she was thinking the same thing. Maybe she wouldn't mind a little romp with me but since her boifriend was in my bathroom, I suspected she would ignore my advances, which were not too nuanced. I stretched my arm further into the cabinet and our faces met. She was near enough to kiss.

Placing the bottle on the counter, I seized three shot glasses from the shelf and came to my senses, deciding to quote from

Double Indemnity. "How could I have known that honeysuckle sometimes smells like murder?" I said.

Sasha's lips parted a millimeter. "Murder sometimes smells like honeysuckle," she corrected me.

"I guess I got the order wrong."

"I guess you did." She licked the rim of her shot glass.

"I guess I'm pretty good at doing that. Getting the order wrong."

"I guess you might be. Then again, you might not be so wrong." Her tongue circled the rim, dipped into the tequila and disappeared inside her mouth.

"I'm not?"

"Not what?"

"Wrong."

"You could be right," she said.

I was imagining sucking on her tequila-laden tongue. "I like to be right."

"Yeah, being right feels good, doesn't it?"

"Feels better than being wrong."

"Better to be right than wrong."

"My thinking exactly."

We each swigged a round that went down like spring rain. I was feeling all crinkly inside like I wanted to take her in my arms. The mood we created from quoting sexy film noir usually made me crinkly and lusty.

"Hey, you two started without me?"

Sasha widened her eyes at me as she answered him. "Plenty left for you, Wally baby. Electra here has plenty to go around. Don't you, honey girl?"

"Yeah, Wally. I saved a shot for you."

"Gee, thanks."

He swigged it back, poured another and swigged that one too, which reminded me that I'd guzzled my evening quota with the exasperating Isabel Cortez.

"Hey, this musta set off the alarm."

Wally held up the half-scorched pink cap.

"Damn, girlfriend. Who you trying to burn out of your memory?"

"Nobody. Why?"

"Only reason anybody takes to burning clothes and shit is to exorcise some ex-lover."

"It's my cap."

"I never took you for the pink cap type, El," said Wally.

"It was a gift for someone else," I lied.

"Quit bullshitting, girlfriend. You're exorcising the lover who gave it to you."

"Sure. Something like that."

I wasn't going to argue, since Sasha had given me a perfectly good explanation for burning the baseball cap. Fortunately, the bloody spot had burned to a crisp and all that remained were the brim and the stringy Velcro band that tied in the back. The band dangled like a limp churro.

Wally handed me the carbonized cap and I pitched it into the garbage can under the kitchen sink. I would finish burning it later. Wait. Not a good idea since the alarm would go off again. Okay, make a note: do not burn remains of cap. Better to wrap it in a plastic bag with other kinds of waste and fling it into a dumpster. A dumpster not in Chelsea.

"Who was she?" asked Sasha.

"Who?"

"The woman you're trying to forget. I know you got a long list of them, girlfriend."

Wally had wandered over to my couch with a full shot glass and put his shoes on the cheap imitation of an Ikea coffee table. "Whoa," he said. "This wobbles. Want me to fix it for you?"

"It's two in the morning, Wally. I think you've helped enough."

"Nah. It'll only take a second."

He exited, leaving me alone with Sasha and a half-full bottle of my favorite spirits. A dangerous recipe.

"Where's he rushing off to?"

"Oh, you know Wally. Off to get his tool set. He's got a tick about anything that doesn't work right."

"Is that so?"

"That is so, honey girl."

"Anything else not working right? In your apartment?"

"There might be a thing or two that's a little squeaky."

"And he hasn't fixed these squeaks?"

"Hasn't even noticed them."

"Anybody else notice them?"

"Well, now, I'm hoping someone else might drop by, say around ten o'clock in the morning once he's off at work. Don't want to bother him with trite, little squeaks that need attention."

"Ten is a good time to fix squeaks that have been neglected for too long."

Wally knocked twice, considerate guy that he was, and entered abruptly. He was wearing a bulky tool belt that made his paunch paunchier. Wally wasn't one of those queer bears but he looked like one when he wore his tool belt and plaid shirts. Add to that a scruffy, unshaven face and any number of bears would take him home. I liked the guy. He was thoughtful and damn helpful around the apartment. Anything that needed fixing, he sprang at the chance. I almost felt guilty about a rendezvous with his girlfriend, but who was I to turn down an invitation from sultry Sasha, who I had wanted to fuck since the day they arrived in the building two years prior. Who was I to wonder why she finally agreed to fuck me? Maybe there was trouble in paradise. Not my problem, I thought.

Wally turned the coffee table over on its side and whipped out his screwdriver. "Here's your problem," he said.

"I have a problem?"

I kept my gaze on Sasha as we lingered beside the kitchen counter next to the bottle of tequila. She looked away.

"What's the problem, sugar?"

"She needs a new screw. This one's bent and rusted."

"You hear that, honey girl? Seems you need a fresh screw."

"One that's not bent and rusted, like the man says," I responded.

"Yeah, yeah, you two are real funny," said Wally. "But I don't see either of you fixing the table here."

"I leave that to you, Wally. You're good at fixing things."

"Yeah, my Wally knows how to fix things with a fresh screw."

"Oh. Does he fix squeaky things too? How about it, Wally? Are you good with squeaky things too?"

"You two are real clever," he said. "I may be an ass sometimes but I'm not an idiot."

He finished screwing in the leg, turned the table right side up, plopped his feet on top and scraped wax from inside his right ear with a house key. "See. Good as new." He mined for more wax from his left ear.

Wally was pleased with himself and I was pleased I had a coffee table that didn't wobble and a date with Sasha in the morning.

"Let's go, sugar."

He leaped from the couch, further inspecting his handiwork. His hands were on his hips and he crooked his neck and nodded, self-satisfied. I wondered if he also nodded self-satisfied after fucking Sasha. I wondered if she invited me over because she was bored with habitual, mind-numbing sex that devastates spontaneous pleasure after a decade of marital bliss.

From what I'd witnessed, couples were in sex heaven for two to three years if lucky. Most only lasted a year. Then monotonous, dreary, uninventive sex reared its ugly head and fantasy life could not sustain what they'd once had. Okay, so I was cynical, but tell me it isn't true and I'll buy you a Mercedes. Better yet, a coffee. Make it a cappuccino.

Sasha bent close to me and kissed my cheek. "Good night, honey girl. Get some rest. Quit trying to burn the past and let it be or you might end up with a scorched apartment and no way Wally can fix that." She pointed her index finger at Wally. "Come on, baby." Sasha sashayed out the front door with Wally following behind.

Damn. Too bad I liked the guy.

A twinge of guilt stunned me and I decided I shouldn't go to Sasha's apartment in the morning. I would be a civilized citizen and arrive in my new dean's office early. But then again, what better way to start the day? A romp with Sasha would improve my mood substantially, helping me to adjust to the damn dean job. Besides, I was only the interim dean. Until they caught the murderer. Sure made me feel confident. I glanced at my watch. Two twenty-seven. I had nine and a half hours to reconsider the prospects before me. Thing is, I didn't want to make Sasha angry and standing her up wasn't cool. I headed for the bedroom, lay my head down on my pillow and knocked out, clothes and all.

I woke to Mocha's stare as she gently pawed my arm. She had a habit of waking me to feed her fresh food despite a full bowl. I peeked at the alarm clock on my bedside table. It was six ten.

Toweling myself off after a cold shower, I reviewed the events of the evening.

The pink cap. I had to get rid of the pink cap. It could still implicate me. Omar said he saw a woman wearing a baseball cap. He may not have seen the color but the cap could still be linked to me, and wasn't that Isabel's plan? And who was that dude in his boxer shorts? What fucking cousin? She didn't have any cousins in town. Well, not that I knew anyway. Probably some ex-lover or current lover who got his rocks off listening to her fuck in the next room, for all I knew. Isabel loved kinky and she more than likely attracted kinky guys too. Okay, why was I so obsessed with the guy in her bedroom? Unless he was the murderer, his reason for being in her bedroom was irrelevant. But what if he had helped her? What if they were in it together? I mean, why leave the pink cap within sight?

I finished toweling off and peered at a tired face in the mirror. This mirror don't have two faces. Just my old wrinkled one. Fuck. I had to stop these late night dalliances with women and liquor. One day. Not today though. I remembered my morning date with Sasha and wondered if I could visit her earlier than she expected. I thought about sending her a text but what if she was asleep and the buzz or ring or whatever sound her text messages made woke her? I wandered into the kitchen, pumped my espresso and burned my toast. Mocha followed dutifully, not something she ever did unless something was in it for her. She reminded me of my ex-lovers. Heck, she reminded me of me.

I finished my buttery burned toast and poured another espresso, waiting for the time to pass as I surfed the web for news. Nothing but the usual Hollywood gossip and disgusting wars this country waged in the name of democracy. Oh, here was something that caught my eye: Goldman Sachs was opening a private bank for the wealthy. Wasn't that redundant? Weren't all their banks only for the wealthy, who stole from the poor to give to the rich so the rich could get richer and luxuriate in the labor of the poor, who worked and worked like poor schmucks, never to be recognized for the blood they gave to the rich who sat around congratulating themselves for devising legalized tricks that stole from common hard-working people? Weren't common hard-working people sick and tired of all the Goldman Sachs who pretended to offer so much to this country? Okay, I'd had too much espresso but still, I was infuriated with disproportionate wealth in the country. I turned from the business page seeking more mindless gossip to get my mind off bitter injustices in the world, most especially in a country that was my home.

Then I saw it. Fuck. I couldn't believe I was staring into President Mike Miller's sunny, stupid face. The headline read: "Another Homicide at Capital College."

President Mike Miller was found dead in his office at Capital College. Police sources confirm the homicide occurred between the hours of three and five this morning.

I looked at my watch. It was eight forty-five. The news story was released at seven. I read on.

When asked to comment on the recent murders on campus, vice chancellor of Academic Affairs, Dr. Justine Aldridge, said, "We will find the person or persons responsible. Capital College will make a comeback from these terrible tragedies."

Damn, Justine. Spoken like a double-talking administrator. No kind words for your best friend Mike? How about condolences to the family? And why say person or persons? Why would she think there was more than one murderer? I read on.

Police Detective Carolina Quinn was pursuing promising leads and possible suspects and hoped to announce an arrest soon.

Hmm. Possible suspects, Carolina? Nothing you've revealed to me, that's for certain.

I hurried to my bedroom closet and yanked my black jeans from a hanger. I also put on my black shirt and black jacket. I wanted to look like I was grieving for poor Prez Like-Me-Mike. At least no one could accuse me of sleeping with the poor fuck's wife. Not that I'd ever seen her but I was sure she wasn't my type quite simply because she was Mike Miller's wife. Nope. Not my type. I unbuttoned my black jeans and changed into black slacks since a certain police detective would probably be visiting me for questioning today. Maybe I needed to affect more remorse for Like-Me-Mike's demise. Yeah, right. And maybe, just maybe, I needed to poke out my eyeballs with needles.

CHAPTER EIGHTEEN

Before heading to campus, I needed to drop in on Sasha to explain why I wasn't available for our morning romp. I tapped on the door and was about to slip a note under when Wally opened it.

"Hey, El, what's up? I mean, besides your college president being murdered last night."

He had a towel around his neck and was wiping shaving lotion from his face. He looked manly.

"Hey, girlfriend, what are you doing here so early?" Sasha widened her eyes as if to send a message asking, *What the fuck? I said ten!* She sat at the kitchen table, watching news coverage of the event. "You want to come in and explain what's up at your college? Isn't that the second murder in less than a week? Damn, girlfriend, if I were you I'd look for another line of work. Or at least another place to work. Somebody doesn't like you folks at that college."

"I'm not worried," I said. I didn't sound convincing.

"Not worried? Who do you think you're talking to, honey girl?"

She motioned for me to come nearer and she pecked my cheek and pinched my arm, whispering, "You're early."

"I know," I murmured.

Wally stood with his back to us in front of the colossal flat screen he'd installed all by himself. The screen was so immense he didn't block our view.

"Hey, look! It's a photo of you, El!"

Wally pointed as he twisted around to face me. Sure enough, a headshot of me illuminated the room. I seemed professorial in a black blazer with a crisp white collar. I remembered the afternoon the campus photographer, a cool brunette, invited me into her lab and I smiled discreetly at the memory of what had ensued—until I heard the newscaster's report.

"The whereabouts of the suspect are unknown to the police at this time."

"Oh, that's funny," said Sasha. "They flashed a photo of you and said they're still looking for the murderer. Sounds like you're the suspect, honey girl."

"That's a mistake. They didn't say that. Wally? Is that what you heard?" Horrified, I flushed with panic.

"Oh, fine, ask the white boi 'cause the black woman ain't possibly gonna be right, huh, Electra?"

"Fuck, Sasha. Give me a break already."

"Gee, I don't know, El. Looks like they made a mistake but folks saw your mug at the same time the news guy said what he said about the suspect and all."

"I've got to get to campus."

"Sure you want to walk the streets alone, girlfriend? Somebody might confuse you for a murderer and all hell's going to let loose once that happens."

"Thanks, Sasha. You're so reassuring." I marched to the door.

"Hospital is open all day and all night if you want to come talk to a professional," she said.

"I've got to get to work."

"Let me drop you, El."

"Drop me? Nobody drops anybody in New York City, Wally."

"Oh, I got my boss's truck for the day. I got a job in Jersey."

"I'm in a hurry, Wally."

"I can be ready in five. Just hold off a second, El."

"He's right," said Sasha. "No reason to go tearing out of here when you're a wanted woman."

"That's not funny, Sasha," I whispered. To dodge more comments from Sasha, I yelled out to Wally, who'd disappeared into the bedroom, "Wally, you've never told me about your work. What do you do?"

"You never asked. I'm in garbage."

"Garbage?"

"As in sanitation."

He reemerged in a pressed lavender shirt, tucked into his chinos, and two-tone brown saddle shoes. I waited by the door far and away from Sasha. Wally walked to her and kissed her on the mouth.

"See you later, baby?" he asked.

"I don't know, babycakes. Depends on how busy we get."

She was turning the pages of the *New York Times*. Sasha was among the die-hards who insisted on old-fashioned newsprint for breakfast. Old habits were hard to break for some. Me, I preferred the inkless, paperless up-to-the-minute news on my computer.

"Give me a call. Or text," he said.

"You know I don't like to text."

"Give me a call."

He headed toward me and as I followed him I had the audacity to glance at Sasha, assuming she was peeved. She blew me a kiss.

"She likes you," said Wally. We were in his borrowed Dodge Ram pickup truck on our way downtown.

"Wally, you could have taken the GW Bridge to get to Jersey. Why are you going out of your way just for me?"

"She likes you."

"Who?"

"Don't act all innocent with me, El. You know who I mean."

"Sasha? She likes to flirt, Wally. You know some women like to know they're desired all the time."

"Sasha's not like that. And anyway, I don't mind. She told me all about it. How you two had plans this morning. I would've gotten out of your way but seems you're in a hurry to get to work today what with all the latest brouhaha."

"Yeah. The brouhaha." I gazed out the window. "You don't mind?"

"Sasha and I have been together a long time. She knew me before." Wally gestured with his head down to his body. "She still hangs in there with me. We're best friends. And we both believe in having our fun outside and away from each other."

"You do?"

"Don't look at me like that, El. Since when are you all conservo about relationships?"

"Me? Conservative? That's not me."

"Well, then?"

"Well, then what?"

"Well, then, I expect you will make my girl happy by the end of the day. Or else."

"Or else? Or else what, Wally? You sound like some kind of wise-guy from Jersey and I'm not one for stereotypes."

He stared out the cab window.

"Wally?"

"Huh?"

"Or else what?"

"Or else I'll hear about it. What do you think, El? That I'm going to get my goons to throw your body in the Hudson? Gee, you've got an active imagination."

He reached for the glove compartment and unlatched it. "Do me a favor, El and look in there for my lighter. It's been missing and I think my boss lifted it."

"Sure, Wally. Anything you say."

I rummaged around and when my fingers pushed further back into the crevices of the compartment, a sharp edge sliced into the tips of my forefinger and middle finger.

"Ouch. What the fuck, Wally?"

I pulled out a knife about six inches long and saw my blood sparkling on the sharpened blade.

"Careful. I told you to look for my lighter, not get yourself butchered."

"Butchered? That's a fine choice of words," I mumbled with my fingers in my mouth as I sucked off the blood. It was a nick, but nicks, like paper cuts, hurt more than a genuine slash.

"Damn, you're a sissy. I don't know what Sasha sees in you."

"Hey, careful. Nothing wrong with sissies." I inspected the blade thoroughly. "What is it with knives these days?" I asked.

"Hey, that's not my knife. Like I said, this is my boss's truck."

"I didn't say it was your knife, Wally. That's funny," I said looking at it more closely.

"What's funny?"

"Looks just like the knife Prez Like-Me-Mike had in his desk. Same pearl handle. Only his had a turquoise bead right here. In the middle. Right where there's a bead missing on this one."

"Oh, that's great. Now you think this is the same knife your president owned? Come on, El. Knives like that are a dime a dozen. You can pick one up at any hardware store. It's a popular design. Don't go accusing my boss of murder before you've even met her."

"Your boss is a woman?"

"Yeah, you got a problem with that?"

"A woman in sanitation?"

"Uh-huh. What's your problem?"

"Nothing. No problem. Just surprised, that's all."

"Damn, El. For being so up on the times, you sure can be a conservo."

"Don't call me that. I'm as progressive as the next lesbian."

"Well, some of you lesbos got a stick up your ass."

"Oh, now, ain't that pretty. Now that you walk around looking like the almighty white man, you accuse us lesbians of being conservative. That's ironic."

"I'm not a white man: I'm a white boi and they don't let me forget it either."

"I'm sure they don't, Wally, just like nobody lets me forget I'm a Chicana and a fucking dyke."

"Yeah, yeah, I know. What are we going on about anyway? We're practically on the same team."

"Well, from what I can tell, we have the same taste in women."

"Seems so."

Wally grinned and double-parked at the entrance of campus. I lingered, hesitant to join the madness. "Thanks for going out of your way to give me a ride. Today of all days. The vultures are out to get me, Wally."

"You're welcome, El." He winked. "Oh and by the way, I don't expect I'll be home early tonight. Sasha usually comes home for a quick dinner around seven." He winked again.

I unlocked the truck's massive door and as soon as I jumped down from the cab, a microphone and a flashing camera accosted me.

CHAPTER NINETEEN

A young woman who behaved like an overzealous journalism student thrust a microphone in my face.

"Dean Campos, is it true you cannot account for your time between the hours of three and five?"

"What? What are you talking about?"

She shoved the microphone closer to my lips. "What can you tell me about Dean Johnson?"

"You mean, other than the fact that he's dead?"

"Well, yes."

"No comment."

"Not even for the family in mourning?"

"I'm sorry for his family and close friends."

"You weren't a close friend?"

"Of Dean Johnson's? He was my dean. That's all."

She blocked my pathway with a fervent body and despite the appearance of a size four frame, the young woman had the spunk of a bulldozer.

"And what about President Miller? What about Mike? "Weren't you friends with President Miller?"

"I was in his employ. Please let me by."

"And you didn't consider him a friend?"

"Look, I know you're scavenging for a good story but you won't find it here."

I bolted before she had a chance to block my path again and ran to my history department office because the Admin building would be crawling with reporters and police. I had nothing to hide but I also had no interest in being accused of murder. Yet again. What was going on?

I snuck into my building through the back door, navigating the bowels of the basement and slunk up the back stairs and saw Adrían speaking to someone hidden behind the archway. Adrían was nodding in agreement.

As I walked toward him, his arm dropped behind his back and he waved me away with two fingers. I waited for him to signal I could approach. Long, cold minutes elapsed and I panicked again. I was being set up. Something wasn't right. Why had my photograph appeared on television? And why had I been accosted by a suspicious journalist and yet hadn't been contacted by Detective Quinn about this latest news, Mike's murder? By now, she should've called me. Hell, she probably thought I was guilty too.

Just as I engaged full throttle panic mode, gasping for air, Adrían shoved me into his office.

"Who was that?" I blew out air, holding my guts as if they were about to fall out.

"David Sloan."

"What's going on, Adrían? Why am I being treated like a criminal?"

"What are you talking about, El?"

"First, my picture on the news this morning and just now, some novice journalist grilled me as if I was a suspect."

"You're paranoid, buddy. I saw your photo on the news too. That was kind of funny."

"Funny? Not to me."

"They cleared up the mistake. Don't get all paranoid."

"They did?"

"I called in and told them you're our new interim dean. That's why they showed your photo in the first place. An honest mistake."

"Honest? Nothing honest about that. And what about that kid outside? She accused me of murder."

"Oh, come on. You're exaggerating. Those kid journalists have just seen too many TV dramas."

"But right now? Why did you wave me away?"

"Sloan's roaming the hallways." Adrían gave me the once-over. "You haven't slept much, have you? Is that why you're acting strange?"

"Me, strange?"

"Well, no more than usual."

"What the heck is going on, Adrían? Are you and Sloan getting chummy?"

"Okay, now I'm getting worried. You sound paranoid again. What's up?"

"What's up? The college president was murdered last night, that's what's up."

"I thought you'd be happy about that."

"Happy? Adrían, a human life, however worthless, has been snuffed."

"Yeah, yeah, I know and it's sad for his family but let's face it, El. The guy was no friend to anyone who actually picked up a book and claimed to have learned something from it. He was all 'Mr. Pick-yourself-up-by-your-bootstraps' as if the rest of us never worked a day in our lives."

"Yeah, I know. 'Mr. Pick himself up by *our* bootstraps' was more like it. Poor schmuck."

"Who do you think did him in?"

"Heck, how do I know?"

"You know what I think?"

"And you're going to tell me."

"I think one of his business partners took advantage of the dean's murder and decided to cash in on Mike Miller."

"Cash in?"

"Well, the guy was worth millions, right?"

"A billion or two."

"Aren't business partners like wolves? Move in for the kill to take over as head honcho?"

"Now you're talking like you've seen too many private dick films."

"Got to love *The Maltese Falcon*. Spade was cool," said Adrían.

"Yeah, he was cool. But Philip Marlowe was a smarter dresser."

"Yeah, huh? That dark blue shirt with a powder blue suit. Hard to pull off that color without resembling an Easter parade."

"I know, huh?"

A knock on the office door saved me from more of Adrían's crazy conjectures about Mike Miller's murder. I stepped forward and swung the door open.

Detective Carolina Quinn, finally making an appearance. "*Buenos dias, Profesora*."

"*Buenos dias*, Detective Quinn."

"May I come in?"

"We've been expecting you."

"We have?" asked Adrían.

"We need you to settle a debate for us."

"A debate? I love a good argument."

"Oh, not an argument per se so much as a preference," I said.

She peered at me and I resisted the impulse to throw her on Adrían's desk. I opted for cool, suave, detached.

"The question before you is: Sam Spade or Philip Marlowe?"

"That's easy. Kinsey Millhone. Or Henry Rios. Yeah, I'd have to say Rios."

"That's cheating. That's a whole other era."

"Call me a cheater." Carolina jacked up the seductive right eyebrow that tugged at my gut, sauntered behind Adrían's desk, plopped onto the desk chair and rested her leather boots on top of his desk.

"Please, make yourself comfortable, Detective," I said.

She looked at Adrían. "Do you mind? It's been a long morning."

"Rest away," said Adrían.

"Long morning?" I asked.

"We got a call at three."

"That early?"

"Well, I was already up. In fact, I'd been in Chelsea."

"Oh?"

"Yeah."

"What's in Chelsea?" asked Adrían.

"You want to tell your friend what or who was in Chelsea early in the morning, *Profesora*?"

"Not me."

"Not you? Are you sure?"

"I left at one. No later than two. I was back in my apartment around two. You can ask my neighbors."

"I know."

"You know?"

"I know."

"Well, why the interrogation as if I'm some kind of criminal?"

"Am I interrogating you as if you're some kind of criminal, Electra?"

"See? You're doing it again. Accusing me without accusing me. Why don't you say what you mean, Carolina?"

"What do you think I mean, Electra? And by the way, why did your parents name you after a Greek tragedy? I've been meaning to ask you."

"And no better time than the present?"

"Well, you are here and it occurred to me."

"Finally, a question I can answer easily."

"Well?"

"My mother loves a good Greek tragedy. That's all."

"But why Electra? The whole daddy complex doesn't suit you."

"You don't know me very well, Detective."

"No, I don't. But what I do know is that you are still frequenting the domicile of one of our prime suspects."

"What? Are you telling me Isabel Cortez is a suspect for Mike Miller too?"

"Maybe."

"Maybe? Is that a big maybe, Detective?"

"Not so big. Just a little maybe."

"But still a maybe."

"Still a maybe."

"Would you two please make sense? I can't follow this crazy shit logic," said Adrían.

We both stood in the middle of his office mystified by the beauty that was Carolina Quinn reclining in his desk chair.

"Why don't you two have a seat? I have a few questions for you."

"For me too?" asked Adrían.

"Sure, why not? Might as well be thorough."

"But I don't even know Isabel Cortez."

"But you knew Mike Miller?"

"Sure, but I didn't want to kill him."

A faint line of sweat appeared on Adrían's upper lip. If he hadn't shaved, the dewy drops would be more apparent. I wondered why he was so nervous. He had no reason to be. But accusations made some people feel guilty even when not. Adrían and I were that type. We both assumed our own guilt until proven innocent.

"I didn't think you wanted to kill him. I asked if you knew him. Why so nervous?" Carolina picked up a lead pencil from the desk and chewed on the eraser tip. I fantasized I was the eraser tip.

"I'm not nervous. Do I seem nervous? I'm just, I don't know, surprised you're asking me questions, Detective."

He paced and bumped my shoulder. Carolina observed his anxiety and tossed her pencil on the desk, then leaned back in Adrían's chair. "Adrían, I'm not accusing you of anything. Just tell me where you were between the hours of three and five."

"But why me?"

"Not just you. We're asking everyone who knew Mike Miller."

"Oh. So you asked David Sloan too?"

"Not yet."

"But you will?"

"I intend to."

"Because if you're just asking the queer folks of color, there's a problem," he said.

"What are you implying, Adrían?" She kept her cool and continued reclining.

"I just wondered," he said.

"Well, don't." She exhibited coolness but underneath appeared seething. She changed the subject and twisted her body to face me. "And where were you, since Adrían refuses to cooperate?"

"*Un momentito*," he said. "I'm cooperating, Detective. I'm not going on record as not cooperating with you."

I wondered why Adrían was acting guiltier than usual. Sweat on his upper lip lingered visibly.

"Well? Where were you this morning between the hours of three and five?"

"I'm thinking I need my lawyer present before I answer any questions, Detective."

I stared at Adrían, shocked at his apprehension. Why couldn't he answer a simple question? To stave off more suspicion, I blurted out my answer. "I was at home, Detective."

"Alone?" she asked.

"Yes, alone. Why?"

"And your visitors at two?"

"Wait a minute. You followed me from Chelsea back to my apartment?"

"I didn't follow you."

"Right. One of your men followed me."

"No, no following. I was in Chelsea and one of my men was stationed outside your apartment."

"Still watching me, Detective?"

"Yes, I'm watching you, Electra. Not for reasons that you believe."

"And what would those reasons be, Detective?"

"I think you know."

"No. I don't. Would you care to elaborate?"

Carolina rose from the desk chair, pushing it back with the back of her legs. The gesture accentuated her hips. Fuck, get a hold of yourself, I thought. She slinked around the desk, braced her ass against the edge and stood inches from me.

"You want me to elaborate? Here? Right now? In front of your uncooperative colleague?"

"*Un pinche momentito.* I'm not being uncooperative," said Adrían.

She squinted and glared at me.

"Well, maybe this isn't the best time," I replied. "We could always have that drink you've been promising me."

"Me? Promise you a drink? I think you promised me one, Professor."

"Okay. Let's go for a drink. This evening. I'll come by your place. Or would you prefer to come to me?"

"I don't believe you two. What the *pinche mierda* is going on here?" Adrían demanded.

Carolina frowned. "I have to go, Electra. More offices to visit, more folks to grill."

She kept her gaze on me as she addressed Adrían. "Detective Swift will want you to drop by the police department to give a statement, Adrían. You can bring your lawyer, but I can assure you this is protocol. We're checking with everyone who knew Mike Miller."

"Only knew him as the president. I can bet you he didn't know me, Detective," said Adrían. He put his hands in his pockets and relaxed into his heels. I knew this gesture. It was his casual yet authoritative demeanor.

"Adrían. No one is accusing you. I'm not accusing you; Detective Swift is not accusing you. We're doing our job. We're gathering information to help us find a killer on the loose at Capital College. For all we know, you or Electra, who is the new dean, could be the next victims. It's our job to protect you."

"And forcing me to go to the police department to determine where I was at three is protecting me, Detective?"

"Fine. Don't come. I'll tell Swift you were at home asleep."

"But you don't know that for sure, do you?" he replied.

"I don't know anything for sure, Adrían, and since you're not willing to answer, I'll rely on my instincts and my instincts tell me you were home alone and asleep."

He rocked forward on his toes and back on his heels, refusing to confirm her assessment.

"Anyone want a cup of coffee?" I asked in an attempt to stop their quarreling. I felt tense enough. "No time for a quick cup of coffee, Carolina?" I asked.

"I'll see you tonight," she said. "Come to my apartment."

We walked outside Adrían's office and Carolina sauntered through the hallway, swaying hips that hypnotized me with their measured cadence.

CHAPTER TWENTY

I barged back into Adrían's office. He faced the window, hands in his pockets, rocking on his heels. I stood next to him and we both studied the chaos outside our building. Police, journalists, students and faculty roamed the quad.

"What a mess, huh?" I said.

"The kind you want to avoid like the plague."

"If only these walls could talk."

"I guess they better take this tiger by the tail."

"Maybe if they just think outside the box."

"Well, every dog has its day."

"Not this dog," I said.

I hoped he would say why he mistrusted Carolina. Something was up. He remained silent.

"What's up, buddy? Anything you want to say to me?"

He scrutinized Carolina as she strolled through the crowd then huddled with other police as if conferring about strategy.

"Hey buddy?" I said.

"Yeah."

"I'll be in my office if you need me."

His silence didn't usually make me uncomfortable. He and I could sit for hours and stare out a window in comfortable, reassuring silence. But this morning, something was different. There were instances when he preferred to avoid, ignore or pretend something wasn't happening to make his life simpler but not necessarily easier. Maybe this was one of those instances. I wasn't sure what to do.

As I walked to the door, he spoke. "It's not fair, El."

I looked into his eyes and waited for clarification.

"No, it's not fair," I offered.

I closed his office door behind me and entered my own, which felt chilly and damp. The window was ajar, which puzzled me because I never opened the windows, fearing eight-legged creatures might crawl through my piles of ungraded papers causing a disgruntled student to get stung with more than a failing grade. Just as I was locking the screens, my office phone rang so loudly I flinched and snatched up the receiver. It was none other than the Vice Chancellor of Academic Affairs herself, the lofty, pretentious Justine Aldridge.

"Electra? I need to see you. Immediately."

"Justine. What an unpleasant surprise."

"How soon can you be in my office?"

"Oh, I don't know. A couple of hours?"

"Not soon enough. You have to come now. I'll be expecting you. Take the back stairs. Be sure no one sees you enter the building."

"How am I supposed to do that? Reporters and police are swarming the place."

"I don't know, Electra. You're smart. Figure it out. Just get here. Now."

She hung up without giving me an opportunity to object. She gave me orders as if I were her flunky. Oh, wait. As her dean, I guess I was her flunky. She was one of my many bosses. Fuck. I hadn't signed up for this. And she expected me to enter her office the back way as if I was the help. Or a criminal.

I meandered through the quad and avoided eye contact with anyone who might recognize me. With so much pandemonium, I snuck through without being noticed. Or so I thought.

"Hey Profe!"

I didn't pause.

"Profe!" The voice screeched. It was Brisa.

"Brisa, I'm in a hurry."

"Oh, yeah, I get it. Now that you're a big-time dean you don't have time for the little people."

"Ay Brisa. What is it?"

"Hey, if you're going to answer me like that, forget it." Brisa stood unyielding before me.

"Okay. What can I help you with, Brisa?"

"Me?" She pointed to her chest with her thumb as she steadied on one leg thrusting her hip forward. Her stance was effective and tantalizing.

"I'm not the one needing help these days, Profe. I'm just a messenger for Omar."

"Omar? You've been talking to Omar?"

"Seems we've both been talking to Omar." She inched closer as if to whisper but didn't.

"And?"

"And he wanted me to tell you he might have made a mistake."

"A mistake? About what?"

"Fuck if I know, Profe. That was the message."

"Oh great. He gives you a perfunctory, ambiguous message to relay to me. What am I supposed to do with it?"

"Hey, don't crap on the messenger, Profe. I didn't have to tell you anything." She turned and stepped away but without conviction. She wanted me to apologize and to beg.

"Brisa. Are you coming to class today?"

"Of course I'm coming to class. Why wouldn't I be in your damn class? When have I ever missed one of your fucking lectures?" She had a hand on one hip as she lectured me with the other hand, jabbing an index finger in my face since she hadn't moved more than one step.

"I guess that means I'll see you later."

"Fuck yeah, you'll see me later." She flipped her hair and swiveled her body to underscore the exit.

Brisa was performance. A beguiling, brazen performance. No matter how rude or insulting she was, I wasn't insulted. Her candid, affected talents made it impossible for me to get angry. I savored her displays and the more outraged she acted, the worthier the exhibition. She turned her head and winked as she walked away, offering a mischievous smile reassuring me everything was fine.

I resumed my walk of blame to Justine Aldridge's office in the Admin building, where President Mike had been murdered. Another crowd of police and yellow tape guarded the area. I veered left toward the Humanities building. When I was sure no one saw me enter the Humanities building, I took a service elevator to the basement and exited through a back door. Shrubs and trees hid the passage between the buildings in the rear. I climbed the stairs two flights to dodge anyone roaming the halls. After gasping for air, having bolted up the steps two at a time for a much needed workout, I opened the door to Justine's floor but when I spotted Detective Carolina Quinn in the hall, I retreated.

"Fuck," I whispered.

I waited until her boot steps sounded faint in the hallway and then raced to Justine's office, knocked and rushed in without warning.

"About time," she said.

"I would've come sooner but a certain Detective was at your door."

"Oh. Her? She's clueless. Nothing to worry about." Justine waved her hand as if she were shooing away a fly, which annoyed me not only because I was fond of Detective Quinn but also because Vice Chancellor Aldridge so airily dismissed such a smart, fetching woman. Then it hit me. Of course that's why she was dismissive. Brilliant, beautiful women threatened Justine. In general, she didn't like women and, like Margaret Thatcher, preferred the company of men.

"What's the urgency, Justine?"

"Sit down, Electra. This isn't going to be easy."

I elected to spread out on her couch instead of sitting rigid on the wooden chairs in front of her desk. She eased into the far corner of the couch and sat erect.

"Electra, when did you last see Mike?"

"You mean dead Prez Mike?"

"Who else would I mean, Electra? Of course Mike."

I ignored her edgy tone. "Yesterday. When he gave me this job. Why?"

"Well, you're going to want to see this."

Justine rose from the couch and smoothed a loose strand back into a tightly knit bun. After unlocking a desk drawer, she retrieved a narrow box probably no more than ten inches in length. She inched along beside me, placing the box on the coffee table.

"Go ahead. Open it."

"Justine, you shouldn't have. It's not my birthday for at least another year."

"Open it, Electra," she nearly growled.

I removed the lid from the box. There it was. The same damn bloody knife. I must have looked puzzled. Justine's silence frightened me so much that I wanted to run from that office but running would incriminate me. What the fuck? I hadn't done anything.

"Why are you showing me this?"

"It has your fingerprints."

"My fingerprints? What do you mean? How can you see my fingerprints?"

"Don't be silly; of course I can't see them. Mike showed me the knife. In his desk. He told me how much you appreciated its beauty and he had planned to give it to you."

"So?"

"He said that when you held it you almost stroked it and he thought you deserved to have something this beautiful. You see, Electra? He liked you."

"Are you setting me up, Justine? Because if you are, I'm friends with a certain detective who won't believe this little stunt of yours."

"This isn't a stunt. This is the murder weapon. But if I hand this over to the detective, she will discover your fingerprints."

"So? The knife will also have the fingerprints of the murderer."

"How can you be so sure?"

"You said it was the murder weapon."

"Don't you think the murderer would've been more careful?"

"Murder isn't exactly a careful endeavor, is it?"

"I'm saying, dear Electra, that the murderer might have worn gloves."

"How would you know this detail, Justine?"

"I'm merely suggesting that it's a possibility, making your fingerprints the ones that will surely be found."

"Unless the murderer wiped the knife clean."

"That doesn't look like a clean knife."

"The handle looks wiped down to me."

"But you can't be sure, can you?"

"Justine, why not hand the weapon over to the police? All this conjecture is making me dizzy."

"My dear Electra, I'm doing you a favor."

"A favor? How is this a favor?"

"By giving the knife to you. Not the police."

"Why?"

"Why? Isn't it obvious?"

"Not to me."

"My dear Electra, I am trying to save you."

"Save me?"

"Why are you making this difficult?"

"Difficult is what I do. Easy is so boring, Justine."

She shook her head and squinted her right eye in her customary style to show impatience while simulating authority. Carolina Quinn often squinted in the same manner, a coincidence I found reasonably disturbing.

"I'll put the knife away. Since you're not interested." She placed the lid back on the box.

I placed my hand on hers. "Justine. What is this really about? I'm no murderer. We both know that."

"The police don't know that, Electra."

"Leave the box. I'll do something with the knife."

"You won't hand it over to the police, will you?"

"Isn't that what you planned to do?"

She squinted her right eye and cocked her head, grinning at me. She was hiding something and I wasn't stupid enough to fall for whatever she planned but here I was, probably doing exactly what she planned, which was forcing me to take this wretched knife off her hands. Not that I thought Justine was capable of murder, but I did think she was protecting someone.

"What do you want me to do with it?"

"Electra dear, *that* is your business. As far as I'm concerned, this meeting never took place."

"That's convenient."

"And you are as cynical as ever, dear."

"You've handed me a murder weapon. Or you want me to believe this is a murder weapon. For the dean? The police haven't said how Mike was murdered. Cynical isn't what I'd call my temperament just now."

"Call it what you will, Electra. The fact is I'm doing you a favor."

"No. You're doing yourself a favor."

She grabbed the box from my hand. "Never mind. You clearly don't see a favor when it's in front of you."

"Okay. I'll bite. Let's say you are doing me a favor. Fine. What happens when the police scour for the weapon? And I'm the trusty owner?"

"Why would you be that stupid? I'm giving it to you so you can get rid of it."

"Why won't *you* get rid of it?"

"I can. If that's what you want."

I stared at her and pondered the cat and mouse game we played. What was my next move? She wanted to confuse me and was succeeding. Thirty seconds passed. Beads of sweat trickled from my forehead. She was double angling and I felt cornered. If I left the knife with her, she might turn it in to the police to implicate me. If I took it with me, she might tell the police, who would hunt me down. My best bet was to take the alleged weapon, hide it or throw it in the Hudson River. Definitely the Hudson. I picked up the box and tucked it inside my jacket pocket.

She smiled, assured she had won this round. "I'm sure if you go out the back way again, you'll be safe."

"Safe? From whom?"

"The police, of course."

"Somehow it's not the police who worry me, Justine."

"You should be thanking me."

"When have you known me to be anything but grateful, Justine?"

I stood and blundered my way to the door. She walked to me and hugged me in that non-touching way when someone places an arm around you without contact. Her body was at a safe distance and of that I was glad. The idea of Justine Aldridge's hands on my person repulsed me. Not the woman herself. Her political convictions and ideologies repulsed me.

I snuck out and dashed to the side door rushing out of the building.

CHAPTER TWENTY-ONE

It was time to be a professor. Interim dean would have to wait. I hurried back to my office and lifted my class folder without mulling about the last time I had perused the same file cabinet and discovered a bloody knife. And now the replicas. Someone was planting pearl-handled, six-inch blades with a turquoise bead embedded in the handle. I even had one in my jacket pocket. I had to toss the knife or offer it to Detective Quinn as an act of good faith. I had no guarantee she would interpret my gift as an act of faith, however. She might think I was groveling. Who was I kidding? I was hot for her body and she knew it.

Sprinting across campus, folder in hand, knife in jacket pocket, I promptly entered the room in which fifty students sat quietly. Unusual for this routinely rowdy group. Many of the students were also in my Anarchy class and they were always a boisterous bunch but the morning's events had probably shocked them sober. My lecture on Latinas who tortured their spouses generally stirred even an unfocused class, but we had already discussed the infamous Lorena Bobbitt who sliced off her husband's penis, as well as Clara Harris, the dentist who flattened her cheating husband with her Mercedes-Benz. I taught the course regularly because I enjoyed tricking students. A title like "The Lorena Bobbitts: Murdering Latinas and the Men who Love Them" made the course trendy each time the topic of murdering Latinas became front-page news.

Sometimes popular culture could be an effortless pedagogical technique. Most students loathed history but when I launched with a present-day tragedy and shifted back in time, their concentration peaked. The class became packed and chairs were brought in to accommodate those who audited. By the third week, after I screened footage from the Bobbitt trial, more students had propped themselves against the back walls, but I'd had to cast them out or be in trouble with the fire marshal and I had enough trouble. The final week, we delved into Malintzin Tenépal, better known as La Malinche to the Mexicans, Mayans and Tabascans in sixteenth century Mexico, when Cortés raided the valley. By then, students were so captivated with powerful Latinas and their hunger to outlive injustices that history became a chosen field for a few initially unsuspecting culprits.

I also transfixed them with Greek tragedy when I discussed Oedipus's daughters as background to the "Latinas Go Wild" section on murderous suicidal women. I impressed upon my students that women's identities were erased in both of Sophocles's versions of the king who blinded himself after murdering his father and having carnal relations with his mother. In neither *Oedipus Rex* nor *Oedipus Tyrannius* are the daughters' names invoked. We know they were Antigone and Ismene but never once did Oedipus the King call them by their names. Instead, he referred to them in the possessive and plural. In the play, he says, "My sisters and my daughters, my daughters and my sisters, I am their father and their brother, their brother and their father." I'm paraphrasing but it's a clear-cut *Chinatown* scene. I wait for Jack Nicholson to walk onto the stage and slap Faye Dunaway as she repeats, "She's my sister, she's my daughter, she's my sister and my daughter." But my cultural references to *Chinatown* are unappreciated by these younger-than-young Facebook, tweeting students.

For this week's discussion, I'd assigned *Refusing the Favor: The Spanish-Mexican Women of Santa Fe, 1820-1880.* The young women in class inevitably loved Juana, the Santa Fe woman who, after being taken to court by her Irish husband for her infidelity, announced *she* owned her ass and would offer it up to whomever she pleased. The historical anecdote usually got their attention and asked that they reconsider stereotypes about passive Mexican women, as well as obliging them to stop underestimating Latinas, or any women, for that matter. I myself was now compelled to consider the prospect of Isabel Cortez as a murdering Latina, realizing I may have underestimated her duplicitous cruelty.

After class, Brisa lingered while students filed outside. When the last student had disappeared, she loomed over me.

"I won't do this anymore," she said.

"Do what?" I crammed my notes into my briefcase.

"Play your games, Profe."

"I don't know what you're talking about," I said.

"See? There you go again and I'm not gonna do it."

"Do what, Brisa?"

"You know. Play teacher, student, mother, daughter, lover—lover thing. I'm done, Profe."

"What are you talking about?"

"I'm done. I want something else."

"What do you want?"

"I don't know. Something else. Not these games between you and me. Besides, I know you're seeing that bitch again."

"What bitch? Brisa, what are you talking about?"

"Profe, I know you don't like me to bring up the past and that you like pretending nothing happened between us but it happened and now you avoid me like we never fucked."

Fortunately, the halls were empty because most students had left campus on their way to jobs and other commitments. This crowd couldn't rely on wealthy parents for a college education. "Brisa. Not so loud," I whispered.

"See? All you care about is your rep. You fucked me and you're done. But I know the last time you came over you weren't done."

"That was a long time ago, Brisa."

"Last summer is not that long ago, Profe."

She crept toward me and rubbed my leg with hers. The slit in her skirt widened and I saw she wore a thin purple thong. I was in trouble.

"Brisa, last summer you weren't my student."

"So?" She rubbed her leg against my crotch.

"Brisa," I whispered, "the door is open."

She closed the door and locked it. She grabbed my hand and led me to a corner of the classroom away from the windows. I intended a counterattack by escaping through a window but when she placed my hand on her thigh, I was done for. I skimmed the flesh with my fingers and lifted her leg, pulling it wide and around my ass. With access to her thong, I ripped it and stretched my fingers inside. Her gasp was sensual and I felt myself wetter and more thrilled. Through her silk blouse, I sucked her nipples, intentionally dampening the cloth; then with my teeth I unbuttoned the blouse nudging my tongue inside the cleft between her breasts. Damn, she felt good and I remembered why I'd spent night after night in her hot, humid apartment in June for almost a week. We fucked for hours, rested briefly and fucked again. Brisa had stamina and savored being fucked, and I couldn't snub a woman who breathed a sensuality that said fuck me now and fuck me again until we're both so fucking tired it won't matter because we'll fuck again.

A bell went off in the building and I jumped unexpectedly. The box with the knife inside my jacket tumbled to the floor exposing the blade. To distract Brisa, I sucked harder on her nipple, drew circles on her clitoris with my thumb and thrust fingers potently until she expanded and drenched my hand. Her breast rose and she breathed faintly and as she was about to come, I buried my mouth against hers and felt her moan into mine. She tilted her head back, eyes closed and sighed.

"Damn, Profe."

"Damn yourself, Brisa."

"You ripped my underwear! Damn, look at my blouse!"

She giggled while affecting aggravation.

"It'll dry by the time you button it."

I picked up the purple thong from the floor at the same time that I tucked the box away in my jacket.

"Sorry. I'll replace it."

"Fuck yeah you'll replace it."

"Hurry up. The bell rang."

"Hurry up and what? Damn, Profe. That's it?"

"What do you want from me, Brisa?"

"What do I want? What do I want? Fuck you, Electra."

Brisa had buttoned her blouse and looked relatively tidy. She picked up her books and purse, unlocked the classroom door and slammed it behind her.

Now what had I done? What was the matter with me? She was in my class and I'd have to see her again, grade her papers and deal with her pouty gestures during class discussion. But still, pouty gestures were not her style. Brisa was combative and self-sufficient. Well, combative was an unfair description. She was assertive and took shit from no one. Including me. Which was why I had stayed away since June but I had also stayed away because of Isabel Cortez. Little had I known that Brisa was the safer of the two options. So when she enrolled in my class in the fall, I opted to be professional and stay away.

Suddenly, the door flew open.

"Your girlfriend is a murdering Latina," said Brisa and slammed the door.

Oh, great. She's doing the old "I'm gonna hook you" trick. Now I'm supposed to chase her down and beg her to tell me how she knows Isabel is a murderer. Damn. I was too exhausted to play those games.

I ran after her. "Brisa, Brisa! Wait. Talk to me."

"Fuck you!"

She sauntered across the quad and I caught up.

"You're unethical, you know that, Profe?"

"I know. I'm sorry. We shouldn't have."

"Shouldn't have what? Fuck? That's not what I meant. I'm not a kid, Electra. Hell, I'm almost forty and I know professors and students shouldn't fuck and I know you know it. But I don't give a fuck about that. I'm talking about Isabel. You dropped me as soon as she came around. That was fucked up."

"Okay. I can see you're angry."

"Don't give me that *mierda*. Don't act all therapist on me with 'I can see that you're angry' bullshit."

She mimicked my words. I stayed quiet, sensing the trap of speaking to someone who was prepared to attack anything I said because she was justifiably outraged.

"You used me and you lied to me."

"I'm sorry."

"Fuck you, Profe."

We walked in silence for about twenty steps. Her anger cooled and finally she spoke.

"Don't trust Isabel Cortez. She's using you and that's something you should know about. Using people."

"How do you know she's the murderer?"

"That's easy. I'm psychic."

"No, really, how do you know, Brisa?"

"I told you. I'm psychic."

"That's great but it isn't going to help Detective Quinn convict her."

"Detective Quinn. Yeah, I get it. Your new conquest."

"You're changing the subject, and besides, a woman like her can't be conquered."

"And I can?"

"You? Yeah, right. Since when are you anybody's conquest, Brisa?"

She smiled and I felt somewhat victorious that she wasn't as livid.

"Look, Profe. All I know is that Isabel Cortez is a user and users like her are capable of anything. Including murder."

"That's it? That's all you've got? I know she's a user."

"You may know it but you're not doing anything about it 'cause you're still after her skinny ass and pussy."

"It's complicated, Brisa."

"Everything is complicated, Profe. Look, I'm just telling you to be careful. That's all. Don't say I didn't warn you. And one more thing. You better unload that box 'cause it's gonna get you into trouble."

She darted into the Humanities building for her next class, late of course but Brisa did what Brisa wanted to do. I needed to make an appearance in my dean's office in the Admin building, which was a few steps down from where I had dropped Brisa. She was sweet to warn me but I mostly wondered what she had gleaned from the box in my pocket.

"Hand it over," a voice behind me murmured. It was Detective Carolina Quinn.

CHAPTER TWENTY-TWO

"Hand what over?" I asked.

"The murder weapon. I know you have it."

"Me?"

"Sure. Why not?"

She elbowed my ribs and lifted an eyebrow mischievously as she walked beside me. We reached the steps of the Admin building and she flashed her badge to a rookie, who drew up the yellow tape that blocked the main entrance.

"This is the freshly appointed dean," she said.

She pointed her index and middle fingers to her eyes, then to his and then to me. He nodded and shuffled aside as we maneuvered beneath the tape and entered the building.

"What was that?" I asked.

"You know what it was."

"Still watching me because I'm a suspect or watching me because I could be the next victim?"

"A little of both."

"You didn't answer my question. Why would you think I have the murder weapon?"

She raised her eyebrow again. "Well, do you?"

"Not evading, Detective. Just waiting for my answer."

We had ascended a flight of stairs and paused in front of an elevator.

"I'd rather walk up," I said.

"Suit yourself."

She disappeared behind the elevator doors and I sprinted to the exit leading up the stairs to my office. I had to get there before her. What if she was serious about my having the murder weapon? Fuck! Vice Chancellor Justine Aldridge was out to get me. I knew it! Bounding two steps at a time on my way up to the fifth floor, I paused to catch my breath. That's when I saw a crevice in the corner of one of the steps on the fourth floor. Without thinking, I plucked the box with the knife from my jacket pocket and shoved it into the gaping hole, pushing it far enough to make it invisible to the naked eye.

When I opened the door to the hallway of the fifth floor, I saw Detective Quinn stationed in front of my office doors, which were frosted glass with my name in gold lettering. It was official. I was the interim dean. I darted over, opened a heavy glass door and watched her stride through. I followed closely enough to smell her perfumed neck. The receptionist, Trudy, was behind her desk doing what she knew how to do best: file her nails. She lifted her head as if to greet me but when she saw me, she returned to her occupation without so much as a hello. I hadn't noticed before but Trudy had exceptionally buff arms.

"Pilates, Trudy?" I paused before her.

She continued filing her thumbnail and as she filed, her right bicep flexed. Without looking up at me, she responded, "Huh?"

"You look like you work out."

Trudy worked her way up to her index finger, still refusing to have eye contact with me. I moved on to the next topic, one she might be able to handle.

"Would you mind getting coffee for Detective Quinn and myself?"

"Yeah, I would."

"Excuse me?"

"Oh, did I whisper? I said I would mind. That's not my job."

"It may not be your job, Trudy, but I'm asking you as a courtesy."

"How's that courteous? Nothing about that is courteous to me or my person."

She picked up a bottle of red polish, uncapped it and smeared red on her thumb with the brush.

"Go home, Trudy. I'm sure you're upset about your Uncle Mike. You shouldn't have come in at all. In fact, don't come in tomorrow either."

"Huh?" She looked stunned.

"No, really. I don't need you here. Please, take the week. Take next week. Take all the time you need."

"But I don't have any vacation time. Already took it all."

"Not a problem. The college gives you a full five days for grief."

"I already took those too."

"I'm sorry. Another family death?"

"My cat. Uncle Mike told me to take grievance days so I did."

"Grievance? Against your cat? You mean grief?"

"Sure. That too."

"Go home, Trudy. You don't work here anymore."

"You can't do that!" said Trudy. Her eyes popped wide open.

"I can."

"Uncle Mike said I could stay here as long as I wanted."

"Uncle Mike is gone, Trudy."

"So?"

"So go home. Or I'll call security to escort you out. This isn't a beauty salon."

"What the fuck?" she mumbled and picked up her purse, a lavish Marc Jacobs blue bag. With that kind of accessory I wondered why Trudy needed this job, then I thought, that's probably why she needs a job. I didn't care. I wanted her off the premises. For good.

Trudy banged desk drawers and emptied their contents into her bag: paper clips, multi-colored Post-its, staples and even a stapler monogrammed "CC" for Capital College in decorative lettering.

"Leave the stapler," said Detective Carolina Quinn.

"It's my stapler. Uncle Mike said I could have it."

"Leave it and don't touch anything else on the desk."

Carolina was serious. Trudy rose from the desk, snatched her bag and flung it, swiping my arm.

"Hey! Careful," I said.

Trudy marched out of the office and shoved the glass door forcefully until the weight of the swing propelled her and she almost tripped.

"Good riddance," I said.

"She's a winner," said Carolina.

"You think the stapler could be the murder weapon?"

"Sure, why not? Trudy stapled her uncle to death."

"Funny."

"I thought so."

"Have you found the weapon?"

"Who said it was lost?"

"You did."

"I did?"

"Well, you implied. I thought since you were being so careful about the stapler…" I didn't finish my sentence, hoping to skirt any suspicion she might have.

"I was helping you out. You wanted to get rid of her, right? "

"I did, but…"

"That's the second time you didn't finish your sentence. Something you want to tell me, Electra?"

Carolina picked up the stapler and twirled it in her hands. I stepped back a safe distance in case the stapler flew out of her fingers and whacked me.

"Me? No. Nothing. I have nothing I want to tell you."

She twirled the stapler so expertly I wondered if she'd twirled batons in high school. She set the stapler back on the desk.

"Your office?"

"Yeah? What about my office?"

Her eyelids were half-shut, observing me suspiciously. "Can we go into your office, Electra?"

"Why? Do you need privacy to seduce me, Detective?"

"I can seduce you here in the foyer if I want, Professor."

"Awfully sure of yourself."

"No surer than you are of yourself."

"I'm too insecure to be sure of myself."

"I'm not buying that."

"Funny, I'm not selling."

"Give it away, do you?"

"Every chance I get."

"You see? You are sure of yourself."

"That's not being sure of myself at all, Detective. That's habit. I'm in the habit of giving it away."

"I see."

"And you?"

"Give it away? Not so easily."

"Not what I meant but thanks for the report."

"May we please proceed to your office, Electra?"

"I've never even been in that office. Why the interest?"

"You were there yesterday, weren't you?"

"Yes, but it wasn't mine yesterday."

"But it is now."

"Was Mike murdered in that office?"

"What makes you ask that?"

"For one, there's no yellow tape. Why all the intrigue, Detective?"

"What intrigue? I want to see your office."

"Fine. Come right in."

In front of the door, I remembered I didn't have the brass key Mike had given me. It was inside my desk in the History Department office. I jiggled the knob and the door squeaked ajar. So much for security.

"What? No lock?" she asked.

"I thought it would be locked but…"

"But?"

"I don't know. It's my first, I mean, only my second time here."

Nothing seemed to have been moved and the bookshelves appeared untouched. No books lined the shelves and instead benign artifacts like whiskey shot glasses from all fifty states were dispersed throughout.

"So Mike wasn't murdered in this office."

"I never said that."

"Why all the secrecy, Detective?"

"No secrecy, Professor. We're just protecting you."

"Protecting me from what? So far, I've been treated like a criminal and then…"

"And then you had a little rendezvous after class with a student? Is that the 'and then' you're eluding to, Professor?"

"Ah. I see. Following me again."

"Not following, just watching to make sure you're safe. Seems to me you're unharmed but not harmless. And with a student no less. Aren't there rules about that?"

"I'm beginning to think you're jealous, Carolina."

"Maybe I am."

She edged closer. So close that her breath was on my lips. I could have tilted forward and kissed her but chose not to. I wasn't going to make it easy for Carolina. She had questions to answer and so far she only evaded my inquiries.

"Jealous? You? I don't believe it. Not for a second," I said.

She hadn't retreated and my breath was on her mouth. She parted her lips a hair and I saw her tongue resting on her bottom lip. She wanted me to kiss her but I refused. If she wanted kissing to be done, she would have to initiate it. Carolina backed away. Damn. I called her bluff and she backed away. Damn, damn, damn.

"You're right. I'm not the jealous type."

"Now I'm thinking you are."

"Of course. You didn't have your way."

"My way? Detective, in this arrangement, I'll never have my way."

"And exactly what does NOT having your way look like, Professor?"

I breathed in, sucking air through my lips and walked to the window that displayed a fraction of sky and grass. Some view.

"Twenty years of schooling and they put me on the day shift," I whispered.

"You."

"Huh?" I turned to face Carolina, who was inspecting a hefty crystal apple on one of the bookshelves. I recognized the venerable apple, that had been sculpted by Simon Pearce for the University of Vermont, because I had one just like it.

A professor at that university had given me a similar crystal weight when we dated. Well, sort of dated.

"They put *you* on the day shift," she said.

"Yeah, I know," I responded. I gazed again at the small piece of blue from my window. "Dylan fan?"

"Who isn't?"

"I've been listening to this guy Rodriguez."

"This yours?" She continued inspecting the crystal apple.

I shook my head. "Feel like he's the real thing. Wish I had known about him back in 1971."

"You haven't moved anything?" she asked.

I shook my head again. "He's got this song that haunts me. Says something like, 'The best kiss I ever got—'"

"—was the one I've never tasted."

"You know the song?"

"Yeah, but these days I find myself listening to Julieta. *Te voy a mostrar.*"

Carolina retrieved a plastic bag from her leather jacket and cautiously released the glass apple into the bag without having touched its parameters.

The sculpted object drooped heavily. I inspected the baggie and that's when I saw a red spot, miniscule but there it was. Blood on the big apple.

CHAPTER TWENTY-THREE

"The murder weapon," I said.

"What makes you think that?" Carolina pocketed the bag with the glass apple and it protruded from her jacket.

"There was blood on the apple."

"No, no blood."

"Carolina, I distinctly saw a bloody spot."

"No, you didn't."

"Why are you gaslighting me? I saw a bloody spot. Take it out of your pocket and let's both have a look."

She retrieved the plastic bag and we both examined the apple through the plastic.

"Right there." I pointed to the spot with a slight bloody smudge.

"Oh, that. Yeah, I know."

"Then why were you denying it just now?" I peered at her. The left corner of her mouth curved into an impish grin.

"Electra. I just don't want you to have more information than you need about this. I'm protecting you."

"By gaslighting me?"

"I'm not gaslighting you. I'm shielding you."

"From what?"

"From your own murder."

"Okay, now you're being overly dramatic."

"Am I?"

As we inspected the glass apple, our foreheads nearly touched from close proximity. She pulled back from me and dropped the bag in her pocket again. "I've got to get to the station." Carolina Quinn's bold brown eyes scrutinized me.

"Are we still on for tonight?" I asked.

"I don't know. I may be held up at the office. I'll call you." Carolina flung the door wide and held it for me.

"Oh, I think I'll stay here for a minute. Collect my thoughts."

"You can't. Not in here."

"It's my office."

"It may be your office but it's not safe right now. I suggest you work out of your other office."

"Thanks for the suggestion, Detective, but I'll be fine."

"No, you won't. Come on. I'm not leaving you here."

"It's not for you to say, is it?"

I was afraid of staying in the dean's office by myself but I was more irritated by Carolina's response to the evening's date, which was probably not a date at all but another one of her ploys to watch me. Her constant vigil of my activities was increasingly infuriating. Never had I been the subject of so much curiosity without getting laid. I was exasperated with Carolina Quinn and concluded she was guiding me to the edge of a cliff to watch me jump off by myself. She was playing me because she could. I guess she could. I guess I had allowed her. I guess I was a fool waiting for Carolina to make up her mind that it was okay to see me. See me? Heck, what I really meant was fuck me. That she would make up her mind to fuck me. Her ambivalence was pissing me off.

"It is for me to say, Electra. I'm under orders."

"You make it sound so ominous."

"It's ominous if something happens to you."

"Why do you care?"

"It's my job to care, Professor."

"Of course. Your job." I sighed and exited the office walking ahead of her. "I'll take the stairs," I said, resigned and morose.

"Be careful, Electra."

"Yeah. Sure."

I was eager to retrieve the box with the knife that could or could not be the murder weapon. All I knew was that vice chancellor Aldridge and Detective Carolina Quinn both knew more than I did. In fact, they may not know much more than I did but they sure pretended as if they did.

On the fourth floor, I found the crevice and poked my hand through, digging for the box. I placed the box inside my coat pocket and descended the stairs, walking out of the Admin building. There was no trace of Detective Quinn. I didn't care. With all the uproar on campus, I decided to call it a day, go home, shower and go to one of my beloved bars: Mamacita's. I sent Adrían a text message to join me.

CHAPTER TWENTY-FOUR

"Not Mamacita's, El. I'll go anywhere but not there."

"Why not, Adrían?"

"The place is transphobic. *No gracias*. Let's go somewhere else."

Adrían and I were having a quick bite at our tapas bar. He'd answered my text and run over to meet me.

"Hey, excitement on campus, huh? asked Mariana. She poured cold sangria into large glasses without squandering a drop.

"Too much," I said.

"Poor ole Mike," she said.

"You knew him?" asked Adrían.

"Sure. He used to come in here. With some of his cheap friends. They always left a lousy tip."

"Which friends?" I asked.

"I don't know. The usual white guys who all look alike to me. Except for that woman who sometimes comes in. She makes a Chanel suit look like it wants a rest."

"Justine Aldridge?"

"I don't know her name."

Mariana set down a big plate of crisp potatoes. I emptied most of them onto my own plate. Adrían pointed to the plate and held up a finger to our waitress suggesting another order because I usually devoured the first portion on my own.

"Chanel suit? Hair up in a bun?"

"Yeah."

"That's Justine."

Mariana tossed her head and her bob bobbled. She was a likeable woman with a slinky, wiry body and I do believe Adrían and I frequented the tapas bar more for the agreeable sight of Mariana than for the food, although the *papas bravas* were crispy perfection.

"When was the last time they were all in here?"

"President Peterson? Hmm. Might have been last night."

She yelled over to the cashier, who was also her brother and part owner. *"Oyes, Raul. Viste al presidente anoche?"*

¿Quien?"

"El presidente."

"Obama?"

"No! Ay, Raul."

Mariana put the tip of her pencil in her mouth and the pencil accentuated the shape of her heart shaped lips. I had never noticed the shape of her lips before today, and I wondered if she had shrewdly placed the pencil on them to call attention to her purple lipstick. I wondered how old she was. Mid-thirties, I guessed.

"I'm sure he was here last night. Yeah, I remember. He came in with a couple of white guys, and the guys left when I left. But I forgot some receipts in the cashbox. I came back and saw Plain Jane sitting with the president. Arguing."

"Arguing?"

"Sort of."

"Mariana, have you talked to the police?" I asked.

"Me? Talk to police? What for? They don't listen to us foreigners anyway."

"But it's important that you saw him here last night. And even more important that he was arguing with Justine Aldridge."

"You mean Vice Chancellor Aldridge," said Adrían. He chomped on bread and swallowed.

"If the police come in here, I'll answer questions but I'm not going to a police station."

"Did you hear what they were arguing about?"

"They weren't really arguing. She was yelling at him and he was sitting back in his chair looking like he didn't like her too much, but she kept right on."

"Did you hear what they were arguing about?" I asked.

"Sure."

"Sure? Well, what was it?"

"Same thing all those types argue about."

"Sex?" said Adrían.

He smirked and Mariana smirked too.

"As if. No, they love something more than that."

"Power?" I asked.

"Money," she said.

"Same thing," said Adrían.

We both stared at him and nodded.

"Yeah, same thing," said Mariana.

"What about money? Was she arguing about her salary or something?" I asked.

"Nah. Nothing like that. I heard her say something about some money she gave one of his friends. I guess he lost it all or something like that. She was pretty pissed."

"Money to invest? That sort of thing?"

"Yeah, I guess so." Mariana looked around and saw that the place was getting crowded. "I've got to take some orders."

"Let us know if you remember anything else, okay?" I said.

Adrían swigged from his sangria and put the glass down.

"Sounds like the vice chancellor has a good motive," I told him.

"Maybe," he said.

"What do you mean, maybe? She invested money with a friend of Mike Miller's and lost it. Don't you think we need to find out who the friend was?"

"We? We? Don't get me involved, buddy. This calls for a visit to your friend the detective."

"I thought you didn't like her."

"Who said I didn't like her?"

"Well, the way you were acting today. In your office. You were awkwardly paranoid."

"So?"

"So? Damn, Adrían, what's going on? Why don't you trust me?"

"I don't know what you're talking about."

"Fine. All right. Never mind. I'll find out on my own who this investment bigwig is. This could lead us to the murderer."

"Us? Us? Like I said, don't count me in."

"What's going on with you, Adrían? You've got a secret you aren't telling me, I know it."

"If you know it then why bother me?"

"Because I want to know."

"Maybe I don't want to tell."

"Aha! There is a secret."

He beamed and blushed.

"It's a woman. That look on your face says woman."

"What if it does?"

"You've admitted it! Okay, who is she?"

"I can't talk about it."

"Huh?"

"I can't talk about it, buddy."

"That's a first. We tell each other everything."

"Oh, you mean the way you've been telling me everything about Ice Queen Isabel Cortez?"

"I tell you the important details."

"Like?"

"Like that I ran into her and I saw her a few times. Nothing else to report, bud."

"Nothing?"

"Nothing. And anyway you're changing the subject. Who is this new woman making my buddy grin like he just had a full serving of you know what?"

"Everything you've told me about Ice Queen Isa I've had to pull out of you."

"*Ay ay ay*, Adrían. What do you want to know? Huh? Okay, so I fucked her a couple of times. Went to her place and fucked. That's it. End of story."

"I think there's more you're not telling me."

"More like what? What are you getting at?" I stuffed my mouth with potatoes.

"I talked to Brisa earlier today," he said.

"Oh?" I mumbled with a full mouth.

"She was full of information."

"Mmm."

"First of all, not too smart to fuck her in a classroom. You could've been caught."

I swallowed. "Yeah, yeah, yeah. I know it was stupid but it happened, okay?"

"El, you know I don't care. And Brisa is old enough to know what she's doing. It's what she told me that worries me."

"She's been talking to Omar and he knows some guy named Dominque. Ring a bell?"

"There was a guy at Isabel's last night with that name."

"I know."

"You know? How do you know?"

"Brisa told me."

"Brisa knows him?"

"No, like I said, Omar knows him. And the guy, this Dominique, said he saw you at Isabel's last night."

"Yeah? So?"

"And that a certain pink baseball cap had blood spots on it."

I swallowed again and a lump of potato colonized in my throat.

Adrían inched closer and whispered, "El, you're getting in deeper and deeper, and you're protecting someone who doesn't deserve to be protected."

"I'm not protecting her."

"She was in possession of the pink cap she wore when Omar saw her on the night of the murder. And it had blood on it!"

His whispers got louder and his face inched closer from across the tiny table. "And it's your cap! Can't you see what she's doing? She's setting you up."

"Yeah. Well. Who isn't these days?"

Adrían tipped back in his chair. "I'm not."

"I know you're not."

I stared down at limp, cold potatoes. Mariana returned to our table and set down two small plates, one with *tortilla de jamón* and another with octopus.

"Did you order this?" I asked Adrían.

"Nope. Can't stand the stuff."

"Mariana, we didn't order octopus."

"You didn't, but she did."

A silhouette from a corner at the bar crept toward us. It was Virginia Johnson. The dead dean's wife. She slithered to our table and sank down next to Adrían. Suddenly, it hit me: the reason for my buddy's sheepish grin and for pinning the murder on Isabel Cortez had just skulked in.

"*Hola guapo*." She spoke to Adrían, not me.

Adrían's cheeks turned crimson. He knew I knew.

"Virginia," I said. "To what do we owe this honor?"

"I was in the neighborhood."

"I thought you didn't like dumps like this."

She ignored me and scooted her chair closer to Adrían.

"Hey," he said. "Feeling better?"

"Much better now that I'm with you, *chulo*."

She wrapped her arm around his. "I've missed you. It's been nine whole hours."

"Ooh boy. Someone has it bad," I said.

"What are you talking about, El? Jealous?" she asked. Virginia pressed her breast against Adrían's ribs. He stared at the plate of octopus.

"Jealous? Of what, sweetheart?"

"Of my newfound lover."

"Not jealous. Just hoping you'll be careful and not use him. He's kind of special to me."

"He's special to me too."

"I can see that. What concerns me is that you don't know how special, Virginia."

"What do you mean? I know all about Adrían."

"But do you know he's a sincere human being who's not deceitful, duplicitous or a murderer?"

"What are you implying, Electra? That I'm a murderer?"

"Are you?"

"I think you know the answer to that."

She rose from the table and Adrían got up with her. Without so much as a good-bye, they both walked out. I was shocked. And hurt. What the fuck? Adrían walked out on me with Virginia Johnson?

Mariana returned to the table and filled my sangria glass. "What was that all about?"

"He thinks he's in love," I said.

"With her? She's trouble. Can't he see that?"

"No. He can't."

I paid the bill and left with a sense of dejection. I settled on dropping in at the Clit Club optimistic that I would find my own trouble.

CHAPTER TWENTY-FIVE

The Clit Club was packed with a crowd too young even for me. Face it, Electra, I lectured myself, you're old and feel older among baby-faced girls and strutting bois, all of whom are no older than twenty-two in years or emotional maturity. But what could I do? I was already here and I needed a drink.

I sat at the bar and signaled the bartender. I sipped my beer and thought about how much I missed Adrían. How could he walk out on me like that? And with Virginia? I didn't care that he was fucking her. I cared that he was under the illusion she loved him. She was nothing but disaster. What was the matter with him? He could have anyone he wanted. If he was here, he'd be making his rounds. Adrían could go into a monastery with celibate nuns and get lucky. He didn't know it but I saw it. He had that gene, that look, that way about him.

A baby butch who reminded me of Adrían lured a femme to the dance floor. She was dressed in a red velvet skirt and a white silk blouse that revealed nubile nipples. The baby butch's confidence and lime green ruffled shirt displayed a message that said she was the center of all universes but she was a crude fledgling with none of Adrían's suave finesse.

"Baby butch won't know what hit her by the time the night is over."

I glanced to my left and observed a not-so-young woman in a low-cut, figure-hugging blue satin dress. She had that Eva Mendes, Rosario Dawson appeal with lips and thighs plump and admirable. She puckered her lips around the tip of a brown cigarette. Nat Sherman's. She has style, I thought.

I claimed a matchbook from the bar, struck a match and lit her cigarette. We gazed into each other's eyes and her dusky brown pools caught me off guard.

"The baby butch. Dancing with the heartbreaker. She's going to be crying tomorrow."

"Why do you say that?"

"You've known women like her, right?"

"Yeah, I have." I blushed, staging shyness, then mustered insincere courage. "Come here often?" I asked with a witty cynicism that she was sure to hear in my voice. If she doesn't get it, that's it I'm going home. Alone.

"Why? Have you been waiting long?" She smiled.

"All night," I said.

Her lips were a twisted smile. The banter had begun.

"What do you do?" she asked.

"Me? I teach. At a college. And you?"

"Me? I don't teach. I mostly learn."

"Do you?"

"Yes. I'm a fast learner."

"I see."

"Would you like to teach me?"

"I've got nothing to teach you, *querida*."

"Ah. How about a test then? If I fail, you have to teach me something. Tonight."

"Okay. What's the capital of New York?"

"New Orleans."

"I guess you failed."

"I guess I did." She winked and crossed her legs, exposing a nice thigh. An anticipatory thigh. The kind of thigh you see on a woman who knows what to do with her thighs at the right moment.

"I don't have anything to teach someone like you."

"Now what kind of teacher refuses a willing student?"

"My kind, I guess." I stood up from the bar.

"Not so fast. Where are you going?" She rested a soft palm on my shoulder. "I thought we were having a nice conversation. Was it something I said? Too pushy, right?"

"No. It's not you. It's me. I'm too old tonight."

"I'm too old tonight," she said.

"That's my line."

"And not a very good one." She took a drag from her cigarette and gave me one of those sideglances, then touched my arm. "Let me guess. You've got a broken heart."

"Aren't you psychic? You can say that about ninety-nine percent of the folks in this bar tonight. Wouldn't we be at home all cozy with our sweethearts if our hearts weren't broken?"

"Don't get nasty with me. All I'm saying is you've been trying the wrong kind of woman. I'm sitting here in front of you, asking you to give me a try and what do you do? You run for the door."

"I wasn't running."

"Weren't you?"

"No. I was going to the bathroom."

"So you could slip out the back?"

"I'm tired. It's been a long day and I have work to do."

"A teacher's work is never done, huh?"

"Something like that." I sat back down and ordered another drink. "What are you having?"

She nodded at her half-empty wine glass. I held up my index finger and pointed to her wine glass then pointed two fingers to the scotch bottle on the shelf. The bartender placed a glass of white wine in front of my friend in the blue dress and set a double shot of scotch in front of me. It was time to drink. A lot.

"Thank you," she said.

"You're welcome." I downed my double shot and held up two fingers for another. The bartender obeyed.

My friend in the blue dress twirled her body on the stool and faced me. "Getting drunk to avoid me?" she asked.

"Everything isn't about you. Why do I feel like we're an old married couple?"

"Because all relationships, even the briefest, go through marital transitions."

"And what might those be?"

"You don't know?"

"I do not."

"Everybody knows. They only pretend not to know. That way, they can have the courage to have more relationships. With the grocery clerk, the taxi driver and especially with our teachers."

She peered at me when she said teachers. And continued, "We have relationships with strangers and the brief interludes are harmonious in a manner that says: I know you exist and I respect that about you, but let's not get too entangled."

"Okay, that sounds like the end phase."

"It's not the end phase. It's the all-the-time phase. After the honeymoon. It's the phase when we take each other for granted because we're too busy to notice our partner, lover, wife, husband, whatever."

"Sounds depressing," I said.

"Is that why you're depressed?"

"This must be the counseling phase."

"Maybe." She sipped her wine. When she set the glass down, creases like rivulets from pink lipstick marked the lip of the glass.

"My place or yours?" I asked. "We might as well move along with this marriage so we can wake up divorced."

"You sure know how to seduce a girl."

"I thought that was where we were headed."

"You ever heard of romance?"

"In a bar?"

"Even in a bar."

"Romance?" I shook my head. "I'm too old tonight."

"I'm too old tonight. See?" She took my right hand and placed it across her heart right above her breast.

"What am I supposed to be doing?"

"Copping a feel. What do you think?"

She offered what I read as a suggestive smile. Must be the Scotch, I thought.

"I'm kidding. You're supposed to feel how sensitive I am. By the beat of my heart."

"I could tell that by the way you sip your wine."

"No, you couldn't," she said.

"Yes, I could. Look. The way you sip your wine shows me how you take something in, then imprint it so that everyone will know you've branded this thing and it belongs to you."

"All that from the way I sip wine."

"Oh, there's more." I picked up the other wine glass, the one that the bartender hadn't removed from the bar. It wasn't empty. It was about one-fourth full. I lifted the glass and held it up to the lamp hovering above the bar. "You see this?"

She gazed up at the glass and seemed engrossed in my philosophical incoherence. Then she adjusted her dress, pulling the length over her thigh. An affectedly shy gesture. I wasn't fooled.

"You like to leave something behind so that your lover won't forget you and she will take this thing and smell you, drink you, have you all over again." I drank the remaining wine. It was cheap, sour wine, probably from a box. No wonder she hadn't finished it.

"You're insightful. And a bit of a romantic."

After more flirtatious, nonsensical exchange, we walked out of the bar and hailed a taxi.

She stayed an hour. Maybe two. Sex was just that. Sex. Sometimes bodies are unsuited. They fit all right but they don't harmonize. After she left, I felt a strange apprehension come over me. One-night stands were typically entertaining, and I didn't care if bodies harmonized or not. Tonight, something was different. I was distracted.

I searched for my iPod and saw my date's peachy-pink lipstick on the nightstand. I tossed the lipstick into a drawer with comparable items from other one-night stands. My book,

The Essential Dogan, about the Zen path to enlightenment, engaged me briefly, but the impulse to call Detective Carolina Quinn nagged at me. Was she going to accuse me of standing her up again when she had made it clear she might, just might, call me? Yeah, when she's ready she calls. I call her and what do I get? Superficial niceties about murders and things. I let my white cotton robe fall to the floor and pulled on a sweatshirt and jeans. Whether she wanted me or not, I was knocking on Carolina's door. I opened the door to my apartment prepared to stride into a cool breeze and there she stood, pursing that fleshy mouth I couldn't have. Detective Quinn.

CHAPTER TWENTY-SIX

Dressed in a form-fitting black dress, leather jacket and black pumps, she propped her left shoulder against the doorframe. Her dark eyes sparkled and her dense tresses spilled over her right shoulder.

"Can't stay away from me, Detective?"

"You'd be surprised."

"I'm sure I wouldn't."

When I held the door wide open, I saw Sasha in the hallway walking to her apartment. Her eyes widened as Detective Quinn passed over my threshold. Sasha and I had eye contact, but I closed the door before Carolina noticed.

"Not at all what I expected," said Carolina.

I thought she might be judging the miniature living room lined with cheap, pressed board bookshelves and strewn with books in no apparent order. Not that I objected to her appraisal. I myself condemned my domestic ambiance.

"Grab your jacket," she said. "There's a chill in the air."

"Are you asking me out on a date?"

"A date?"

"Well, you're dressed for a date."

Her right eyebrow arched faintly and she scowled at the bookcases, avoiding eye contact. Aha! She had been on a date. I knew it.

"Was your date fun?"

Her lips curved at the left corner of her mouth, but in a split second she was composed and officious. Damn. I thought we'd had a moment. I'd almost managed to unlock a furtive look. Her spine straight, she folded her arms and bent her right knee so that the folds of her dress creased her skin. She must have been aware of her sensuous stance. I know I was.

"Electra, please. Get your coat. We're going to the station."

"The station? The police station? At this hour?"

"We're open all hours, Professor."

"Ah. I guess this means you're not here for our date."

She didn't smile, but I noted her eyes twinkle a teeny-tiny bit. Or I hoped they had.

"Why the station, Detective?"

"I can't say. You'll just have to come with me."

I lost all fortitude once she became bureaucratic.

"Is it about the bloody apple? I knew there was blood on that apple."

She hitched up her right eyebrow again and this time her eyes refused to twinkle. I wasn't going to get an answer from Detective Carolina Quinn. I chose not to wear my jacket to defy her order. When I saw her Buick double-parked in front of my building, I understood she'd been confident she wouldn't be delayed in my apartment. My ego deflated.

The streets were nearly deserted at three in New York City, yielding a speedy ride to the police station near Capital College. When we arrived, Detective Quinn led me into a musty room with a rectangular window as its central focus. Two police officers munched on donuts and clasped paper coffee cups while they observed activity on the other side of the glass. Carolina shoved the two behemoths aside and sidled up next to me. She grazed my arm and I could have sworn her breast was pressed against the flank above my waist. As I was about to feel self-satisfied from the faint impression of her breast, Detective Swift, on the brightly lit side of the window, stepped aside and Adrían's face appeared.

"What the fuck? What's going on here?"

"We brought him in," said Carolina.

"Brought him in? For what? And where's his lawyer?"

"He won't need one."

"What kind of game are you running here, Detective?" I demanded. I shifted, abandoning her body's heat and edged closer to the one-way mirror.

Carolina seized my arm. "He'll see your shadow if you stand too close," she said.

"I don't care. I want him to know I'm here." I wrenched out of her grip. The Neanderthals sneered. "This is about today, isn't it? Because he wouldn't tell you where he'd been the night before?"

She nodded to the two men in the room and they both wandered out the door snickering. Carolina clutched my arm and squeezed me close. Despite her slight frame she was persuasive. I have to admit that the darkness, her breasts and the overall mess were a turn-on but I had to focus on Adrían, who, for some unjust reason, was in an interview room without a lawyer and without me. Without anyone who had his back.

Her face was millimeters from mine. "Grow up, Electra. I brought you here for him. And he's not being held against his will, so stop it."

I inhaled her breath and whispered into her mouth. "Oh. Sure. I see. The same way you brought me in. Is it legal, Detective? You and Swift seem to be in the habit of harassing perfectly innocent people."

She hadn't released her grip and her breath on mine in that murky room was excruciatingly arousing. I wanted to wrap my leg around hers and kiss her cruelly for about an hour.

"Innocent, Electra? You? Really?"

Her breasts heaved as she whispered into my ear and I thought I felt her tongue lick my lobe's flesh. I had to stay cool.

I veered aside, not sure why I had, except that I was preoccupied with the interview room.

"How long are you going to make him suffer in there with that cretin?" I didn't whisper this time.

Carolina relaxed on her right foot and crossed her arms. That stance again. So damn self-contained. "He's done. Come on."

She opened the door and I trailed her into the narrow passage. Adrían wandered out of the interview room and when he saw me, he avoided eye contact.

"Hey, buddy, are you all right?"

I patted his arm and he jerked away. Damn, I guess we're all in the mood to play hard to get tonight, I thought.

I held my hands up and stepped back.

"Sorry, bud. I thought you needed a friend right about now."

Adrían shrugged. "Are you done with me, Detective?" he asked.

"For now," she said.

"Does that mean I'm free to go?"

"You've always been free to go," said Swift and he rushed through the dank hallway without so much as a hello to me—not that I expected a dinner date.

"Why these games, Carolina? What are you and Swift up to? My buddy and I aren't your prize Chihuahuas to haul in at all hours."

"Prize Chihuahuas? That's funny," she said.

Adrían's face was red and sweaty. He twitched his body, more from anger than apprehension.

"I'll give you both a ride home," said Carolina.

"We'll walk, Detective Quinn," I said.

"Don't be foolish, Electra. It's late."

I nodded to Adrían and he nodded back. Good, he's feeling better, I thought. As I ushered him out of the precinct doors, I heard Carolina yell to me.

"I'm checking in on you tomorrow, Professor."

"No need, Detective. I can take care of myself."

Adrían and I descended the stairs and turned the corner, heading toward his apartment in Chelsea. We plodded for four blocks in silence. Finally, he spoke.

"It was Virginia's fault."

"That they took you in?"

"No. I mean, yeah. I'm not sure. I'm confused."

"Confused?"

"Yeah."

"What happened after you left the restaurant?"

"Same as always. We went to her place."

Adrían had his hands buried in his trouser pockets. As he strolled, his shoulders crumpled and he straightened the collar of his suit jacket. He wore a navy herringbone jacket with matching wide-legged trousers that had apparently wrinkled from his having sat for who knows how long on a cold plastic chair.

"What happened, Adrían?"

"Like I said, we went to her place. But something wasn't right. I mean, I guess I kinda knew when she showed up at the tapas bar looking for me. She doesn't like to be public. You know how she is."

"Yeah, I know Virginia."

"We got to her place and it was crowded with her crazy-ass friends. I mean, the dean's barely been dead less than a week and she's got a party going on."

"She likes her parties."

"She's got some crazy-ass friends."

"Yeah."

"You know any of them?"

"Maybe. Did you get any of their names?"

"Not really. We were kind of busy if you know what I mean."

"Yeah, sure."

"So Ginny and I—"

"Ginny?"

"Yeah. What of it?"

"Nothing. I just never heard anyone call her Ginny."

A fine mist fell and we paused to contemplate the night sky twinkling not from stars but from high-rise buildings with lights shimmering. On the horizon, through twin buildings, I glimpsed an indigo beam emerging from the shadows. The mist fell on Adrían's hair and the glimmering from the street lamps formed a halo on the circumference of his head. I despised those who wanted to crucify him because he was who he was, and I knew I couldn't protect him but that didn't stop me from trying. We bowed to each other with a fleeting, trusting glance as if to approve of the night sky's mood. I dug my hands into my jeans pockets and regretted not having my coat. The sweatshirt I was wearing was getting damp. We must have looked like a distinguished pair—Adrían in his elegant, wrinkled suit and me in my hoodie sweatshirt and jeans—traipsing the streets of Chelsea with the late-night crowd heading home from bars and primal morning trysts.

"As I was saying, Ginny and I were keeping to ourselves. It was weird, El, kinda like it wasn't even her party, like she didn't even plan it but there were all these crazy-ass friends drinking up her booze and sloshing around in the hot tub, smoking weed in the kitchen, dancing in the dining room. I think I saw some babe on the dining room table, stripping."

"Damn. And you didn't call me?" I quipped.

"I didn't think you wanted to be at Ginny's place, especially, well, you know."

"You want to say it out loud, Adrían?"

"You might be a suspect."

"Not you too? She's the suspect and you know it. Stop trying to protect her."

"I'm not so sure she is anymore."

"But you're sure I am? Great. Thanks for the vote of confidence."

"I don't mean you're guilty of murder. Fuck, El, I just got dragged to the police station for questioning, so don't go getting all sanctimonious on me."

I took a calming breath and heard him do the same. "Hey, did you ever see that indie lesbian film about the professor who runs away with the circus?" I asked.

"The one with that African-Canadian babe? Heck, I'd run away to the circus to be with her any day."

"Yeah, me too."

"Was kind of a bizarre film though, don't you think? I mean, why do us queers always end up being the circus?"

"It's a metaphor."

"I get that but still, I get tired of being considered the bizarre circus, you know?"

"We're not the bizarre circus. People with no imagination just don't know what to do with those who don't fit their damn categories and pigeonholes. As if life is that simple."

"I guess."

"And anyway, life is a circus, Adrían. And we're the lucky ones because we not only crave the erratic and erotic, the sensual and extraordinary but we also choose it all—all the ridiculousness with the intensity. And we don't hold back. What for? Life is too damn short and I, for one, will take the circus over so-called 'normal' any day. Wouldn't you?"

"Sure, if it will get me a woman like the one in that indie lesbian film. Or, better yet, America Ferrera. Damn, she's so sexy smart. And she has great lips."

"Yeah. Smart, sexy women with full lips." I said. "Our downfall."

"And down we do fall," he said. "But you can't give up, El."

"I didn't say I was giving up. I don't know. Just tired, I guess. Tired of finding myself right back in the same weary circumstances with every woman I've dated or loved. Worn out by the same *mierda*. Do you know how many times women have told me I'm too intense? I mean, what the fuck does that mean? How can anybody be too intense about loving the woman you worship, admire and desire? But our flaws keep us from loving fully, Adrían. Our own mistaken ideas about what love should be keeps us from sustaining the real thing but that's not my point. You and I, we'll do anything for the woman we love. Anything she asks—get a dog when we don't like dogs, have a baby when we think we'll make lousy parents, move wherever we've got to go to be with her and yeah, even join the fucking circus if that's what it takes."

"Yeah, I know. We do crazy shit for women," he said.

"Especially sexy, smart women who make us crazy."

"Yeah."

I was so immersed in my cogitating I didn't notice we were poised at his apartment building's steps. Adrían punched in a code, shoved open the door to a skinny hallway and we rode the elevator to the third floor.

In his apartment, I flung myself down on the couch, which also served as my bed.

"Hey, El, you want to get some sleep? I don't think I'm up to telling you the rest of my police precinct adventure."

"Whatever you want, bud. Just throw a blanket and a fresh toothbrush my way."

"Whatever you say, buddy." He paused. "Hey, do you have to go in early tomorrow? I mean today?"

"I'm the new dean. I can do whatever I want and anyway tomorrow's Saturday."

"Interim Dean," he said and shut the door to his bedroom.

"Yeah, yeah, interim," I mumbled.

After I washed up in the half-bathroom, I rested my head on an overstuffed bolster and felt a crick in my neck. Damn. Weren't there any decent pillows around here? I tossed the bolster on the floor and rummaged around the couch for a flat pillow. When a sharp object pricked my fingers, I pulled my hand out from the pile and saw that my middle finger was bleeding. I sucked on it to stop the blood from seeping into Adrían's fine, navy blue cotton couch. Without thinking, I shoved cushions and pillows to the floor and beneath the mountain of fabric and cotton, I saw it: another damn bloody knife.

Fuck, Adrían. What the fuck?

CHAPTER TWENTY-SEVEN

"Adrían!"

I heard him scrambling to the door.

"*¿Qué pasó*? You all right, El?" He flung the door open and it slammed against the wall.

I held up the six-inch blade with a turquoise bead in the middle of the pearl handle. Sasha's Wally was right. These things seemed to be a dime a dozen.

"What's this?" I punched the air with the blade. "It was hidden. Here. Inside this mountain of pillows."

"It's yours."

"Don't bullshit me, Adrían."

"I took it. From your jacket. At the restaurant. You took off your jacket when you went to the bathroom. I snuck it out of your jacket."

I scrunched up my forehead. "But why? And how did you know I had it?"

"Brisa."

"Brisa told you?"

"She said it fell out of your pocket at an inopportune moment."

"Are you and Brisa colluding to save me from this knife?"

"Somebody has to. You're running around all over the city with it in your jacket pocket like it's a fucking lucky charm."

"But when did you bring it back here? You said you went to Virginia's after you left me."

"Oh. That. Well, we stopped by to pick up some toys." He blushed and gazed at his feet. Adrían still got shy when he talked about sex. "Well, anyway, we left my place and went to hers. I didn't want to carry that thing around so I buried it in the pillows when she wasn't looking."

"She didn't see you with it?"

"No. I don't think so."

"What I want to know, and I know you're tired—heck we're both tired—but can you please tell me how you ended up in that room being questioned?"

"Oh, yeah." He slumped on the couch next to me and tossed a stuffed pillow to the floor to give him more room. He folded his arms behind his neck and stared at the ceiling. "The party got a little rowdy. Neighbors must have called the cops, 'cause before I knew it, people were running out the back way and some of us got hauled in."

"Virginia too?"

"Nope. She disappeared. Last I saw, she was, well, you're not going to believe this part. I'm pretty sure she left with Isabel Cortez."

"What? They don't even know each other. Are you sure it was Isabel?"

"Pretty sure, bud. I saw them on the back porch. They looked pissed like they were arguing and before I knew it, a couple of cop cars drove up and both Ginny and Isabel were gone."

"Damn."

"Damn is right."

"I know what you're thinking. You're thinking that Isabel is the prime suspect for the dean's murder. Aren't you?" I asked.

"It looks suspicious, bud."

"Looks to me like they both know something."

"I'm putting my money on Isabel," he said.

"Why didn't the police pick her up? If she's so guilty?"

"I told you. She disappeared."

"But so did Ginny." He shrugged off my accusation. "Did the police question the others at the party?"

"Nah. Just me."

"But why?"

"We both know why."

"They let the others go? Just like that?"

"Well, someone made a phone call and a shiny, Armani-suited lawyer showed up. You know these folks have money. Before I knew it, about nine or ten partiers were walking out the door of the precinct and they took me to that back room and made me wait about an hour before that Swift dude came in and asked me if I wanted any coffee."

"And no sign of Virginia?"

"Not a one."

"Fuck her. Now you see what I meant when I told you she's dangerous?"

"She didn't know I'd been taken in."

"Oh, she knew all right. In fact, she probably orchestrated the whole thing."

"Nah. She wouldn't do that, El. I know her."

"Yeah, the way I know Isabel?" I wasn't getting through to him. "Adrían, you've known her for all of what? Four days? No, you don't know her. I've seen how she operates and believe me I was infatuated too. Sure, at the beginning she makes us all feel special."

Adrían's face dropped with disappointment.

"She made you believe that, didn't she?"

"Yeah. I guess."

"Oh, buddy. I'm so sorry. I thought you were in it for the fun."

He raised his head and stared at the knife I had set on the couch's navy cushion. The six-inch blade with the turquoise bead on the pearl handle glinted probability but offered no solutions or clues to what the heck was going on.

"Something's not right," he said.

"No kidding."

"Why'd you take it?" His head bobbed toward the knife.

"I didn't."

"How'd you get it?"

"Vice Chancellor Justine Aldridge."

"Huh? When? How?" Adrían sat up straight on the couch. He was in his navy blue boxers and navy blue T-shirt. He picked up an overstuffed pillow and placed it on his lap.

"In her office. Earlier today. I mean, early yesterday." I gazed around the room for a clock, curious about the time.

"It's four forty-seven," said Adrían.

"She called me in and put the knife in front of me. Said it was the murder weapon."

"Damn." Adrían stared at the knife then looked back up at me. "Is it?"

"I don't know. I thought it might be. But here's the thing: she said it had my fingerprints on it."

"And did it?"

"If it's the same knife that was in Mike Miller's office on the day he showed me the office that is now my interim dean's office, then, yeah. He asked me to hold it so I did. Here's what's a little weird. I think he saw a spot of blood on the inlay. Where the bead is."

Adrían got up and went into his bedroom. He returned with a white cotton handkerchief embroidered with his initials, A.F. for Adrían Fuentes. His grandmother had embroidered them for him. What a guy. He was enduring the wrong century. Some of us wanted to be far into the future in another century, heck, even another planet, but not Adrían. He wanted to revert to the 1940s and '50s despite the knowledge that the 1950s were brutally suffocating but he insisted he would've been fine so long as no one ever guessed his assigned sex at birth allowing him to traverse his chosen gender. But the bashing and murder of non-white, non-heterosexual folks was common back then. Almost as common as in the 21st century.

Adrían folded his handkerchief over the blade and held it beneath the light of a mid-century orange and beige lamp on the side table that was also orange and beige.

"Hmm," he said.

"What?"

"Well, someone has done a good cleaning job but I still see something."

He rose from the couch and held the blade directly under the orange lampshade and continued to examine the bead. He folded the knife inside the white cotton hankie and placed it on top of the side table. Adrían sprinted to his bedroom and returned with a magnifying glass.

"You're such a Boy Scout," I said.

"Yeah, well, too bad the Scouts are so damn homophobic and transphobic."

He inspected the inlay. I could see his eye magnified and spiderlike on the side of the glass facing me.

"There is something here. Looks like dried blood to me."

"But it can't be Mike's blood if he's the one who was inspecting the blood on the knife in the first place."

"Well, you're right but maybe it's the dean's blood. Have they found the murder weapon for Johnson's murder?"

"Maybe. I don't know."

"I thought you and Detective Quinn were chummy."

"Yeah, real chummy. She leads me on, seduces me with questions and drops me when she has the answers she wants. Next she reverts to superficial, nuanced behavior, which could be confused as flirtation. When I steer closer, she runs. Or says she's busy with the case."

"Sounds like your type of woman."

"Yeah, the kind who only calls to chat about work or some other shallow nonsense and pretends we're friends when it's convenient. That the type you mean?"

"Hey, your choice, not mine."

"Not my choice at all. More like I'm her lackey when she's damn well ready, if she's ever ready because I don't think she is. I think she'll lead me on until this whole circus is over, then I'll never see her again."

"And you think she's keeping information from you?"

"What information?"

"About the murder weapon. What else?" Adrían sounded exasperated.

"Like I said, she doesn't tell me anything. I ask and she flatly refuses, saying she can't tell me because it's classified information and she's protecting me."

"Yeah, the old 'I'm protecting you' ruse."

"Very funny."

"Look, here's what I think: I think this could be the knife that killed the dean or an elk."

"An elk? In New York City?"

"Maybe Mike went hunting." He smirked, self-satisfied with his joke.

"Yeah, right. All he knows about roughing it is wearing those cowboy boots and faking a western twang."

"All he knew."

"Oh, yeah. Poor Mike."

"Poor Dean Johnson. Now no one will remember the poor schmuck. I wonder if they'll take his murder as seriously?" mused Adrían.

"Heck if I know. One guy had millions and the other had billions."

"Dean Johnson had millions?"

"Well, his daddy did. Or does. But the dean was still worth a lot."

"Oh."

"You read mysteries, Adrían. The femme fatale is always the guilty one 'cause she's after some poor schmuck's money."

"Spoken like a crafty academic."

"Me? Crafty? Wouldn't that be businessman Mike Miller and his trusty regents?"

"Yeah, huh? The guy didn't even have a PhD and he ran a college."

"Not reason enough to kill the bastard, unfortunately."

"Hey, ever met his wife?"

"Nope. You?"

"Once. She wasn't bad either. Loves the opera too, I hear."

"All those types love to say they love the opera."

"She's a real aficionada though. Especially loves *Faust*. Seems it's her favorite."

"*Faust?*"

"Yeah. Never misses a performance. Goes every night and likes to sit in all areas of the Met to get a better perspective or something like that."

"How do you know all this?"

"She and Ginny are sort of friends."

"Wait. Let me get this straight. Virginia Johnson, formerly Mendez, whose husband is dead—murdered, that is—is friends with Mike Miller's wife, whose husband just so happens to be dead too—murdered, that is."

"Wow. Now that you say it that way, it is a little suspicious."

"More than a little, Adrían. What does she look like?"

"Oh, she's young to be with an old guy like him. I mean, she's probably in her late forties, early fifties. Wears her brown hair down in a kind of Jackie O flip. According to Ginny, she likes girls every now and then too."

"Fuck."

"Yeah, that's it. To fuck girls. But really to get fucked by them. Especially at the opera. Seems that's why she likes to sit in the cheap seats. Inevitably, she finds some cool idiot dyke who'll fuck her right there in her seat."

"Fuck, fuck, fuck, Adrían!"

He saw the look of despair on my face. "No. Please tell me you didn't, buddy."

"You're looking at a cool idiot dyke."

"*Pinche mierda*, El. What were you thinking? The college president's wife? When?"

"Remember the night I was supposed to meet Isabel at the opera?"

"Oh. Yeah. *Pinche mierda*."

"*Pinche mierda* is right."

"Well, fuck."

"What if she sees me? She'll recognize me and tell the police. I'm fucked."

"Why would she see you?"

"Well, why wouldn't she?"

"I don't know. Wait a minute. We're approaching this all wrong. You don't have anything to worry about. You didn't do anything."

"No, I just so happened to have fucked the wives of both the dead dean and the dead president."

"Well, that could happen to almost anyone."

"Really?"

"Okay, not really, but I know you, you're not a murderer. You'd like to have sex with women every day if you could and from what I can tell, you do and then you wonder why someone like Carolina Quinn isn't interested? Really, El. Have you thought about the fact that she's waiting to see when you stop fucking a different woman every day?"

"Right now, the last thing on my mind is why Carolina Quinn isn't interested in me."

"Oh, she's interested all right. Just a little gun-shy, that's all."

"Do you have to use metaphors that refer to murder weapons?"

"You know, that reminds me. How was Mike Miller murdered?"

"I just assumed it was a knife, but you know they haven't released that information yet as far as I know."

"And again Detective Quinn won't come to your rescue."

"My rescue will be more than information at this point. Once she finds out about me and Mike Miller's wife, I'm a dead man." I paused. "Mike Miller's wife. What's her name anyway?"

"You don't even know her first name, El? Damn. That's cold."

"Look, I know she likes M&M's. Peanut. And that someone who wasn't Mike escorted her to the opera."

"And you didn't bother to ask her name?"

"No. Why would I? It was a quick rendezvous. Her name, please, Adrían."

"Oh. Clarissa, I think."

"Clarissa? As in *Mrs. Dalloway*'s Clarissa?"

"Sure. Why not?"

"Not a name you hear often."

"I guess."

"And don't you find it amusing? Virginia and Clarissa. Friends. It's as if they made each other up."

"Huh? Why?"

"Virginia and Clarissa, get it?"

"Get what? If you mean Mrs. Dalloway and Virginia Woolf, sure, okay, but who cares?"

"You're right. Never mind. All I know is that as soon as Detective Quinn or Swift get a clue about Clarissa Miller and me, I'm in big trouble. Really big trouble."

"Well, maybe they won't."

"Yeah, and maybe the sun don't shine in Florida."

"And the rain don't fall mainly on the plains in Spain."

A text message buzzed on my phone, which I had left in my pants in the guest bathroom. I got up and retrieved the phone.

"Damn, buddy. It's already six forty-five. How'd that happen?" I said.

I checked my text message and there it was: a message from Detective Quinn and all it said was *Clarissa*.

CHAPTER TWENTY-EIGHT

I put the phone in front of Adrían. He read the message out loud. "*Clarissa*. Wow. It's as if Detective Quinn has been in the room with us. You think we're bugged? Maybe they put something on me when I was at the station. Or on you. Don't say another thing."

"Quit being all *Mission Impossible* on me, Adrían. We haven't been bugged. She's a detective doing her job. She probably questioned the wife. Her husband was just murdered."

"Don't tell me you trust Detective Quinn, buddy?"

"I never said I trusted her. I don't think she's going to waste her time putting a bug somewhere in our vicinity when all she has to do is ask."

"Yeah, but ask what?"

"Ask. Just ask whatever she needs to ask."

"And you'll answer? With the truth and all?"

"Do I have a choice? She knows about me and the President's wife."

"You don't know she knows and even if she does, that doesn't prove anything, El."

"Doesn't it?"

"Okay. What does it prove? That you like women, particularly the wives of high-level administrators at our specific college."

"That's not entirely true."

"Isn't it? I mean, first Virginia and it sounds to me like that went on for over a year. Then Clarissa, and who knows how long that might have gone on if…"

"No, Adrían. I wouldn't have run into her again and if I had I wouldn't have continued anything with her. It only happened that night. Remember, Isabel stood me up."

"Of course, Isabel."

"Yeah. Isabel."

"She probably set you up. I bet she sent you to the opera that night," he said. "Think about it, bud. Isabel was obviously friends with Ginny, who was friends with Clarissa. Maybe Ginny just mentioned something to Isabel about Clarissa's love of *Faust*. I bet Isabel knew you'd run into her. And fuck her."

"Oh, right. Let's pin it on Isabel and let Virginia off the hook when she's probably the murderer all along. Remember, she has a lot to gain from her dead husband."

"She's got her own money, El. She doesn't need his and anyway, they signed a pre-nup."

"Virginia may have signed a pre-nup but I can guarantee you that it only holds up in the case of divorce and not in the case of death."

"Now you're just making stuff up because you don't want Isabel to be the killer."

"Okay. Let's say it was Isabel. What's her motive? Why would she want to kill the dean? Or the president?"

"Heck, I don't know. Maybe she was fucking them both and neither one of them would leave their wives for her, so she got her revenge."

"Wait a minute. We've got this all wrong, bud. Virginia, of course! She's Vee! Virginia and Isabel were more than friends. I heard Isabel on the phone pleading with a lover she called Vee. It had to be Virginia. Adrían, what if Virginia set up Isabel? And promised her money if she killed Johnson?"

"But why would Ginny want him dead, El? I'm just not convinced this was her plan. With or without Isabel Cortez."

"Well, I know for a fact that Ginny and the dean were getting a divorce."

"You know for a fact?"

"Didn't Ginny tell you that? I thought you had become pretty damn close in the last few days."

"Don't call her Ginny. Only I can call her that. And yes, we've gotten close. She's not who you think she is, El. She has a whole other side to her that no one sees. She's sweet and funny and bighearted and—"

"And left you to get picked up by the police at her own crazy-ass party while she ducked out with none other than Isabel. There it is! And you refuse to see the obvious. She's so bighearted she'll set someone up to take the rap for her husband's murder so she can get off free. Nope. Sorry. Too many fingers point at Virginia. And now I'm thinking that Isabel was her accomplice. Johnson had lots of money. I bet they both planned to cash in on it. His father was in the inner circle of Goldman Sachs."

"So?"

"So? What have I been trying to tell you? We're talking millions, Adrían. And not the low millions but triple digit millions put away in Swiss bank accounts. Virginia wasn't going to let that kind of money get away. Made her crazy. Her inheritance from her family was a pittance compared to the stash dean Coxwell Johnson had."

"I don't get it. If he was so loaded, why was he working at a Podunk college?"

"Heck if I know. Maybe he was trying to prove to daddy that he could do something. Coxy was a disaster during his college days. The guy's biggest claim to fame was that he was a cheerleader at Yale. And he didn't just drink; the guy was a big-time cocaine addict. And daddy didn't like spending his money that way."

"And Ginny confessed all this to you."

"Made for great pillow talk." I shrugged.

He narrowed his eyes.

"Sorry, bud. I'm just being honest," I said.

"Why'd she marry him anyway?"

"That's easy. Drugs and money."

"Come on, El. Give her a little more credit."

"Oh, okay. True love. She married him for true love of drugs and money, parties and pussy."

"You're cold."

"You're pointing the finger at the wrong person. Virginia's the cold one."

"I tell you, El, you've got it all wrong. She's changed. I think his murder has really affected her."

"Of course it's affected her. She gets to keep a chunk of his cash. Coxwell's daddy will buy her off. Just watch."

"What do you mean?"

"Well, Virginia knows Coxwell's daddy doesn't want to go to court and if she wants Coxwell's money, she'll have to do some battle. So instead of any court mess and publicity, daddy will buy her out for more than just pocket change. She'll be set for life, that Ginny of yours. I wouldn't be surprised if she finally took off to Buenos Aires."

"Buenos Aires?"

"Yeah, her first love is in Buenos Aires. She's never gotten over him."

"Her first love?"

"Oh, I guess she's never talked about him?"

"No, she hasn't."

"Well, none of this conjecture matters, because when Detective Quinn gets her act together, she'll discover that the dean's murderer is his wife. Come on, bud. Motive is almost always money. Just follow the money."

"Okay. Okay, so let's follow the money. From what I remember, Isabel Cortez has her own romance with money. It makes sense Isabel was involved but I don't think she was only an accomplice. What she didn't tell you is how close she and Dean Johnson had become."

"Huh?"

"You heard me."

"Wait a minute. Pillow talk with Ginny, right?"

"She didn't just tell me; she showed me. A letter."

"And this letter is important because…?"

"Because it was from Isabel, the Ice Queen herself, to Coxwell Johnson."

"Okay. I'm waiting. What did it say?"

"That she wasn't going to wait much longer for him to get the divorce he had promised. That she wanted to be Mrs. Johnson soon."

"Isabel? And Coxy? Mr. and Mrs. Johnson?" I laughed until I slid off the couch.

"I saw the letter."

"I'm sure you did. I'm sure Virginia crafted a convincing letter to show you knowing you'd tell me and I in turn would tell Detective Quinn. No, wait, she probably assumed we'd both tell Quinn. She's crafty, that Virginia."

"The letter was signed by Isa."

"Isa?"

"Yeah."

"And what did the letter say?"

She signed it off with, "*Te quiero, te adoro, mi amor, soy totalmente tuya, Isa.*"

"Gee, I used to write exactly that to Virginia in my letters to her."

"Why would you sign Isa's name?"

"I didn't sign her name and I never signed my name. I'm not that stupid. Ginny probably filled that in herself."

"You told Virginia you loved her?"

"It was part of the game."

"What game?"

"Oh, please. Don't act so innocent. As if you don't tell women you love them when you're fucking."

"No, I don't."

"Never? Not once?"

"Nope."

"Adrían, you mean to tell me you have never ever told a woman you love her while fucking her?"

"You mean, in the act of fucking?"

"Yeah, what did you think I meant?"

"Okay, maybe once or twice, but I never wrote it in a letter."

"Oh, really? Never once declared a semblance of love to a woman in a love letter?"

"Only the ones I loved."

"How many women have you loved, Adrían?"

"Only two."

"You're kidding, right?"

"Only two."

"Virginia better not be one of those two or I'll be worried for you."

Adrían was silent. We sat quietly, having resolved nothing after another hour of speculation and dispute. The sun had peeked its way through the thin curtains in the living room. I needed coffee.

"I can't help it," he said. "I think she's cool. And so fucking sexy in bed, El. Damn. How'd you ever let her go?"

"She wasn't mine to let go of, Adrían. She's her own woman, I told you. Virginia gets what she wants when she wants it and you, my friend, are her latest boi toy. She needs you for fun and to prove a point."

"What point would that be?"

"That she's not the murderer. You with your blind love will plead her case better than anyone. She knows that."

"How do you know her so well?"

"Let's just say Virginia and Isabel are made from the same mold, and I've been hanging around that creeping mold too long."

"You make them sound so sinister."

"Nah. Not sinister. Clever, but not sinister."

"You see? Even you admit that Ginny isn't sinister enough to be a murderer."

"Okay, fine. Maybe you're right, Adrían. Maybe it's someone else and not either of the women you and I seem to be foolishly in love with."

"You're still in love with Isa, buddy?"

"Did I say that? No, no I meant I *was*. But that wasn't love. That was captivity."

"Captivity, huh?"

"And habit. Just habit with her."

"Habit?"

"Yeah, you know, habit. The body remembers some quest for desire and she's the closest thing to satisfy that quest but it's not true or kind or lasting. It just is."

"Wow. Maybe you are over her."

"Yeah, I guess I am."

"Well, that's good, because when they cart her away for murder, you won't be upset about it."

I got up from the couch. "I'm taking a shower. Can we please make some coffee?"

"Don't you want to sleep a couple of hours first?"

"It's already after eight."

"So? I'll close the blinds. Turn off your phone and I'll turn mine off too."

"Thank the goddesses for Saturdays."

"What a week, huh?" Adrían walked to his bedroom.

"Hey, bud, just one more thing before we take our nap," I said.

"Yeah?"

"What am I supposed to do about Carolina's text message?"

"Oh, shit. I guess we forgot all about that."

"I didn't."

"Tell you what. Let's get some sleep. Everything will seem better in a couple of hours."

"What if she comes knocking?"

"If she comes knocking, we'll open the door and offer her some coffee."

"Sounds like a plan."

CHAPTER TWENTY-NINE

We slept longer than we had anticipated because when I awoke, the moon had found its way inside the apartment, reflecting shadows of bare tree branches on the wall. Despite my best friend sleeping in the next room, I felt lonely and alone. I was disillusioned about what I'd become. Despondent and hopeless. Childless and loveless. I felt sacred and profane, like Charles Ryder in *Brideshead Revisited* when he arrived at that spiritual punctum in his life, conceding he had nothing and no one. Only memories of what might have been, what almost was and couldn't be and then left to wonder if anything was the way we remember. We reinvent the past to fit a present that won't make us crazy. I spent each day performing rituals that kept me from going crazy. Or acting crazy. Meaningless sex was one of those compulsory rituals. Enough. These philosophical musings were depressing me.

I got up, sprang into the shower, dressed in the same dingy jeans and sweatshirt and made espresso and toast.

"Hey buddy!" I called to Adrían. "It's after nine. We slept twelve hours! Get up, get up! Time to party!"

He stumbled out of his bedroom, hair disheveled, wearing his signature white T-shirt and Perry Ellis boxer shorts with his robe's belt hanging loose. He sank down next to me on a barstool at the kitchen's bar, which also served as his kitchen table. I don't think he entertained much. The life of an assistant professor, I thought.

"Here. Drink this." I placed a mug of black, thick espresso in front of him. He sipped slowly and relaxed his head on his arm, which was stretched across the counter.

"Time is it?" he mumbled.

"I told you. It's after nine. Actually, it's almost ten p.m. on a Saturday night! We're going out."

"I'm too tired to go out, El," he muttered into his arm.

"You're too young to be tired. Come on. And I have to borrow some clothes. I can't run around in these stinky jeans and sweatshirt."

"Sure. Go ahead. But most of my clothes fit you a little baggy."

"That's okay. Where we're going tonight, it won't matter. I just need to make a good impression when we arrive."

"Where're we going, El?"

"The Down Under."

"The Down Under? Not me. Uh-uh. Last time I was in that place, well, never mind. Mostly, I swore I'd never go back. Not my style. Uh-uh. You're on your own, El." He propped his head up and it bobbled animatedly.

"Oh, come on. What's the worst that can happen?"

"I don't know. Someone will confuse me for a bottom and not hear when I scream my safe word."

"That doesn't happen in these places, Adrían. Boundaries are honored."

"What about Detective Quinn?"

"Nah, I'm not inviting her."

"That's not what I meant." He narrowed his eyes. "Clarissa, remember?"

"I'm not inviting her either."

"Okay. Now I'm worried. A few hours ago, you were agitated about Clarissa Miller and what Detective Quinn would think about your rendezvous with the dead president's wife."

"It is a little messy, huh?"

I rose from the kitchen counter holding a mug of espresso with steamed milk and strolled into his bedroom. The walk-in closet was impeccably organized. His shoes, polished and inserted with shoe trees, were lined on shelves. He must have owned at least twenty pair and not a one had a scratch. His suit jackets hung according to color, material and season, the linen shuffled to the back of the closet to make room for his fall and winter line. Brown corduroys and navy wool were prominently positioned up front. Pants on a lower rack matched each suit jacket above. I grabbed a wool navy sports coat and concluded I'd wear my jeans again since his trousers were pleated and not my style. I also found a clean, sharp white shirt with thin ruffles on the bib.

I tucked the shirt inside my pants and tugged on the sports coat, admiring my somewhat lean look. Maybe I wore too much black. Maybe navy wasn't a bad change.

I burst out of Adrían's closet. "Come on. Let's get to the club before it's too crowded."

"El, what's up with you? Suddenly you're not worried anymore?"

"Worried? About what?"

"Okay, fine. If you're not worried, why should I be?"

"That's exactly what I'm talking about. Now put on some of your fancy clothes."

Adrían must have been in his room for over an hour before he emerged coifed and ironed in a dark tan wool suit with pleated, loose-fitting trousers. His red silk tie was wide and clasped to his black shirt with a gold tie clip.

I pointed to my watch.

"I know, I know but I had to press my shirt." He smoothed his hand over his silk tie and pursed his lips.

"It's under your jacket. No one will see it. And anyway, no one is going to be looking at your shirt at the Down Under."

"Do we have to go there? Can't we drop by another bar? I'll even go to Mamacita's with you."

"You will?"

"Yep."

"Okay, *vámonos*."

I figured after a few drinks he'd soften up and accompany me to the queer sex club and anyway the cool queer bars were in Adrían's Chelsea neighborhood.

We walked two blocks to Mamacita's and sat at the bar. That's when I heard a voice from the past.

"Well, well, well, if it isn't the one, the only Electra Campos, heartbreaker and soul robber."

It was Brandy. She was dressed in her leathers, which meant one thing: her motorcycle was outside and she was on her way to the Down Under.

"Hey, Brandy, happy to see you haven't outgrown the sex club phase." I inspected her while she flaunted her black leather chaps.

"Outgrown it? Hell no!" She grinned. "The missus and I like to spice it up on Ladies' Night, if you know what I mean."

I returned the grin. I had a soft spot for Brandy. Unlike me, she had the skill to make a meaningful relationship with a woman last for longer than a month.

Brandy elbowed me, ordered a drink and parked herself on the stool next to me.

"Hey, you want to go on over with me?" asked Brandy. She elbowed me again.

"Way ahead of you. We just stopped in for a drink."

"We did?" asked Adrían. "I never said I was going."

"Who's *Leave it to Beaver*, El?"

Brandy sized up Adrían, inspecting his vintage 1950s dark tan suit.

"Brandy, this is Adrían. My best friend. Be kind."

"Come on, son, you'll love the place."

"I thought you said it was Ladies' Night?" Adrían asked.

"Indeed it is and I can think of at least two ladies who would love to get their hooks in you."

"No, thanks. I'm going home."

"Going home? What the heck for? To sulk? No sireee, sir. El, tell your friend here he can't go home yet. He's got to go with us. It'll be like old times."

"Yeah, Adrían, old times and new times, we're all going." I motioned for the bartender. "Have a stiff drink for courage, bud."

Catriona, the bartender, glided toward us in her heels. She poured us each a hefty scotch. "On the house." She was in her red stilettos, appearing tall and refined. What was it about high heels that made femmes look like sexy intellectuals?

"I don't care for scotch much, bud. You know that."

"Fine." I guzzled both mine and his, hoping to hear the "click" Tennessee Williams described so accurately in *Cat on a Hot Tin Roof.* The click hurled you to that place of forgetting, and tonight I wanted to forget Isabel Cortez, Virginia Johnson and especially Clarissa Miller. I rattled the ice in my glass and the bartender slid over and poured another double, then hustled to the other end of the bar poised comfortably as she conversed with some *papito*.

"Take it easy, El," Adrían whispered to me.

Brandy downed her Scotch and stood up. "Are we going or what?"

"We're going all right." I slammed the empty glass down on the bar. "We'll meet you there, Bran."

CHAPTER THIRTY

Brandy stood at the entrance of the Down Under and drew back a black leather curtain that separated the entrance from the main room. The scent of moist leather, K-Y jelly and bodily fluids inundated the foyer.

After reassuring the bouncer of our credentials, we proceeded through the curtain to a main room with such dim red lighting I was afraid I might stumble on a body or two. When my eyes focused, I saw leather swings with couples swaying back and forth. In a corner, a big, broad beauty was tied by the wrists and ankles to a giant steel cross. In front of her, a tiny, lean woman, dressed in a black leather corset, leather hat and red leather boots that reached her hips, held a cat-o'-nine-tails and swept it gingerly across the broad beauty's breasts, then increased the force of the whip by striking broad beauty's hips. I imagined blood on the surface of the skin, shiny and dripping in petite drops. The sight captivated me for a number of reasons but mostly because I thought I recognized the participants. Instead of lingering longer to attempt to remember if I had ever exchanged bodily fluids with either of them, I advanced to one of the back rooms, passed an orgy of about five naked bodies, encountered more swings and heard moaning coming from the private rooms. My preference. Anonymous sex in dark rooms always sucked me in. No lights. Just someone reclining on a tiny cot and you could walk in, fuck your brains out and walk out never having to ask, "Hey, what's your name? Can I have your phone number?" No obligations and pretentions. Tonight, I skirted past the private rooms.

I staggered over naked bodies and when hands grabbed my ankles, tripping me, I fell on top of breasts and fluffy Venus mounds as well as slick waxed ones. Hands unbuttoned my shirt and unzipped my jeans and more hands caressed and groped me and I felt restored by their fluency. The groping and caressing was unceasing and idyllic but I had to piss and since I'm not the type that enjoys golden showers—yeah, I'm a boring hygiene freak—I squirmed and thrashed to my feet until the hands released me and resumed prying and stroking other bodies on the floor's mattress.

I picked up the remnants of my clothing strewn across the floor, slipped my jeans over my underwear and tossed my shirt across my shoulder where someone had bit me. The blood wasn't so bad but the teeth marks had left an indentation that would surely bruise by morning.

I found a bathroom and waited until two women filed out of the small space with one toilet. They smiled and I returned the courtesy, entered the bathroom and sat on the toilet. I thought I wanted to piss but really I had to get out of that mound of bodies because I felt numb. Absolutely numb. The sensation of nothingness had made me want to run to the bathroom.

Okay, Electra. What the fuck?

It was time to have a serious talk with myself. I hadn't come to this place of debauchery and bliss to sit alone in a bathroom. At the sink, I ran the faucet and splashed water on my face, moistened a paper towel and dabbed a few tiny drops of blood from my shoulder. It was tender but I barely felt it. Too bad. I guess I wanted a more vicious bite, one that was lasting, one

I could whimper about, one that would prove my life was dangerously profound. Who was I kidding? Adrían had been right about this place. What were we doing here?

I walked out of the bathroom to search for Adrían and passed Brandy on a mattress in a threesome with her wife. I waved to be polite but doubted she saw me. Still wearing only my jeans with the same white, ruffled shirt strewn across the bloodless shoulder, I began to search the environs for my jacket and boots, which were probably somewhere in the first big room with the massive mattress where I'd been groped and grabbed. I wanted my boots and I wanted to find Adrían and I absolutely wanted to leave. A heavy, harsh loneliness crushed me.

I wandered to another area with couples on various twin beds or on floor cushions and that was when I saw Adrían, fully clothed, pumping vigorously with his strap-on dildo jutting from his trousers. He crouched over a cute redheaded woman with a short pixie haircut who moaned, steeped in ecstasy. She was lying on her back with cushions holding her up high for Adrían's reach, and I stopped for a moment of voyeurism to soothe my soul. Adrían's eyes were closed and because he publicly straddled the pixie-haired redhead, I didn't think he'd mind that I observed. Her moaning grew louder until she let out a shrill cry, and Adrían pulled out and pulled off a condom, then stuffed his dildo back in his pants. He saw me and lifted his head, grinning. The pixie rolled over on her side and grabbed his arm, seemingly wanting cuddle time. He took her hand, kissed it, smoothed back his hair and marched over to me.

"Hey," he said.

"Hey yourself."

The pixie stared at him.

"Sure you're done there, bud?"

He turned around and went to her, kissed her on the mouth, whispered something and returned to me.

"Okay," he said.

"Ready to go?"

"So soon? We just got here, El."

"Damn if you haven't changed your tune."

"Well, I didn't think I'd get lucky. And there's another femme who asked me to join her in one of the private rooms."

"Damn. Well, Brandy said you'd be popular."

"Not that popular. Just a little lucky. These women are awesome."

"Yeah, I guess so."

"What's the matter? Haven't found anyone you like?"

"It's not that."

"What's the problem?"

"No problem. I don't know."

"You don't know? What's to know?"

"I feel kind of empty, Adrían."

"Empty? What do you mean empty? Isn't that why we came? 'Cause you didn't want to feel empty? This is no time to philosophize, buddy. Just have some fun."

We whispered to keep from disrupting the couples, threesomes and orgies. Brandy must have been on a break because when she found us she grabbed Adrían's wrist, pulling him away from me.

"Get on over here. One of those women I told you about wants to meet you, son."

Adrían stood firm and looked at me. "Nah, I've got to keep El company."

"El, what the heck are you doing standing around at the Down Under? Plenty of women who like a popper like you, and there's a few who want a turn with Adrían here. Let me borrow him for about twenty minutes."

"Hey, I'm not keeping him," I said.

"Are you sure?" Adrían asked me.

"I'm not your damn mother. Go. Have some fun."

They strolled into another dark cavern of blurry sexual bliss, making me that much more determined to find my boots and Adrían's jacket and take a taxi home. Neither of them would notice I left. I wasn't in the mood for new prospects and what I craved was a hot cup of tea and a good novel. Or a good film. And if I wanted to engage in fantasy by myself, that was okay with me. Tonight, I wanted my own company.

I wandered back to the main room and found my boots lined against the wall but I couldn't locate Adrían's jacket, which I had to recover because he was prudent with his vintage clothes and I couldn't lose one of his prized possessions. Back in the central shadowy room of sexual paradise, I tiptoed, exploring for the jacket and when I looked up again, I observed the same two women on the main stage. The broad, voluptuous one was still tied up to a steel cross and the tiny one was marching about on the stage in thigh-high red boots. She brushed the cat-o'-nine-tails across the tied-up woman's back and ass and each time she brushed softly, she lifted the whip, gained momentum and struck the curviness of her ass cheeks with such vigor that the voluptuous one moaned louder with each thrashing. I was mesmerized by the finesse of the flagellation as well as the desire expressed from each moan. The tiny one inched closer to the voluptuous one and rubbed the red ass with a red leather-gloved hand that grabbed pubic hair and pulled hard. Then, Tiny slipped her gloved fingers inside voluptuous one's vagina, drew out and shoved again, thrusting from behind with a red-gloved hand. With the other gloved hand, Tiny pinched Voluptuous's left nipple and tugged steadily on a nipple ring. Okay, I was getting a little aroused and thought about taking a detour to one of the private rooms.

I forgot about Adrían's jacket and found a room with the door ajar, exposing a woman lying on her stomach. Her ass was propped up slightly and invitingly. I remembered I had packed one of Adrían's butt plugs knowing he wouldn't mind. We were both safe-sex hygiene freaks and knew that if we borrowed toys from each other they would be well-sterilized. The strapped-on butt plug popped out from my indigo underwear and I swathed the black plug with a condom I retrieved from my back jeans pocket. I reached for the K-Y jelly on the shelf and dabbed the plug until smooth and silky. She was already on her knees offering easy access but before probing, I teased her clit with my fingers, then pushed gently into her ass waiting for her groans to guide me.

Then it hit me: no wonder they looked familiar, the women strutting on the main stage! Justine Aldridge, the Vice Chancellor of Academic Affairs, was tied up and Trudy, the receptionist I fired, who happened to be President Mike Miller's niece, was whipping Justine! I jerked back, only to have my current sexual colleague turn around and stare at me as if to ask, "Really?"

"Oops. Sorry, I forgot something," I said.

"You forgot something? Now?"

"Yeah, I got to go."

"Did you leave something cooking on your stove?"

"Something like that."

I buttoned my pants and returned to the massive room. I noted a huge mirror on the stage that allowed me to spy unseen. I hid in the shadows, figuring neither would see me because of dim lighting and even when your eyes adjusted, you couldn't focus unless you concentrated. I didn't want them to see me. Who was I to spoil their fun? They would probably be far more embarrassed than I could ever be since their secret would be revealed, so to speak. Vice Chancellor Justine Aldridge at a sex club, engrossed in activity reserved for someone other than her type—the type who wore Chanel suits and hair in a bun. And then what about Trudy? Okay, seeing her here surprised me, but only because she resembled more a pushy cheerleader with a football captain boyfriend. I would never have guessed that Trudy had a proclivity for a woman old enough to be her mother. Of course, pushy cheerleader Trudy was the one who whipped. Maybe that was the attraction. I guess Trudy and Justine had their own Freudian fixations and complexes. I wasn't alone. A warm, fuzzy feeling of sisterhood and its nascent camaraderie flooded me.

As I stood observing, my mind raced and I pieced together fragments of a puzzle. Was there a connection between these two women and the two murders on campus? Why would there be? Was that why Justine had been attempting to set me up? She placed the alleged murder weapon in my hands—but for whose murder? And what about Trudy? Trudy was a rude young woman accustomed to being pampered and probably had to pretend to have a job so she could get her allowance from her wealthy uncle, who was now dead. Why would they want both of these men dead?

Wait a minute. What did Mariana at the tapas bar say about an argument between Justine Aldridge and Mike Miller? And that money was involved? I knew Justine didn't come from money and she was working to move up the administrative ladder at the college, but she also wanted big money. And according to Mariana, Vice Chancellor Justine had been duped by President Mike because thanks to him, she had lost a chunk of change. I didn't know how much. The amount might help determine if she was capable of murder.

Wait a minute. Was Trudy going to inherit money from her uncle? Were these two in this together for Mike's money? As far as I knew, Mike had no children and his latest wife was the only one who stood to inherit his wealth and if I knew Mike Miller, she too had signed a prenuptial agreement. None of these guys went into second or third marriages anymore without a prenuptial contract.

Trudy raised her whip and let it fall hard on Justine's thigh. She moaned so loudly that I wanted to run and untie her. Again, Trudy raised her whip and let it fall on the same thigh and again Justine moaned loudly. The couples and threesomes in the room ignored the two women, which made sense since everyone came for their own pleasure and most assumed those attending abided by rules, which held explicitly that safe words were honored. So far, I hadn't heard a safe word coming out of Justine's mouth. I was a wimp when it came to serious play.

Tired of standing in the shadows, I wanted to leave but couldn't risk being seen. I slid down the wall and just as I sat, I heard Brandy yell, "Hey, El, quit hiding!"

She sprinted toward me and I didn't move from fear of being seen.

"Electra! I'm coming to get you!" shouted Brandy.

What I feared occurred and in that split second, Justine Aldridge opened her eyes, tore her wrist from the leather bind, which must have been wrapped loosely, turned her head and peered at me. I froze. Trudy was oblivious, because she picked up momentum with her whip and let it fall, but Justine caught it with her hand and yanked so firmly that Trudy lost her balance and toppled over in her red leather thigh-high boots.

"Fuck," I whispered.

"Fuck is right, Electra. Now come on. I got someone who wants to meet you," said Brandy.

Brandy had bare, tiny breasts and assumed the appearance of a cute, self-assured hard-ass with a big frame and wide hips. She was still covered with leather chaps over her jeans, making it possible for me to hide behind her, hoping to be shielded from Justine's gaze. Fortunately, Brandy was in a rush and we zoomed out of the main room. I didn't want to turn around and not until we were hidden from sight in a lesser room with mattresses on the floor did I feel protected from Justine Aldridge's wrath.

"Brandy, sneak back into the main room and tell me if the two women on stage are still there."

"Huh? Which two women, El? Plenty of women in that main room."

"They were on the stage. An older one. Tied at the steel cross. She's with the young, tiny one in red leather thigh-highs."

"Okay. Be right back."

I grabbed her arm. "Don't be so obvious."

"Huh? What do you mean? You told me to go check them out for you. I'm thinking it's 'cause you want a thing with them. Now do you or don't you?"

"No!" I heard how loud I sounded. "I mean, no," I whispered. "I just want to know if they're still there."

"What for if you don't want a thing with them?"

"Brandy, dammit. Okay, never mind. Where's Adrían?"

"Oh, don't go bothering him. He's got about six soft hands caressing him right about now."

"Six?"

"That's what I said. Three solid, divine beauties."

"Damn. The boi is lucky."

Suddenly, anxiety engulfed me. "Bran, please go see what those two are doing. Let me know if they're still playing or if they left. That's all. And don't let them see you."

"Damn, you sure are bossy, El. Okay, okay, I'm going."

Brandy tiptoed to the arched doorway, which had no door but instead a gossamer curtain that was pulled back. She peeked from the archway and tiptoed back to me.

"Gone, baby, gone."

"They are?"

"I don't see anybody up on that stage."

"But you saw them before, right?"

"Of course I did. Everybody loves it when they show up."

"What?"

"And they love to include a third in their game. Hell, El, why didn't you join them?"

"How long have they been coming here?"

"Hell, I don't know. I've been coming for about six months now. Hell, you probably saw them the last time you were here. Don't you remember? You and that cool Isabel had that rip-roaring fight." She chortled and rubbed her eyes with the back of her black leather-gloved hand. "Where is that cool, long woman in a black dress named Isabel?"

"Bran, is it the same two? Tiny and Voluptuous?"

"Huh? Tiny and Voluptuous?"

I could practically see the cogs in her mind spinning.

"Oh, yeah, sure, El. Same two. Tiny and Voluptuous. Good names, by the way."

"How do you know they weren't someone else?"

"Well, I guess they could be but I'm pretty sure they're the same two 'cause they always go straight to the stage with the steel cross and sometimes they reverse roles but most of the time the taller one, I mean, Voluptuous, likes to be tied up. That's what it looks like to me anyway. Let me tell you, she sure looks sexy when she lets that bun down and her beautiful gray hair falls on her shoulders."

"Bran, stay focused. You're sure it's the same two?"

"Pretty sure. Why? You want me to go ask?"

"No! And I thought you said they were gone?"

"Well, I could ask around to see if anyone else knows something about them. Thing is, lots of folks don't use real names in here."

"Never mind. I know who they are."

"You do? Well, then why are you bugging me about it? Damn, El. Did one of them break your heart or something?"

"It's not what you think. Look, I'm tired, Bran. I just want to go home."

"But why, El? Where's the partying El?"

"I've got some things I need to sort out. Tell Adrían I'm going to my own place and tell him thanks."

"Okay. Whatever you say, El. Come here first and give me a hug. You seem to be needing a hug."

Brandy enveloped me in her broad chest and her tiny nipples pressed against me felt comforting. I guess I needed a hug. I guess I wasn't much for the Down Under after this week's harrowing events. Damn. I hated how my life was transforming.

I returned to the central room and found Adrían's navy wool jacket hanging on a wooden knob near the entrance. Funny, I didn't remember hanging it up. I grabbed the jacket and pulled it over my shirt, stepped outside and hailed a taxi. It was barely midnight and I was going home.

CHAPTER THIRTY-ONE

The taxi ride was bottlenecked in traffic from late-night theater crowds, and the sight of clutching couples made me nostalgic, but I was content to return to my own apartment, having been gone for over thirty-six hours. At the curb near my street, I darted out of the taxi and sprinted up the sidewalk into my building on Overlook Terrace. In the elevator, I examined my face in the chrome button fixture and glimpsed wrinkles and sagging eyelids warped and heightened by the distorting surface.

As I neared my apartment door, I remembered I'd forgotten my keys at Adrían's but since I kept a spare under the fake plant in the hallway, I wasn't worried. I lifted the plant and found no key. Damn. Now what? I'd have to wake the super. Just as I was about to tap in the superintendent's phone number, I saw that the door to my apartment was ajar. I crept closer. I couldn't help myself. I did what I knew I shouldn't and entered a sinister room alone.

"Hello?"

I'm not sure why I was friendly. There could be a mass murderer in my apartment and I'd greeted him with a simple hello. What did I expect? For the murderer to spring out from darkness and declare, "You had me at hello?" Okay, get a hold of yourself, Electra. The intruder is probably a thief. Or a former lover. Come to think of it, a thief might be less destructive.

"Isabel? Is that you?" I yelled out.

I felt a blow to my head and pitched forward.

I was out maybe a few seconds. After crawling to a floor lamp, I pressed the on button and blinked. When I focused, I saw kitchen chairs knocked over, utensils scattered on the floor, emptied drawers strewn across the kitchen and the couch cushions ripped open. Why did thieves insist on ripping couch cushions when it's unlikely that anyone has slit them open, hidden something inside and sewed them back up?

The door flung wide and exposed the sight of me sprawled on my living room floor to none other than the ubiquitous Detective Carolina Quinn.

"That was quick," I said. I rubbed the back of my head to soothe a budding knot. "Somebody knocked me out."

"Let's get some ice on that," she said, "but let me see first." She came over to me. "I should call nine-one-one."

"Forget it. What took you so long?"

"Sorry about that. I was about to knock on your door and here you were. Sprawled out. Ready and willing." She lifted her right eyebrow seductively.

"You like your women sprawled and semi-conscious, Detective?"

"No, just placid."

"Excuse me? You didn't really say that."

I rose from the floor and she attempted to assist me but I had to prove I was capable and not placid. Dizzy, I fell back on the stiff, cushion-less couch.

"What a mess," I said.

I rubbed the back of my head and wanted to throw up.

"You okay?"

"No, I'm not."

Carolina walked to the refrigerator and snatched a bag of frozen peas, sat next to me and pressed the frozen bag to the back of my head.

"Here, hold on to that. I'm going to look around. The place looks like whoever did this was looking for something specific. Robbers go straight for the jewels or silver, and it doesn't look like you had much of that around here anyway."

"I keep all that in the family bank's vault."

My head was pounding but the bag of peas was starting to freeze my fingers. I placed the sack on my lap.

"Good you've got a sense of humor."

She sank down next to me, grabbed the freezer peas and put the cold plastic against my head's bump. With her free hand, she massaged my neck.

"Feels nice," I said.

"Anyone you know who might be angry at you? Besides the string of women you string along?"

"There's no string of women, Detective. And if any of them are pissed at me, believe me, they let me know."

"Aren't you tired of this kind of life, Electra?"

"What kind of life? Teaching? I like to teach. Research? Love that too. Writing? That's my all-time favorite."

"You know what I mean. What's the point of going to places like the Down Under? At your age?"

"For your information, all ages can and do go to the Down Under. Given that you followed me, why didn't you come inside for some fun? Maybe I would've stayed."

"What makes you think I wasn't inside?"

"You were?"

"Why were you so shy in there?"

"I wasn't shy, Detective, just meditative."

"You go to a place like the Down Under to meditate? Unusual."

"What can I say? I like to be unusual."

"You're actually pretty common, Electra. You're 'homeless, childless, middle-aged, loveless' and you don't have the good sense to despair over your future and from looking around this place, you haven't secured much of a future."

"Ouch. That hurts. Are you always this judgmental?" I wasn't going to acknowledge out loud that she had quoted from *Brideshead Revisited* with astute precision. "And anyway, what's a secure future, Detective? You put yourself in the line of fire every day. You call that secure?"

"Sure it is. I made a conscious choice. Are you making conscious choices? Or taking what comes your way?"

"What comes my way isn't so bad."

"But it's not the best you could possibly have."

"Are you the best I could possibly have, Detective?"

"Well, I guess you'll never know, Professor."

We sat quietly until she stopped massaging my neck and rose from the couch. "I've got to go. Whoever did this won't be back. He's looking for something and it probably wasn't here."

"You're leaving me alone?" I felt like a cowardly candy-ass.

"You'll be fine."

I must have looked pathetic, because Detective Carolina Quinn came to me, bowed and kissed me, delicate and earnest, until our tongues collided and the depth of her mouth felt overpoweringly perfect and the kiss persisted even as I dreaded she might pause and break away. The pain in my head receded as my tongue enveloped hers. I puckered my mouth and sucked tenderly until the sucking became a fierce rhythm and the ardor of drinking her tongue dazed me and besieged my arms and legs until I could stand no more. I wanted to pull her closer to me and taste every pore of her flesh but I didn't move, sensing she might retreat and I'd lose her. I didn't care that she kissed me because she felt sorry for me. What I cared about was that we were engaged in a mouth-to-mouth armistice, a truce of sorts. A treaty that spoke this could, would occur again. I didn't even care that I was at a disadvantage because she was bending over me and I was sitting with my face up toward her. Not the stance of someone in control. Fuck. I was doomed.

"You're not used to being on the bottom, are you?" she asked.

"I'm not?"

"No, you're not."

I gazed up at her, not wanting her to go but aware that begging her to stay would make me look weak. She wasn't one to welcome begging. Her kiss had been that good and I started to get angry because it had been that good. Damn her. She'd waited all this time and then when I was most vulnerable, *zas!* Just like Adrían said. I watched her walk out the door.

"Come chain the door, Electra."

I hobbled from the stiff, cushion-less couch and chained the door noting what Carolina must have seen. The bolt was broken. The intruder had clearly broken down the door to get in. Great. I'll sleep well tonight.

I pressed my cheek against the cheap metal and listened to her footsteps grow faint. Then I freaked.

CHAPTER THIRTY-TWO

"Mocha? Mocha? Come out, please!"

I stumbled into the bedroom, checked under the bed and found her inside the mattress lining, her preferred hiding place. She sauntered out, brushed against me and walked away.

"I guess that's all I'm worth to anyone tonight."

I took aspirin for my head and went to bed, tossed, turned and woke early, too early for a Sunday morning. All that sleep at Adrían's had been good for me but clearly had disrupted my intention to sleep late.

I got up, showered, dressed, drank two cups of espresso, looked around at the mess in my apartment, fed Mocha and resolved to leave to avoid the ransacked chaos. It was early to drop by Adrían's, but I wanted a firsthand account of his adventures, meaning I wasn't going to let him off the hook by talking on the phone.

I took more aspirin, then caught the subway and rode down to the West Village, got off and strolled, observing the lazy bodies leaning into each other after a long night of parties and hot sex. I was confident everyone in my path had had hot sex last night except me. Although that kiss from Detective Quinn still tickled my mouth.

I stopped in a local coffee shop, ordered a cappuccino and sat down at the counter to peruse the *London Review of Books* and the *New York Times Book Review*. Neither faired well statistically when it came to reviewing female authors. But what did I expect? White "Dudeville" was alive and well in arts and entertainment. Still, I couldn't help myself. I read most book reviews religiously anticipating the moment when queer women of color made the cover.

After another cup of decaf cappuccino, I made my way to Adrían's in Chelsea, which was a nice brisk walk on a November morning. Lazy Sundays could be so depressing when spying upon Sunday brunch couple-dom. I wanted to scream at couples sitting in their comfy restaurants drinking mimosas and eating eggs benedict, "Enjoy the moment, fools, because in a few years, a break-up will burst your lovers' bubble."

At Adrían's building, I slipped into the foyer and buzzed his apartment. I waited. No response. I buzzed again. Finally, an unfamiliar voice answered. Female.

"Oh, sorry. I'm looking for Adrían Fuentes."

"Yeah, hold on."

I heard voices mumble, static and then Adrían. "Hey, buddy, where'd you go last night?"

He sounded hoarse, as if he had just woken up.

"Did I wake you? Sorry. It's almost noon. Thought it was safe to come over."

"Sure, come on up, but I got to warn you."

"What's her name?"

"Well, it's not just one."

"Two? Good for you."

"Well, you may not think so once you see who they are."

My thoughts raced to Carolina. Then to Isabel.

"Okay, I'm listening."

"Come on up and see for yourself."

"I don't like surprises, Adrían."

"It'll be fine. Come on up."

Just then, Virginia knocked on the glass door of the building's foyer. She cradled a cardboard tray with two cups of coffee and a paper bag.

I released my finger from the intercom button. "Early delivery, Virginia?"

Donned in her customary Jackie O sunglasses, she smirked.

"Good morning, Electra." She glanced at her designer watch encased with diamonds. A new purchase, I thought.

"It's twelve eleven. Officially Sunday afternoon," I said.

"Why are you standing here? Isn't Adrían home?"

"Oh, he's home all right."

"Well?" Virginia reached for the intercom button.

"Wait. Let me buzz him. He might be in his underwear and I know he wants to look his Sunday best for you, Ginny."

"Very funny, Electra. Go ahead, buzz him."

"Would you mind standing over there? I want to speak to him privately."

"Why?"

"No reason. Just two buddies needing private time."

"Fine."

She walked to the end of the foyer and rested the tray and paper bag on a table adorned with plastic flowers.

"Still waiting for you, El. What's up?"

"Virginia's here."

"Yeah, sure, of course she is. El, get up here and quit fooling around."

"Adrían? Adrían?"

I buzzed again but he didn't pick up. Oh, well, I thought. Here goes nothing. I signaled to Virginia and we rode the elevator to his apartment.

"You do the honors," I said.

Virginia knocked once and the door flew open.

"It's about time you get your cute ass up here, Electra."

I peeked around from behind Virginia, who wore a look of shock and disdain.

"Justine?" said Virginia.

"Justine?" I repeated.

"Virginia?" said Adrían.

In his bathrobe, Adrían peeped from behind Justine.

"Virginia who?" asked Trudy.

"Trudy?" I said.

"Hello Virginia," said Justine.

Justine sauntered away from the threshold and collapsed on the couch. Her hair fell around her shoulders and I thought Brandy had been right. She looked quite fetching with her gray hair wavy and full on her shoulders. She wore one of Adrían's robes and it fell open in the front, revealing an incredibly sexy left breast. Damn, when the girl let her hair down, she really let her hair down. I guess even the Vice Chancellor of Academic Affairs had to let loose every now and then. I was still in shock from having seen her at the Down Under, but now this? And Trudy too? Okay, this was going to be fun.

"Virginia, I..." said Adrían.

"Don't say I didn't warn you," I said.

I wasn't sure why I was getting so much pleasure from the scene unfolding before me but I was. I moseyed behind Virginia who set the coffee and bag on the kitchen counter.

"You brought cappuccino," said Trudy.

Trudy grabbed a cup but Virginia seized it and handed the foamy cappuccino to Adrían, who looked handsome with his tousled hair and ruffled robe.

"I guess you weren't expecting me," said Virginia.

"No, he wasn't," said Justine.

Justine Aldridge sounded officious despite her half-dressed garb.

"Never expected to run into you, Justine."

"No, Virginia, I guess our paths don't cross that often, do they? How is the grieving widow? Collected all of Coxwell's millions yet or is his Goldman Sachs daddy giving you a hard time?"

"My lawyers are taking care of it, Justine. Not that it's any of your business. Oh, wait. You did lose a bit of revenue during your last investment, didn't you? Gee, so sorry about that.

I'm sure you'll be fine, though. I mean, Trudy here should be inheriting a few million from Uncle Mike. Maybe, if you're real good, she'll share."

Trudy was munching on a pecan-laden sticky roll and her mouth and hands were pecan-laden and sticky.

"Trudy dear, isn't that true?" asked Virginia.

"Huh? Isn't what true?"

"That your Uncle Mike left you money. Lots of money."

"Uh, well, not really. He left it to my half-wit cousin who's off in la-la-land building ditches or something, I don't know. Anyway, my aunt told me my nitwit cousin says it's blood money and doesn't want it. That means I'm next in line, I guess."

She spoke with her mouth full and I wondered how anyone as pretty as her could be so dim but then I remembered to whom she was related. What didn't make sense was why she was a receptionist when she clearly didn't need the money; unless of course she was cozying up to Uncle Mike to be assured a place in his will. Maybe Trudy was smarter than she pretended.

"Trudy, how've you been?" I asked.

"Huh?" She peered at me. "Fine. No thanks to you." She wiped her mouth with the palm of her hand and the blood red nail polish on her nails gleamed.

"Trudy dear, don't be rude," said Justine. "You're speaking to our new interim dean. And who knows? If she does a splendid job we may keep her in the post."

"Not me, Justine. And anyway, Mike said I'd be done with this little stint by the end of the academic year. In May."

"Poor Uncle Mike." Trudy covered her face with her hands, began to cry and ran to the bedroom, slamming the door behind her.

"She wasn't this upset a few days ago," I said.

"Why did you fire her, Electra?" asked Justine.

"She wasn't exactly doing her job."

"What job is that? Retrieving coffee for you and that detective?"

"Oh, I see. You're defending Trudy."

"Poor girl's lost her uncle."

"Yeah, and isn't it funny she only gets all broken up about it when she knows she's about to inherit his millions?"

"Some people have delayed reactions."

"Is that what that is?"

"Electra. Come." She patted the cushion next to her.

I wandered to the couch and sat a safe distance from vice chancellor Justine Aldridge. Again she patted the cushion beside her.

"Closer, Electra. I don't bite."

"Don't you?"

"Well, if you'd like me to."

The prospect of the vice chancellor coming on to me crammed me with anxiety. She hadn't pulled the robe over her breast and it was too alluring for me to ignore. I looked around the room, hoping Adrían would rescue me, but he and Virginia were standing in the kitchen whispering loudly in their own comedy act. And Trudy was behind closed doors in the bedroom. Fuck. What was I going to do? Nothing.

"I'm fine here, Justine."

She crept closer until her thigh was pressed against mine. "Electra, I never noticed you had such beautiful brown eyes."

"Light brown," I responded.

"Ah. Light brown."

She stared into my eyes and I got nervous from the proximity of her body and her breath. She smelled like oregano. Or cloves. Or both.

"You don't like me very much, do you, Electra?"

"I never said I didn't like you, Justine."

"No, you didn't." She paused, gazing doggedly into me, then smoothed her robe over her breast, covering every inch of that flesh. "We used to be such good friends."

"That was a long time ago, Justine."

"Yes. A long time ago."

Justine reclined on the couch and gazed at the ceiling. "I didn't kill Mike," she said.

"I didn't know you were a suspect, Justine."

"Oh? That's not where you're going with this?"

"With what?"

"With this little investigation of yours, Electra."

"What investigation? You're paranoid, Justine."

"Why were you at the Down Under last night?"

"Same reason you were. To have some fun."

"I find it strange that you left shortly after seeing me."

"Call me old-fashioned. I guess the sight of my vice chancellor with my receptionist, both of whom seemed firmly heterosexual, in an embrace at the queer sex bar, well, it sort of threw me off."

"I can't imagine anything throwing you off, Electra."

"Well, that sight did."

"Why? Because we were there or because we were engaged in foreplay you don't approve of?"

"Why wouldn't I approve? That's a stupid question. Do what you want. I just didn't want to see it."

"Oh, I see. So perversion disturbs you? And you went to the club anyway?"

"No, I never said that. There are some people I'd rather not see in the throes of sexual abandon."

"And I'm one of them."

"You. And Trudy."

"Anyone else?"

"I'm sure there are others but none come to mind at the moment."

"Electra, Electra, my dear, I never figured you for such a prude."

"I'm not a prude, Justine. Anything but."

"Well, then it must be the burden of your name. Who names a child after a Greek tragedy? I assume you and your father are close?"

"Why would you assume that?"

"Your mother then?"

"What about my mother, Justine?"

"No clear answers from Professor Electra Campos."

"What do you really want to know, Justine?"

"Why that name?"

She sidled up closer and seemed to think distracting me with a discussion about my name would help her endeavor, which, at the moment, was to seduce me. At least, that's what I thought she was up to.

A loud crash from the kitchen disrupted the pending seduction.

CHAPTER THIRTY-THREE

"Ginny, *mi amor*, take it easy," pleaded Adrían.

Virginia flung dishes against the walls, the floor and at Adrían, who shielded himself with a sizeable frying pan.

"Take it easy? Take it easy? You two-timing fucker!"

"It's not like that, Ginny. Let me explain."

Briefly, I felt guilty for not having told Adrían that Virginia, who did what she wanted with whom she wanted, was the jealous type. I guess I had more pressing things on my mind and besides, I had warned him about her.

"Fine. Explain, you two-timing piece of shit."

Virginia stopped flinging her arsenal, or maybe she was running out of ammo, but in any case, she hesitated while Adrían recovered himself and tied his robe around his waist.

"You left me to get arrested," he told her. "And then you left with someone else. What was I supposed to think?"

Here it was. Virginia's confessions were sublime. She defended herself so expertly that you never knew what was true, what was fiction and what was unadulterated fantasy.

"You mean with Isabel? We just talked for a minute."

"You just talked? For all I know, you two are an item."

"Sure, accuse me. I find you with an orgy of women and you accuse me."

I got up from the couch, unwilling to observe Virginia's master performance of evading truths. Virginia and Isabel were hiding something. "I'm leaving," I said.

"Not a bad idea, Electra," said Justine. "I'll be in the bedroom changing clothes."

Just as I was headed for the front door, I felt Justine's hand on mine. "Electra, please, come into the bedroom and assist me," she said.

"But Trudy's in there. She can *assist* you." I emphasized assist.

"Oh, I think we'll both need *assistance*." She was equally emphatic.

She winked and I followed, not that I had any intention of engaging in any activity other than zipping zippers or buttoning buttons. Mostly, I had a penchant for watching women dress. Who knows? They might have a little rendezvous and I had front row seats. I convinced myself I was doing research. One or all three of the women in the apartment this morning had to be the killer. I was about to find out which one. Okay, maybe I wasn't really going to find out but I thought that by monitoring them all closely, I would surely come up with some clues.

Justine shut the door behind me and Trudy shoved me onto the bed. I was surprised to see that Trudy was already in her S/M attire, meaning thigh-high red leather boots, a black and red leather bustier and red gloves. She had also donned a red and black leather mask that covered her eyes, which pleased me because I didn't want to look into Trudy's eyes, having just concluded she was the suspect with the most to gain from President Mike Miller's death.

Vice Chancellor Aldridge dropped her robe, stepped up on the bed and stood over me, nude and magnificent. There was something so alluring about an older feminine woman with long gray hair and vast, shapely hips, especially when she was poised above me in glorious stature. Fuck, I thought, Justine was seducing me and I was allowing it. Oh, well. I was about to be pampered by two enchanting, possibly homicidal women. Could be worse.

While Justine hovered above me smiling self-satisfied, Trudy removed my black boots and socks and without wasting any time slapped the heels of my feet with a leather stick. She began gently, gaining momentum and force.

"Ouch," I said.

"Careful, Trudy. We have ourselves a virgin here."

"I'd hardly call myself a virgin, Justine."

"For our level of games, believe me, Electra, you're a virgin. Which makes this initiation that much more pleasurable."

"Initiation, huh? Do I get a safe word?"

"Of course you do. Let's keep it simple, shall we?"

"Simple is good," I responded. "Is that the word? Simple?"

"Oh, this is going to be fun. Isn't it, Trudy?"

Trudy wasn't exactly into it, which should have slighted my ego but I didn't care, because she wasn't my type. She was too young and I didn't mean in years. She had the personality of a cheerleader who had never appreciated the meaning of her task. And at this moment, she still wasn't doing much cheering or leading. Vice Chancellor Aldridge clearly led.

"Trudy, get me my bag of tricks."

"Sure."

"Sure? Sure what? Is that how you address me?"

"Sure, Mistress."

Trudy picked up a bulky leather bag and tossed it on the bed at Justine, who proceeded to pull out black fishnet stockings that she donned leisurely while standing above me. Her balance was superb and she only tripped once, forcing me to catch her as she landed cagily on my lips. Just as I was about to wrap my mouth around the crevices of her labia, she knelt and again was above me. Okay, this is taking too long, I thought. Maybe I wasn't made out for the seriousness of these games. Without my having noticed, Trudy had taken off my black jeans and suddenly my T-shirt was on the floor. Not until she tugged at my tight jog-bra did I see myself naked. Wow. They were good.

In one fell swoop, Trudy tied my ankles with a leather strip and Justine locked my wrists in handcuffs. I was a nude, flopping fish on the bed. I felt silly and slightly aroused. Okay, maybe more than slightly. Trudy held a leather strap and brushed my thighs and legs while Justine spread her body beside me and with fuchsia leather-gloved hands, she smoothed over my torso, pinched my breasts and probed my mouth with her gloved middle finger.

"Suck," she said.

I didn't hesitate. I sucked the thick, leather-clad finger with deliberate conviction, bringing a smile to Justine's face. Trudy stung my thighs and legs with a leather strap as I immersed myself in the sensation of Justine's throbbing finger. They were dressed in their costumes from the night before and they staged similar play, except that I was now their object of play, which suited me fine.

"Suck harder."

I sucked harder and felt leather scraping my tongue despite the smooth texture. Okay, let me focus on something sexy, I thought. Justine's hefty breasts burst out of a black lace and leather bustier. That's it. I'll focus on Justine's breasts. Trudy slapped my thigh so ruthlessly I was sure she drew blood.

"Simple!" I cried out. "Simple, simple!"

"Oh, don't be such a wimp, Electra," said Justine.

"I'm not a wimp. Would you please tell your assistant to go easy on the leather strap?"

"Trudy, put down the strap. Come here and help me with this."

I lifted my head up. "With what? What's she going to help you with?"

They searched in the leather bag and I couldn't make sense of their whispers. Where was my buddy when I needed him? At that moment, the bedroom door sailed open and Adrían stormed in, sprinted to his closet and dressed in navy slacks and a powder blue shirt.

When he saw me splayed on the bed, he winked. "Hey, El, I'll be back in a couple of hours. Ginny and I, well, never mind."

"Don't leave me, bud," I called.

"Play-acting, huh? Have fun."

"Where you going?" I asked.

But he didn't hear me.

"Hey, Adrían!" I yelled but the front door slammed shut. Things were getting ominous. Adrían was gone and Justine and Trudy, possible homicidal maniacs sexily clad in leather bustiers and leather gloves, sat on the edge of the bed whispering. Their whispers fluctuated from muffled to faint and fainter.

"I told you to..." said Justine.

"I know, I know but..." said Trudy.

They continued in this vague manner and I couldn't make sense of what they were saying or to what they referred. In the meantime, I was laid out in bed naked and feeling more and more like a flopping fish tied at the ankles and handcuffed at the wrists. I felt a chill too. This wasn't a pretty sight, and I was getting more and more afraid of the possibilities.

"Uh, hello, excuse me," I said. "Justine, I'm getting a little cold here."

Justine whispered to Trudy as they scoured the bag for something inside it. Then, without warning, Justine slapped Trudy across the face. Hard. This wasn't play. Trudy palmed her reddening cheek and peered at Justine in shock. She seized a paisley red and blue dress from the floor, slipped it over her costume, snatched the leather bag, stomped out of the bedroom and slammed the front door. Justine repositioned her right leg over her left, then rose from the bed's corner, slid her pink and black Chanel skirt past her thighs and put on a pink silk blouse with a matching Chanel jacket over the blouse, hiding her costume. She pulled her hair up in a bun and stood up straight, ironing the skirt with her palms.

"I have to go, Electra."

"Okay. I can see that but I'm a little tied up here, Justine."

"Oh, sure." She untied the leather string around my ankles. "That should help some."

"Uh, my wrists, please?"

"Trudy pilfered the bag of goodies, I'm afraid."

"So?"

"I mean to say she took the bag with the keys."

"What am I supposed to do, Justine?"

"You're a big girl, Electra. You'll figure it out."

Justine lingered in front of the long mirror hanging from the closet door, daubed orange lipstick on both lips and then strolled out of the apartment. I was alone. I was handcuffed. I couldn't move. Damn. Now what?

I must have stared at the ceiling for almost an hour before I stumbled out of bed and I do mean literally stumbled to the floor face first. I had the brilliant idea that if I could get up on my feet, I could find my cell phone and punch in a phone number. But whose? Adrían would probably see me calling and let it go to voice mail. Brisa, well, Brisa was my student and I couldn't make that mistake again. Of course the likely candidate was Detective Quinn. Damn. I didn't want her to find me like this but I had no choice.

After locating my phone in my jeans' front pocket, I attempted to turn the pants upside down so the phone would fall out. That didn't work. I scrunched to the floor and used my foot to dislodge the phone from my pants. Don't ask me how, but after twenty minutes or so of playing footsie with my jeans, the device finally dropped out.

I stared at the face, attempted to wake it from its slumber until I figured out the battery was dead. Great. I didn't want to call anyone anyway. I struggled to put on my jeans but it was nearly impossible because my hands were bound in handcuffs that fortunately were not at my back but allowed me to maneuver both arms in front of me. The cuffs squeezed tight and each time I wrangled my wrists to tug on my pants, both hands throbbed. With my pants halfway up my legs almost to my thighs, I fell back on the floor. The rug felt itchy on my back but I was too worn-out and frustrated to care. Daylight shrank outside and odd shapes fell on the bedroom walls.

When the front door opened, I was elated.

"Adrían, I'm in here!"

Silence. Then I heard footsteps in the living room.

"Adrían? I'm in the bedroom." This time I whispered.

Footsteps approached the bedroom door and I could see a shadow come closer, then stop. I couldn't move. I held my breath. I wanted to run but couldn't get up. Fuck, fuck, fuck. Then I heard a bewildering sound. The shadow had retreated and whoever was out there was probably in the living room again. The sound was soft and constant until I realized someone was slicing cloth with a knife. Strident punctures preceded methodical cutting. Someone was ripping up something. The cutting was much too methodical, leading me to believe the thieving vandal was more than likely combing for a lost item.

Then it hit me: the knife. Where had Adrían hidden it? When we went to the club he buried it between the cushions but not inside them. It would've been easy to find. Someone was looking for the knife. Fuck. Could only mean one thing: the killer was in the room with me. Now I was scared.

CHAPTER THIRTY-FOUR

I was frozen, immobile. Not because I was handcuffed but because I couldn't move from downright fear. The room grew quiet. No more ripping. Footsteps shuffled away and the door opened and shut. I held my breath, terrified of that trick—the one when the killer pretends to leave by opening and shutting the door to fool the victim. I held my breath until I couldn't. My heart was pounding out of my chest and panic engulfed me.

I waited. Okay, so maybe he or she had left. I took a deep breath and let it out to relax my body. I felt tense and my wrists felt raw. Now I was angry. Where the fuck was Adrían? What time was it? I wasn't wearing my watch. I didn't like to wear it on Sundays to remind myself that I needed to quit staring at the hours at least one day of the week. Some plan I had. I played with my cell phone again but it was dead. Dead. At least I wasn't. Who the fuck had been in the apartment and how did they get in so easily? Maybe Justine neglected to lock it behind her? Maybe this killer thief was a master at breaking in? It didn't matter now.

The door opened again. Fuck. They were back. Whoever it was, is back. The bedroom door slid open.

"El, what the fuck? Why are you lying on the floor like that?"

"Where the fuck have you been?"

"Why are you half-naked, handcuffed and on the floor? And where are the dominatrix twins?" He bent down, wrapped his arms around my torso and helped me sit up.

"They left."

"They left you like this?"

"Evidently." I grew angry at the obvious observations. "It gets worse."

"Worse than this?"

He got up and went to a dresser drawer, shuffled things around and came back with a set of keys.

"You've got the keys to these handcuffs? You mean they were in your dresser all along? That damn Justine."

"Oh, they're generic. These aren't the serious kind of handcuffs that your Detective Quinn has." He grinned. "But I thought you would know that by now."

"Don't bring her up. I'm pissed at her."

After he unfastened the cuffs, I rubbed my wrists. I felt good to be free again. I stood and stumbled, suddenly dizzy. I was still feeling the effects of the blow to my head last night.

"Hey, careful. You okay?"

"I had a scare, bud."

"Yeah, I guess lying around handcuffed and naked for hours can be scary."

"Worse than that." I sat on the edge of the bed and pulled my pants past my legs. "Someone broke in. They ripped something up. Maybe your couch?"

"My couch?"

I got up from the bed and rushed into the living room. The couch wasn't ripped up. What the fuck had I heard? Something in this room had to be torn to pieces. Then I saw the cushions in a corner, shredded.

"My new cushions!" yelled Adrían. "Damn! What happened?"

"I told you! Someone broke in and tore these apart. I think it was the killer looking for the knife. Where is the knife, by the way?"

"I hid it in one of these cushions."

"What? You mean to say that you ripped apart a cushion, put the knife inside and then sewed it back up?"

"Not exactly."

"Not exactly?"

"Well, no. All I had to do was this."

Adrían picked up one of the torn cushions, reached for the zipper and unzipped it.

"Why didn't the thief do that?"

"I don't know. Too easy, I guess."

"Which one of these had the knife?"

"Hard to say. They all look alike. It was the one in the middle of the couch, but I can't tell anymore."

"Well, it's gone."

"You didn't get a look at the thief, buddy?"

"I was a little tied up."

"Oh. Yeah. Sorry."

We stood silent for a few minutes. I sensed we were each trying to get our bearings. Finally, I couldn't stand the silence any longer.

"What's up with you and Virginia?"

"Nothing."

"Nothing? Excuse me but you left me here with two dominatrix types who are potentially dangerous. You've got to give me a little more."

"It's the usual. She's available when she wants something."

"What did she want?"

"Sex. What else?"

"Not your mind?"

"Very funny."

"Don't you think it's suspicious she shows up today?"

"No. Why?"

"Does she ever just show up?"

"No. Why?"

"I don't trust her."

"I know you don't trust her."

"And you do?"

"Not really."

"I wouldn't be surprised if Virginia, Justine and Trudy were all friends who staged this little scenario this morning."

"You're so damn paranoid, El."

"Oh and you're not?"

"Sure, I am but…oh fuck, never mind."

"Are you getting pissed at me?"

"No, it's not that. I'm just tired."

"What time is it?"

"After five."

"I'm going home, which, by the way, got ransacked last night too."

"What?"

"Yep. Somebody broke in and ransacked the place looking for something, then bopped me over the head."

"Why didn't you tell me?"

"Well, your apartment was a little busy and then you left."

"Yeah, I guess so."

"I've got to go home."

"Should you go alone? Is it safe?"

"Carolina said since they didn't find what they were looking for they probably wouldn't be back, which may be why they came here."

"Oh, Carolina. Of course."

"It's not what you think."

"Oh. What do I think?"

"I don't know. What do you think?"

"Nothing, buddy. Not a thing."

"Fine." I stared at him for a moment but he didn't speak. "I'm out of here."

I left his apartment and when I arrived at mine, I fell into bed and slept until my alarm rang at seven ten the next morning.

CHAPTER THIRTY-FIVE

My apartment was in shambles and I was in no mood to clean. I dressed in a pair of black, light wool slacks, a crisp Hawes & Curtis purple shirt and one of my many black suit jackets. I pulled on my wool peacoat, not wanting to get caught in a cold night again. It was Monday morning, a week since the first murder and I was determined to work as interim dean even if I didn't know what I was supposed to do. I'd begin by answering emails.

I arrived at my office building, climbed the stairs to the fifth floor and was surprised to see Trudy composed at the receptionist station polishing her nails.

"Trudy. You're back."

"I'm back."

"Did the vice chancellor ask you to come back?"

"Nope."

"Oh. I see."

She resumed polishing her nails and lifting the ringing phone receiver only to hang up. Messages wouldn't get through to me but that wasn't a bad thing today. In my office, I sat behind President Mike Miller's lavish desk and realized I didn't have a computer. President Mike hadn't been the type to answer his own emails or browse the web. The guy was old school. He used landlines and carried a cell phone that went straight to voice mail. I had tried reaching him more than once on his cell phone back in the day, when the college was still a place of academic rigor. But shortly after he was appointed, President Mike transformed the academy into an anti-intellectual money mill.

I buzzed the receptionist's phone hoping Trudy would pick up but of course, she didn't. I got up, walked to the office door and saw Assistant Professor Hugh Roberts, Jacksonian specialist, hovering above Trudy.

"Everything all right?" I asked.

Startled, he turned around. He looked taller and scrawnier than ever, with a large mass of light brownish-blond hair that poked out in numerous directions as if it hadn't been combed or washed in weeks. The boy was disheveled with bloodshot eyes. His shirt was wrinkled and partially tucked into chinos. Hugh narrowed his eyes and half grinned.

"Good morning, Electra. How are you?"

"I'm fine, Hugh. Can't say the same for you."

"Why not?"

"You look like you haven't slept in weeks."

"Just working on an article and can't seem to get it to do what it's supposed to do." He gazed at Trudy and back at me. "Would you mind having a look? I have it right here."

Assistant Professor Hugh Roberts, Jacksonian specialist, wasn't the type of young scholar who needed my approval or support in any venture but because I was the interim dean, the boy probably thought I'd have a say in his pending tenure case. He was right.

"Sure, why not?"

He pulled out a grubby file folder from a worn, brown leather book bag. I'd seen that book bag before but then again, it resembled all book bags that aspiring and non-aspiring professors owned. He strode three steps to my door and placed the file folder in my hands. The title, "Andrew Jackson's Peculiar Lament," struck me as odd and academically reckless.

"Okay. I'll have a look."

"Thanks, Electra." He gazed down at the floor, hands digging in his pockets. "Trudy, I'll see you later?"

"I don't know, Hugh. I told you I'm busy."

"Oh. Okay."

He sounded dejected and I almost felt sorry for the guy. I mean, did he have any inkling who and what Trudy really was? She would make mincemeat of him. Assistant Professor Hugh Roberts skulked away, shoulders bent, gazing at the floor. I wondered if he was going to fall over from not watching where he was going.

"Trudy, I know it's none of my business, but what was that all about?"

"It's none of your business."

She plugged away filing her left index finger and I returned to my office. I tossed the file folder on the edge of my desk and plunked down to check email on my smartphone. A cryptic email from Detective Quinn piqued my interest but I refused to call her.

"Electra. Must see you. Soon. Please call me."

Was this work related or kiss related? I wasn't going to venture forth. Instead, I put my feet on the desk and decided to take a nap. A long one. Just like President Mike Miller would do. When I awoke, the building was quiet and dark. I got up and went to the front reception area and saw that Trudy had left for the day but not without lining up her nail polish neatly on her desk. She obviously had plans to return the next day. Lucky me. The phone rang and I picked it up.

"Electra, good you're in your office. I'll be right over."

"It's late, Justine. I'm leaving."

"Just give me a minute. I'm taking the elevator up to your floor now."

"Can't this wait, Justine?"

"No, it can't."

Fine, I thought. The offices are empty, it's dark outside and a potential homicidal dominatrix is on her way to my office, the same office that had been occupied by the murdered president. I hurried to my desk, picked up my briefcase and I was about to run down the stairs, when Justine popped out of the elevator.

"Caught you," she said.

"Justine, why can't this wait? It's late and I'm hungry."

"Come inside. It will only take a minute."

I walked behind her. She entered the corner office, sat down on the tan leather couch and pulled a balled-up handkerchief from her beige Chanel bag. I recognized the hanky. It had Adrían's initials on it.

"I thought you'd want this back."

She placed the turquoise-beaded, pearl-handled dagger on the glass table in front of the couch.

"What the fuck, Justine? You took this from Adrían's apartment yesterday?"

"No, I didn't take it."

"Trudy?"

"Yes."

"Why?"

"She's protecting someone."

"You?"

"Don't be silly, Electra. You don't think I have the capacity to murder, do you?"

My face must have flushed at that moment and, I have to say, I thought I *was* talking to a pathological mind capable of murder. I wasn't sure why but I thought she was. For Money. Money and greed.

"It is you."

"Oh, Electra, you have an active imagination, dear. Just because I like to dress up in leather attire doesn't make me a murderer."

"I don't think your dressing up has anything to do with it, Justine. It's the money, isn't it? Both Mike and Coxy. They convinced you to invest in their little venture capital and everyone lost money but you're the biggest loser."

"Why would you say that?"

"Oh, come on, Justine. They can afford to lose a million here and there. You can't even afford to lose a few thousand."

"They *could have* afforded to lose, Electra. Past tense."

"So it was you. And you've been trying to set me up. With this bogus knife. Is it even the murder weapon?"

"Who knows? And no, I'm not trying to set you up, Electra. Be reasonable."

"Oh, I am being reasonable, Justine. And right now, I'm leaving, thank you."

I got up from the couch and didn't touch the dagger. I left it lying on the table and hoped it no longer had my prints just in case Justine was determined to prove I was guilty.

"You're not going anywhere," said a voice from the shadows.

"Huh?"

I turned around and from the corner of my office a figure emerged.

It was Assistant Professor Hugh Roberts, Jacksonian specialist.

"Hugh?" I said.

"Yeah," he responded.

"What do you want?"

"What do I want? What do I want? I want you out of my way. I want you both to leave Trudy alone. I want all those disgusting men to quit thinking she's gonna give them blow jobs just 'cause she works for them."

"Mike Miller made his niece give him blow jobs?" I asked.

"She's not his niece," he said.

"No?"

"She's his daughter."

"Fuck! That's so sick," I said.

"Well, he didn't make her give him blow jobs but that other guy did."

"What other guy?"

"The dean. Fucking Coxwell."

"Hugh dear, put down the knife," said Justine.

"No, Auntie. You can't make me."

"Auntie? You two are related?"

"Hugh's my nephew."

"Your nephew? You two are in this together?"

"Don't be silly, Electra. Why would I want to kill Coxwell? Or Mike?"

"They deserved to die," said Hugh.

"Hugh, we've been through this," said Justine.

"Been through what?" I asked.

"Nothing. Don't listen to her," he said.

"Don't listen to her?"

"Hugh, put down the knife," said Justine.

As it turned out, he was brandishing yet another dagger that resembled the one on the table. In fact, it was identical.

"She deserves to die. After the way she treated Trudy."

"Who, me? I didn't treat Trudy to anything," I said.

"You fired her!" he screeched.

"But she's back. You saw her here today."

"I told her to come back," he said.

"You?"

I looked at Justine, who seemed unaffected by her nephew's behavior.

"I thought Justine had told her…"

I stopped talking when Justine shook her head at me. Assistant Professor Hugh Roberts focused on me and didn't see his aunt shaking her head.

"I know about you too, Auntie," he said.

Oops. Too late, I thought. Oh no. The *mierda* is going to hit the fan now. If this guy was capable of killing men just because Trudy gave them blow jobs, he was capable of killing women who had engaged in rather racy sexual activities with her. Auntie or not.

"I don't know what you mean, dear," she said calmly. "Have you been taking your medication, Hugh? You know your mother and I are concerned that you may have stopped."

"Shut up! Shut up! Shut up!" he screamed.

Oops again. The guy was getting upset and now I hear he's not on his meds. Great. We're never going to make it out of here alive. Where's Detective Quinn when I really need her?

"Hugh. Sweetness. Calm down."

"I won't calm down. I won't calm down. I won't calm down."

Assistant Professor Hugh Roberts stalked to a corner of the office and slid down, his back against the wall. His knees were propped up and he placed his head between them as he pulled a gun from the back of his pants. Assistant Professor Hugh Roberts pointed the gun at me, not his aunt. "I guess blood is pretty thick among lunatics." I spoke too soon—he shifted the gun between Justine and me. I couldn't tell what kind of gun he was flaunting since I was no expert but it almost looked like an antique Luger. Why would he have such a thing? Did it even work? I guess this wasn't a time to find out.

"Hugh dear. Put the gun down."

"Shut up, shut up, shut up," he murmured.

It was as if he was calming himself with repetition. I remembered that students had written on his evaluations that Assistant Professor Hugh Roberts had a proclivity for repeating himself when he was challenged in class. His repetition was like a self-soothing tic. I wasn't sure if his self-soothing was good or bad for us, his victims.

"I know about you and Trudy, Auntie."

"There's nothing to know, Hugh. Now put down the gun."

Hugh fought back tears that streamed down his cheeks. He wiped his face with the back of his hand, the same hand that wielded the knife. He held a knife in one hand and a gun in another. The boy was resourceful.

"I know, I know, I know," he repeated. "Why does everyone mistreat her? She's just an innocent, sweet girl. I love her. I want to marry her but she won't marry me, and it's all because of you perverts. You made her like she is, you made her like she is, you made her like that."

Oh, fuck. This was going from bad to worse. I was being blamed for something I hadn't done. I mean, me and Trudy? Okay, there was that little incident yesterday morning in Adrían's apartment but nothing transpired and how could he know about that?

"Don't think I don't know about you too," he said. "I know about you."

"What about me?"

"You're a pervert, you're a pervert, you're a pervert," he spat. "And you want to make Trudy a pervert. But she's not. She's a sweet girl. She can't help it if her fucking father never claimed her. I know what that feels like. Having a father who never says he's your father. And having a mother who never says she's your mother but instead makes her sister take you and pretend that she's your mother but you know, you know, you know they're all lies. All lies. All lies."

Hugh muttered into his knees and whimpered.

"What's he talking about, Justine?" I whispered. "Are you his mother?"

Her eyes widened and she shook her head.

"I can hear you," he said. "Yes, she's my fucking *birth* mother. She fucked Sloan. They both gave me up and now they think they can make up for it. By bringing me here. After all these years you think you can do that to me? Well, here's a newsflash: you can't. You can't. You can't."

Hugh sputtered through tears and conviction. I felt sorry for him. I wasn't sure why he had turned to murder but it was clear the boy was a tad unstable.

Quickly, he rose to his feet and waved the gun at me. "Take off your clothes, Electra," he said.

"Huh?"

"I said take off your clothes, take off your clothes, take off your clothes! Now!"

"No. I won't."

Without a moment's hesitation, Assistant Professor Hugh Roberts, Jacksonian specialist, lifted the Luger, aimed at the ceiling and fired. A bullet shot through the ceiling and chunks of plaster crumbled to the floor, covering him in white plasterboard.

"I'm serious, Electra. Take off your clothes."

Having fired the Luger seemed to calm him but his eyes looked crazed and bloodshot. I wasn't taking any more chances. I removed my boots and socks, hoping someone who may have been in the building heard the gunshot and called the police.

"Faster," he said. "Don't think I don't know what you're doing. Go faster, faster," he sputtered. "Auntie, go help her."

Justine sat relaxed on the couch as if nothing unordinary occurred. The gunshot hadn't frightened her.

"Auntie, I said help her! Help her now! Help her, dammit!"

Vice Chancellor Justine Aldridge wasn't accustomed to orders and even a gun directed at her person didn't budge her.

"I mean it, *Mom*."

He said mom so sarcastically that she got up from the couch and stood in front of me, calmly discarding my peacoat and my suit jacket, tossing each on the couch.

"Now the shirt," he said.

Justine unbuttoned my shirt methodically while staring into my eyes with a look of patient curiosity, as if she and Hugh had gone through this comedic tragedy before. She was acting much too casual and confident. But come to think of it, I'd never seen Justine lose her cool, except when it came to money and I'd never seen her lose her cool over that either. I'd only heard about it.

After unbuttoning my shirt, Justine folded the sleeves and the shirttail and set it on the coffee table. She was stalling. My compression jog bra was going to be much too difficult to negotiate without my help but then again, we could both stall for time. She struggled pulling it off and I allowed her until the impatience on his face frightened me. Finally, I pulled off the bra myself. The guy was aiming a gun at us. What did I care if he saw my breasts? I stood in bare feet, shirtless, wearing only black slacks.

"Off. Take them off. Now."

Hugh leveled the Luger at my legs. I unzipped my pants and let them drop to the floor.

"Underwear too."

"But it's chilly in here, Hugh."

"I don't give a fuck if it's the fucking North fucking Pole. Take them off. Take them off, take them off!"

"Okay, okay, I'll take them off. Fuck, Hugh. What do you want anyway?"

"I want *Mom* here to eat you out."

"What? *No gracias.* I'm not giving you a fucking show, asshole."

Assistant Professor Hugh Roberts, Jacksonian specialist, who denied the massacre of indigenous people, wagged his Luger to prove a point. I got the point.

"Hugh, why did you really kill dean Johnson?" I risked asking him questions while I eliminated the last item of clothing on my person.

"I told you. He made Trudy give him blow jobs. I caught them at it once. He made like it wasn't really happening but I saw. That's when I decided. Enough."

"Did you think you'd catch them again?"

"Maybe."

"It was that morning, wasn't it?"

"Maybe."

"Was Trudy here? With Dean Johnson?"

"It was some other girl. I waited until she left. Then I surprised him."

"Who was the other girl?"

"Just some girl."

I paused for a moment. I was standing in the middle of my new dean's office butt-naked with the vice chancellor and her nephew, or alleged son, who was our newly hired Assistant Professor in my Department of History. Can't say I didn't warn them. Andrew Jackson apologists are a bloodcurdling bunch if you ask me, but no one asked me.

I felt awkward standing naked before a murderer but not awkward enough to stop pursuing the truth while delaying his plot.

"Oh, I get it," I continued. "This was premeditated, wasn't it? Trudy was having a thing with Coxy and you got jealous. I bet she used to meet him often and you thought, heck, why not get rid of the deceitful asshole."

He sneered. "You think you're so smart. You and your kind. Well, you're not. You're all a bunch of perverts. That's who you are. Perverts perverts perverts. Perverts."

"I might be a pervert, Hugh, but I'm not a murderer."

"They deserved to die. Both of them. They deserved it."

"Did you stick that same knife in the president's heart?"

"Maybe."

"How many of those same knives do you have, Hugh?"

"This?" He held up the knife in his left hand. "Fuck, I don't know. They're cheap and sharp."

"Sharp knife, huh?"

"Shut up shut up shut up, you pervert. You think you know everything. That's not how I killed the president. I bashed his head in. He deserved it. But first I made him change his will. He left it all to Trudy. All of it. That bitch wife of his won't get a dime. I made sure of that."

I felt sorry for Mike. Even though he was a duplicitous clown, no one deserved to die that way.

"In this office? You bashed his head in here?"

"Nah. Not in here. In there."

Hugh pointed the gun barrel toward a closed door.

"What's in there?"

"The bathroom. I washed away all the blood. And my fingerprints. They'll never suspect me."

"Uh, excuse me, Hugh but they're on to you."

"You're just saying that. To scare me. I know better. That Detective? She's a fucking twat. She's never suspected me. I fooled her. Made sure she'd go after you. And that bitch you fuck."

"Who?"

"That bitch. She sucks off the dean too. Or used to anyway." He snickered.

"It was her that night, wasn't it? With the dean?"

"Yeah. It was your girlfriend." He snickered again. "All I had to do is plant that computer near her apartment. It was easy. Idiot cops."

I wondered how Coxy Johnson got his johnson serviced so much by so many women. Oh, wait. The guy had millions. Of course. Money. Some women are attracted to a guy with money and Isabel was no exception. Fuck you, Isabel. I continued my line of questioning to distract him. I was praying to Buddha and the *Virgen de Guadalupe* for divine intervention. I couldn't believe the building was empty. At least fifteen minutes had passed since he'd fired the gun. From the corner of my eye, I saw Justine fingering her jacket pocket. It looked as if she was trying to make a call on her cell phone but without seeing the name or number, who could she possibly reach? Butt dialing wasn't an exact science.

"What are you doing?" He pointed the Luger at her jacket pocket. "Take your hand out of your pocket, Auntie. Stop it now or I'll shoot it off. I mean it."

Leisurely, she slid her hand from her pocket. "I'm not sure what you think I was doing, Hugh dear."

"Give it to me," he said.

"Give you what?"

"Your phone, your phone, your fucking phone, Auntie. Give it here now!"

Justine pulled the phone from her jacket and handed it to him. Evidently, she had managed to reach someone because a voice on the other end repeated, "Hello, hello, Justine? Is that you?"

Hugh snatched the phone and smashed it against the wall. Pieces of plastic and tiny metal flew into the air. The boy was serious and he was seriously angry. I was feeling progressively hopeless except for the butt call that might bring someone to the Admin building. I didn't recognize the voice on the other end but I hoped Justine had a concerned friend.

"Sit," he said. "And you, Auntie, on your knees. Now!"

"Hugh, is this about your tenure, dear? You're going to get it. You realize that both Electra and I will ensure your tenure. Don't worry about that book you have to publish. We will be sure you get your job security. Without the book."

"I can finish my book. I'll finish it."

"Of course you will, dear. I'm simply saying that you will have your tenure."

"Fuck you, Auntie. I don't need you and your fucking favors. Get on your knees. Now!"

Justine stared at her nephew, who stared back. They seemed to be in a staring contest. More delaying tactics. Good. I was sitting bare-butt on the couch and saw the knife within my reach. Fully aware that knives are not as powerful as guns, I took a chance and inched my butt closer to the coffee table. I wasn't sure what I was going to do if I retrieved the knife. In an instant, I grabbed the dagger and lunged forward at Hugh's scrawny body and we both toppled, but I was on top of him, giving me a marginal advantage. We struggled and he gripped the gun tighter, firing at the ceiling. More plaster crumbled on us both and I found myself spitting out fragments of white dust as I held him down with my knees pressed firmly on his chest. I held the knife on both ends and smashed the flat part of the blade on his right wrist, thinking that enough pressure would force him to release the gun.

"Fucking cunt! Get off me! Auntie, get her off me!"

I pushed down harder on his wrist with the knife's blade and he still wouldn't let go of the damn gun. I kicked his chin with my knee and he bit his tongue. Blood seeped from his lips and blood seeped from my left palm where I clutched the sharp end of the blade but I refused to let go until I incapacitated him.

He peered at me, beady-eyed, and I bore rage fuming from his eyes and his bloody mouth. Luckily, he was a scrawny, pathetic half-wit making my job of overpowering him relatively easy, except that I couldn't get him to release the gun. I pressed harder and the blood on my left palm squeezed out, making my grip slippery. I wasn't going to be able to hold him down much longer.

Where the fuck was Justine? Just then he wrapped his legs around my ass and tipped me over with such force that my head banged against the granite tile. I felt myself go faint but I was too scared to allow myself to pass out. I still had a grip on the knife's handle with my right hand and without thinking, I impulsively stabbed his back, which probably only nicked him but he squealed and his body collapsed on top of me. Blood trickled from his back onto my naked torso and I felt dizzy.

At that moment, I saw Detective Quinn's face hovering over mine, frowning and saying my name out loud, but I couldn't really hear her. I passed out.

EPILOGUE

"To long for the woman who returns longing—that is complete, lucid pleasure."

Now that the case was closed, I was mustering the courage to send a text message to Carolina Quinn. I continued with: "Love your breasts without having touched them, but in my mind a thousand times I've kissed each one."

But I hadn't sent the message yet. It was too corny and she wasn't the type to appreciate turgid clichés. Two days had passed since Detective Carolina Quinn barged into the dean's office, tipped off and ready to arrest authenticated, crazy-ass murderer Assistant Professor Hugh Roberts, expert on President Andrew Jackson, Indian killer. And with Hugh permanently behind bars, I could relax. As I perused various news sites on my computer, a photo of Carolina popped out at me. She was being honored for having solved several cases in one brief year, including the murder of the dean and the president of Capital College. In the image, Carolina was in emblematic uniform drag I'd never seen her wear. She looked officiously ridiculous before the mayor and her police chief, her eyebrow arched as if to mock the tribute.

I compared it to another photograph of her, one I had found online on her Skype page. This image I'd memorized. She sat unassumingly in an overstuffed wingback chair upholstered in gold velvet cloth. She wore a sleeveless summer dress, short enough to show legs crossed casually, the right over the left, and with her right hand she caressed the soft flesh of her leg. In the other hand she held a phone, staring into its face, a slight grin at the corner of her mouth. She probably smiled for a lover who had sent a text message. An overwhelming sadness shrouded me. I wasn't that lover. Or was I? I tapped "send" on my smartphone and promptly regretted it.

I refilled a cup of coffee and sat down again in front of my computer, engaged in both images of Detective Carolina Quinn. The news item reported how she had been suspicious of Hugh Roberts and had been trailing him but hadn't had the evidence she needed until she discovered the crystal apple in President Mike's office. It seems the apple had a fingerprint that linked Hugh to the it, but that wasn't enough to charge him. She waited and knew he would mess up. She had told me none of this.

Just as I was settling into studying her Skype photograph, I heard the doorbell of my apartment buzz.

"Hey, buddy, I know you're in there."

It was Adrían.

"Door's open, bud."

Adrían walked into the kitchen, poured himself a cup of coffee and sat down across from me. "When are you going to get a new lock on that door, El?"

"I don't know."

"Hey, guess who I ran into at the Down Under last night?"

"Looks like you're a regular there now. Better not let Ginny find out."

"Aren't you going to guess?"

"Nope. Don't care."

"Our very own vice chancellor."

"I'm thinking I don't care."

"She was with Trudy and, get this, Isabel too. The three of them. Having a good old time. Makes you wonder, doesn't it?"

"Nope."

"No, really, El, doesn't it make you wonder if the three of them planned the murders? And that they put poor Hugh up to doing the deeds for them? You know all of them have inherited a chunk of change. Did you know that?"

"Yep. Heard that Ginny got a little bit of cash herself. Millions, in fact."

I scanned the news online without reading. Mostly I didn't want to get angry all over again. Adrían was probably right. Justine had sat back when I was being attacked making me think she had orchestrated the whole affair but I had no way of proving any of it. Not until Brisa dropped by to give me the details she had heard on the street did I realize my suspicions hadn't been too far off target. The gossip mill was churning. Seems Trudy inherited millions and Justine had profited as well. Trudy had given money to Justine because she was Hugh's aunt and Trudy felt sad for Hugh. Or so she claimed. Justine had her ways. Isabel had been awarded her own chunk of change mysteriously. She wouldn't say where she got the money but I still suspected Virginia and Isabel had been up to something.

What had been revealed was that after servicing the dean, Isabel slipped into a bathroom, showered and even put on fresh makeup. She hadn't seen Hugh at all, but she had seen me and said she was protecting me when all along she was gaslighting me with the pink baseball cap, which only had menstrual blood, Dominique told Oscar, who told Brisa. These students were efficient. Isabel wanted to confuse me about having been in the building by alleging she wanted to protect me but she was protecting herself.

"I told you she was a fucking lying bitch, Profe," said Brisa.

The kicker was that Hugh went to the dean's office early hoping to catch Trudy with the dean but instead saw skinny-ass Isabel and he still went homicidal.

"Ginny deserved to inherit the dean's millions, buddy. She put up with a lot from that fucker."

"Yeah. Well. I guess." I looked up from my computer. I wasn't going to burst his happy bubble with my suspicions about Virginia sending Isabel to kill the dean. Knowing Isabel, she convinced Ginny that she had put Hugh up to doing the deed. "Where's she taking you?"

"We're off to Buenos Aires for Thanksgiving break. Want to join us?"

"No, thanks. And I don't think Virginia would want me along."

"Sure, she would. I mean, you tackled the murderer." He studied the gauze wrapped around my left palm. "How's your hand?"

"I'll live."

"Damn, El. What's up? You're a hero and you're in such a funk. Come to Buenos Aires with us. You'll meet some sweet tango-dancing women."

"No thanks."

The doorbell buzzed again.

"Grand Central in here," I said. "It's open!" I shouted.

In strolled none other than Detective Carolina Quinn in her usual attire of tight black skirt and knee-high leather boots. She wore a cream-colored silk blouse underneath a white wool coat. My demeanor changed so much, I myself noted a bearable lightness yielding inside me. My eyes probably sparkled and twinkled. I was that predictable.

"I think I'll be going," said Adrían.

"Professor Fuentes."

"Detective Quinn."

They greeted each other with such formality that I wondered if either of them would ever warm up to each other.

"Going so soon, bud?"

"Yeah. I'm meeting Ginny for lunch. She also wants to take me shopping before our trip."

"Ah. Must be nice," said Carolina.

Adrían hoisted both eyebrows and tightened his lips into a pucker. "See you later, buddy."

I could tell he was peeved with Carolina's comment. He walked out and as he closed the door behind him, he yelled,

"Maybe your friend here can help you replace the bolt on your door!"

Carolina poured coffee and hovered over me. I immediately closed my laptop.

"Something private?" She sipped her coffee and her bottom lip protruded in an enticing manner. I had to focus. On something other than her bottom lip. I lifted the laptop cover and let her see a photo of herself at the ceremony.

"Looks like you're a hero," I said.

"I guess."

"You have doubts, Detective?"

"No, no doubts. The guy was sprawled on top of you by the time I showed up. Sorry."

"Yeah."

"How's your hand?"

"Fine, Detective. Although my hand would be better if you'd arrived a little sooner."

"Ah. So you are angry."

"A little. I mean, you could have warned me about Hugh."

Carolina raised her eyebrow and blinked coolly as if annoyed. "No, I couldn't."

"Can I at least ask a few questions?"

"You can. I might even answer."

"Was Sloan involved?"

"Sloan? Ha. He's a wimp."

"Is he really Hugh's bio-dad?"

"Seems so."

"And Justine? His mother?"

"Nope. His aunt. Her sister and Sloan are his parents. Justine was just taking care of her family. Can you believe that?"

"Was she taking care of him? Seems to me she set the guy up."

"No proof of that, Watson."

"One more thing is nagging at me."

"Just one?"

"Well, two. Maybe two."

"Let's have it."

"Who planted the bloody knife in my office?"

"Oh, that's easy: Hugh."

"Why was it gone when I woke up?"

"Who knows? He doesn't even know."

"He confessed?"

"Also said he broke into your apartment."

"Was he looking for the knife?"

"Nope. Said he wanted to scare you. I get the sense the guy never liked you much."

"Did he also break into Adrían's?"

"That was Trudy."

"For Justine?"

"They were playing tricks on each other and on you with those damn knives."

"Cat and mouse?"

"Something like that."

"One more thing."

"Go ahead. Why stop now?"

"Was the knife planted in my office the murder weapon?"

"Nope. We had that knife all along."

"You did?"

"We did."

"And you didn't tell me?"

"Nope."

"Thanks."

"You're welcome."

"I think Justine and Trudy were in on all of this. Virginia and Isabel too."

"No proof, Professor. I do, however, have proof of something else."

"And you're going to share with me? Do tell, Detective."

"I got this text message about thirty minutes ago."

"You did?" I felt a pang in my stomach.

"I did. And I was wondering…"

"About?"

"Well, not wondering exactly."

"Not wondering?"

"No. I was hoping."

"For?"

"I was hoping you had a few days off."

"You were?"

"Yes."

"Why?"

"Your hand needs tending."

"I've been tending to my hand, thank you, Detective."

"I hoped you might need someone else."

"Someone else?"

"To help you."

"Help me what?"

"Tend to your injury."

"I wasn't assigned a nurse, if that's what you mean."

"Lucky me," she said.

"Lucky you?"

"Lucky me."

With her eyebrow irresistibly ascendant, Detective Carolina Quinn clutched my uninjured hand and led me to my bedroom and closed the door behind us.

We didn't leave the room for three days, other than to raid my refrigerator and change the dressing on my hand, which healed so thoroughly that I felt better than my old self. A new Electra emerged from a tragically complex week.

Lucky me.

Bella Books, Inc.

Women. Books. Even Better Together.

P.O. Box 10543
Tallahassee, FL 32302

Phone: 800-729-4992
www.bellabooks.com

CPSIA information can be obtained
at www.ICGtesting.com
Printed in the USA
LVHW050002140922
728272LV00003B/327

9 781594 934407